必學

Business English
Writing Essentials

英文商業書信寫作
快速上手

- 主題關鍵字心智圖，透過圖像強化字彙記憶效果
- 圖解商業書信基本元素與格式，重要架構一目了然
- 剖析商業書信常見用語與下筆重點，掌握商務書信寫作原則
- 如何運用「8C」寫作原則，打造清晰簡潔商用信件
- 多篇情境範例，快速套用各類商用信件
- 多樣化課後練習題，仿真實情境書信寫作演練

作者 • Owain Mckimm / Michelle Witte
譯者 • 黃詩韻／陳依辰　審訂 • Helen Yeh

　　本書囊括完整的英文商業書信寫作架構、範例教學，內容充實實用，涵蓋各種商務情況會使用到的商用英文書信。全書內容豐富、主題多元，是學習商用英文書信的入門首選。

　　每課後皆附練習題，配合相關主題信函實例練習，有效複習重點商用書信字詞與常見句型，提供學生更多機會熟悉與應用所學，同時自我檢測學習成果，並讓教師能夠評估學生是否真正理解，且能靈活運用課堂所學內容。

　　本書共分 9 單元、17 課學習內容，並含一章節附錄做為補充資料，依照使用情境，收錄 49 種實用商務書信。各單元課文架構及其主旨如下：

1 **關鍵字 Key Words**：根據各課學習主題，列出相關關鍵字彙或片語，依照單字／片語間的邏輯關聯，圖解串聯成圖像化心智圖，幫助透過圖像與意義連結，強化字彙記憶效果，同步吸收同一主題的相關字詞。

2 **單元課文**：詳細介紹英文商業書信的寫作原則、方法與技巧，並依使用情境收錄十多種實用商務書信，涵蓋共 17 課，每課並適時提供情境化的寫作範例，讓學生完整了解寫作理論，並理解如何應用於實際寫作。

3 **範例書信 Examples**：主課文結束後，提供有一至五則的主題書信範例，呼應課文所介紹的寫作理論，有助加深學生對課文內容的理解，同時也提供學生可以參考的寫作模板。範例信件並搭配核心字彙片語表，標註中文字義和 KK 音標，提供完整的學習。

4 **常見句型及用語**：針對每課書信主題，整理出實際商務情境中常用的英文書信句型及用語，搭配中文參考翻譯。學生可以背誦用語，或以此為基礎進行變化和靈活運用，以在未來商業書信寫作中實踐，逐步提升寫作能力。

5 **課後練習 Exercises**：每課結束後皆附一回練習題，兼顧理論與實作，幫助即時複習所學內容，仿造真實情境的實作練習，能讓學生將課堂知識應用於實際場景中，使學生能夠自我檢視學習成效，也讓老師能驗收學生是否確實將上課內容融會貫通。

目錄 Contents

Lesson 1 商業書信的特性 Features of Business Letters

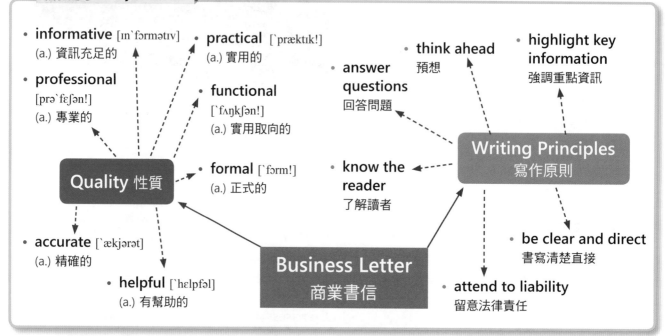

關鍵字 Key Words

- informative [ɪnˋfɔrmətɪv] (a.) 資訊充足的
- professional [prəˋfɛʃən!] (a.) 專業的
- practical [ˋpræktɪk!] (a.) 實用的
- functional [ˋfʌŋkʃən!] (a.) 實用取向的
- formal [ˋfɔrm!] (a.) 正式的

Quality 性質

- accurate [ˋækjərət] (a.) 精確的
- helpful [ˋhɛlpfəl] (a.) 有幫助的

Business Letter 商業書信

- think ahead 預想
- answer questions 回答問題
- know the reader 了解讀者

Writing Principles 寫作原則

- highlight key information 強調重點資訊
- be clear and direct 書寫清楚直接
- attend to liability 留意法律責任

1 What Is Business Writing?（什麼是商業寫作？）

商業寫作（business writing）是用於**專業職場情境**的寫作。使用商業寫作的**原因**有很多，舉例如下：

- 向他人建議做事的方法（如員工手冊〔employee manual〕）
- 說服他人採取特定行動（如企劃書〔proposal〕）
- 呈現重要資訊（如年度報告〔annual report〕）
- 協助採購或銷售過程（如請款帳單〔invoice〕）

商業寫作必然會設定寫作**目的**（purpose），而且目的要盡量**清楚精確**（clear and accurate）。

本書將主要探討一種使用相當廣泛的商業寫作類別：「**商業書信**」（business letter）。

2 What Is a Business Letter?（什麼是商業書信？）

商業書信是一種**正式**（formal）書信，用於**商務用途**，而非出於個人因素。當一家公司希望循專業方式向特定對象溝通時，就會利用商業書信聯繫往來，聯繫對象可以包括其他公司、客戶、或是公司內部員工。商業書信的寫作形式，包含：letters（書信）、emails（電子郵件）、faxes（傳真）、memos（便函／備忘錄）、presentations（簡報）、reports（報告）、resumes（簡歷）/ CVs（履歷表），以及其他各種文件等。

商業書信**須注意的事項**有以下幾點：

1 **Be Informative**（著重資訊提供）：閱覽商業書信是**為了取得資訊（information）**，而非消遣取樂。讀者不會期待在商業書信中，看到引人入勝的故事或嘉言美句，而是希望盡快抓到信件要傳達的**重點**。

2 **Be Functional**（商業書信旨在發揮功能）：商業書信常用以**達成工作任務**，例如僱用新員工、開發新客戶、採購產品等，一定會設有特定目的。因此，查看或是撰寫商業書信時，一定要了解這封**商業書信的目的**是什麼。

3 **Be Helpful**（幫助忙碌的商務讀者）：商務人士往往時間有限，所以讀信時通常會快速瀏覽掃讀，有時只會**大略瞥過（skim）**各個段落，希望快速找到跟他們切身相關的細節資訊。因此，商業書信的**格式要一清二楚**，段落必須言簡意賅，也可使用**小標題（header）**和標有**項目符號或編號（bullet points or numbers）**的清單，引導讀者找到重要資訊。

4 **Use Professional Tone**（使用專業語氣）：商業書信不同於私人信件，使用的**語言通常以正式禮貌用語為主**，較少使用太過口語化的俚語（slang）。

雖然商業書信通常使用正式用語，然而正式程度（formality）需視**對象**、情境（context）、**目的**調整，例如寫給地位（status）較高的主管時，用語要盡量正式，對平輩的同事或下屬則可以較不正式。此外，也需考量和對象的**親疏關係（familiarity）**、**年齡**、**性別**等條件，若用太過正式的用語寫給熟識的對象，可能顯得疏遠（distant）、冷淡。

溝通情境也會影響書信用語的正式性，例如討論重要公事時，宜採用正式用語，而在推銷信中則可使用較非正式、活潑（lively）的語句。另外，現代商業書信經常使用**電子郵件**，撰寫電郵時常因講求**溝通效率（efficiency）**，用語漸趨**口語化（colloquial）**，追求簡單、直白，反而應避免過多過於正式的用字。

下方對照表列出了數個非正式、正式用語的例子：

非正式 vs 正式用語	
Informal 非正式	**Formal 正式**
• Hi, John, 嗨，約翰	• Dear Mr. Smith: 親愛的史密斯先生：
• It was great to . . . 能夠……很棒	• It was a pleasure to . . . 能夠……實屬榮幸
• I'd like to talk to you about . . . 我想跟你談……	• I am writing in regards to . . . 此次來信是針對……
• Can you tell me . . . ? 可以跟我說……嗎？	• Please could you inform me . . . ? 能否請您告知……？
• Thanks for . . . 謝謝……	• I very much appreciate . . . 我非常感激……
• I'm sorry to tell you that . . . 很抱歉要跟你說……	• I regret to inform you that . . . 很遺憾要通知您……
• Bye! 再見！	• Yours sincerely, 此致，

商業書信範例 Example Business Letter

Deco Design Company
5723 Morgan Ave
Los Angeles, CA 90011

May 21, 2023

Jacob Blau
Blue Moon Consultants
155 E 29th St
New York, NY 10016

Dear Mr. Blau:

1 商業書信重要目的為**提供資訊**，而非閱讀取樂，因此信件開頭建議直接切入重點，點出**書信主旨**（subject）。

1 Subject: May 20 board meeting summary

Thank you for attending our board meeting on May 20. **2** For your records, here is a summary of the points discussed.

2 商業書信應發揮**預設的功能**，並能協助讀信者執行業務，因此需向讀信者表明這封信的**用途**為何。

3 Goals for the next six months
- Reach out to new markets in Mexico.
- Create an employee handbook.
- Continue to seek out government contracts.

3 商業書信的讀者相當忙碌，因此可將重點列為**清單**或以**編號**排序，以便快速消化吸收。

3 Lessons learned during the past six months
1. Allow more time for government bids.
2. Have our finances checked before making any government bids.
3. Provide training for staff in the newest design software.

4 商業書信自始至終應保持**專業口吻**書寫，避免俚語等太過口語的用法。

4 Thank you again for your valued input. We hope to have positive news to report to you at our next meeting.

Sincerely,

Layla Kim

Layla Kim, President

3 **Well-Written Business Letters**（如何寫好商業書信）

當代全球化（globalized）、數位化（digitalized）的商務環境下，商業書信常以**電子郵件**等電子溝通方式寄送，**傳統紙本書信**的使用頻率逐漸減少，但無論是紙本或電子形式的書信，**最重要的考量都是要能達成溝通目的（purpose）**。在寫信時，應顧及下列五點，以確保信件能成功達成目的：

1 **Know the Reader**（了解讀信對象）：為使信件發揮預期功能，寫信者必須了解誰會看這封信，以及對方為什麼要讀信。下筆前，必須考慮以下問題：

- 誰會查看信件？
- 對方的觀點和對信件主題的既有了解。
- 對方會如何處理信件（例如依照信中的指示辦理、回覆等）？

假設**寫信者相對資淺**，而**讀者地位較高**，更需要仔細考量讀者身分和需求，並以正式語氣撰寫書信。請參考以下信件摘錄：信中，寫信者提到收信者 Mr. Jones 為餐飲服務業的資深專業人士，因此可發現其採用正式且非常禮貌的用字，回覆 Mr. Jones 先前對於餐廳服務的建言（有關何謂建言信 suggestion letter，請參見本書 Unit 6）。

Dear Mr. Jones:

Thank you very much for your suggestion about the service situation in our restaurant. We very much **❶** appreciate the views of people like yourself with many years of experience in the service industry. We will work on our staff training and **❷** hope you will feel more satisfied the next time you visit us.

❶ 展現對讀信者身分的了解，尊重讀信者意見，以及顯示對其經驗和職涯背景的認識。

❷ 預想讀信者需求，在信中提供對讀信者後續行動有幫助的資訊（告知對方可再次來店體驗）。

2 Think Ahead（預想對方會有的疑問）：預先設想對方讀到這封信時可能會有什麼問題。好的商業書信會**預想讀信者的疑問並提供答案**。

讀信者的疑問可能有：

> ● 為什麼要看這封信？
>
> ● 發生了什麼問題？
>
> ● 會面、會議或活動中發生了什麼事？
>
> ● 接下來應該怎麼做？可以採取的措施為何？

通常，這些問題將牽涉對方會如何回應這封信，請把這一點考慮在內，並設想對方讀信時可能會出現的所有疑問。

有關此點，請參考以下信件節錄。本封範例中，**寫信者為公司主管**，**收件者為全體員工**，信裡**以上對下的角度**向員工說明問題並提出要求，然而用詞依然**客氣**、**禮貌**、**專業**。

Dear Staff:

❶ Attendance at our monthly meetings has been low recently. This is a friendly reminder that **❷** attending the monthly meeting is one of the major requirements in this company. It is also important for attendees to be there on time. Otherwise, the flow of the meeting will be disrupted. Meetings begin at 9:30 a.m. on the first Monday of each month. **❸** Please set a reminder in your calendars.

❶ 明確告知讀信者這封信件欲討論的問題為何。

❷ 向讀信者表明為何需要知道信件討論的內容，顯示信件和讀者切身相關。

❸ 告訴讀者接下來可以進行什麼具體行動。

3 Answer Questions（回答讀信者的問題）：考慮完對方的問題後，需在信中清楚地加以回覆。**最重要的問題必須最先回答**，次要問題留到後面。例如：

● We will refund the purchase price. We are very sorry for the inconvenience.

最重要資訊先行　　　　　　　　　次要資訊在後

4 Highlight Key Information（協助對方從信中掌握資訊）：人在忙碌時會選擇略讀而不是詳讀，因此**凸顯關鍵資訊**非常重要。寫作時可透過下列方式，**讓重點「跳出來」（pop）**，協助讀信者找到重點：

> ● 將相關資訊分段（section）呈現，以清楚的標題來標示不同重點段落。
>
> ● 用**數字**或**字體大小**（font size）來顯示不同段落的關聯以及資訊的重要程度。
>
> ● 用**項目符號清單**（bulleted list）凸顯重要資訊。如果這些資訊有前後順序，請以**數字**標明。

可參考以下信件摘錄：

❶ 用小標題將
資訊分段呈現。

❷ 使用項目符號
將資訊分項列出。

❸ 以數字清單將
前後有關的資訊，
按照順序排列。

> ❶ **Goals for the next six months**
> ❷ ・Reach out to new markets in Mexico.
> ・Create an employee handbook.
> ・Continue to seek out government contracts.
>
> **Lessons learned during the past six months**
> ❸ 1. Allow more time for government bids.
> 2. Have our finances checked before making any government bids.
> 3. Provide training for staff in the newest design software.

5 **Be Clear and Correct**（書寫應清楚直接）：句子要直截了當，方便對方迅速了解。另外，務必使用**適合溝通情境的禮貌用語**，避免用艱深的文字和複雜句型，並以**主動語態敘述**為主，少用被動句型。

主動語態 vs 被動語態	
✔ Active 主動	✘ Passive 被動
• We <u>received</u> your order. 我們收到您的訂單。	• Your order <u>was received</u>. 您的訂單已經收到了。
• We <u>decided</u> to . . . 我們決定要……	• The decision <u>was made</u> to . . . 已有決定要進行……
• I <u>attempted</u> to . . . 我試圖……	• An attempt <u>was made</u> to . . . 已有設法從事……

需注意的是，在部分情境下，主動語態會帶有**批判的**（critical）口吻。此時，則可以採取**被動語態**以維持**中性**（neutral）的語氣，例如可比較以下兩個例句：

- **You sent the package to the wrong address.** (Active voice, critical tone.)
  <u>你把包裹寄到了錯誤的地址。</u>（主動語態，語氣帶批判）

- **The package was sent to the wrong address.** (Passive voice, neutral tone.)
  <u>包裹送到了錯誤的地址。</u>（被動語態，語氣中性）

6 **Attend to Liability**（留意法律責任）：當今社會法律觀念普及，因此撰寫商業書信時，應意識到若未來出現相關法律糾紛，無論是紙本還是電子通信、代表公司或是個人寫的信，都可**能成為白紙黑字的證據**，因此下筆時若內容有法律疑義，務必**請教專業人士再三確認**。反過來說，**收到信件後也應皆妥善留存**，以備未來不時之需。

1 The principles of composing a well-written business letter are listed on the next page. Choose sentences from the following email to illustrate each point. Discuss your answers with a partner.

From: mleblanc@beautypro.ca	
To: cslee@beautybyching.com.tw	
Subject: Speaker Invitation	

Dear Ms. Lee,

As head of the Beauty Pro Conference organizing committee, I am writing to invite you to be the keynote speaker at our 2024 event. We believe your expertise and experience in Taiwan's competitive health-and-beauty industry will make your speech the high point of the conference.

About the event:
Beauty Pro Conference is Canada's largest health-and-beauty conference. The 2024 event will be held on March 13 in the Charles Ford Business Center in Vancouver. It will be a full-day event, and we expect roughly 3,000 health-and-beauty professionals to be in attendance.

We will provide:
We are pleased to be able to offer you a speaker's fee of $2,000. We will also organize and pay for your flights from Taiwan and your hotel in Vancouver.

What we require:
We would like you to prepare a 40-minute speech containing your thoughts on how to succeed in a highly competitive beauty market. We would also like to dedicate 20 minutes at the end of the speech to questions.

Please let us know by January 15 if you would be interested in accepting this invitation. You can do so by replying directly to this email.

We very much look forward to hearing from you.

Kind regards,

Marie Le Blanc
Organizing Committee Head
Beauty Pro Conference

❶ Know the Reader

❷ Think Ahead

❸ Highlight Key Information

❹ Clear and Direct

Lesson 2 商業書信的種類 Types of Business Letters

關鍵字 Key Words

1 sales letter 推銷信
2 invitation letter 邀請信
3 thank-you letter 感謝信
4 congratulation letter 恭賀信
5 complaint / suggestion letter 客訴／建言信
6 apology letter 致歉信
7 cover letter / resume/CV 求職信／簡歷／履歷表
8 email 電子郵件
9 memo 便函
10 letter of inquiry 詢價信
11 letter of quotation 報價信
12 order letter 訂貨信
13 letter of resignation 離職信
14 reference/recommendation letter 推薦信

Types of Business Letters 商業書信種類

1 Types of Business Letters（商業書信的種類）

　　在職場上，商務人士會需要撰寫各類信件。根據工作職位的不同，亦會有特別較常處理的信件種類，例如客服部的人員可能需要處理很多客訴信，而業務部的人員需要撰寫產品推銷信來開發新客戶。為了因應未來可能所遇到的各種情境，全面了解及學習撰寫不同種類的商業書信是十分重要的。

　　本書將介紹下列各項書信類別：

Lesson	書信種類與內容說明
6	Sales Letters（推銷信） 推銷信是用來**推銷業務內容**的信件，信中會**說明自家銷售的產品和服務（goods and services）**，並向對方闡述這些產品和服務能創造什麼效益（benefit）。寫信者必須分析讀信者的**性別（gender）**、**年齡（age）**、**經濟狀況（economic status）**等身分資訊，從顧客的需求著眼寫信，並以搶眼的標題和文案**引起讀者注意（attention）**。

7	Invitation Letters（邀請信）
	邀請信的目的為**邀請（invite）**其他商務人士來參加公司活動，例如宴會、舞會、茶會、慶典等正式場合（occasion），信件務求**真誠懇切（sincere）**，並須向收信者提供**該如何回覆的細節資訊**，以期對方如願應邀出席（attend）。商場上，邀請信是拓展人脈（networking）、建立關係的重要媒介。

8–9	Thank-You Letters（感謝函）
	感謝函可用來表達**對於對方付出的時間（time）**、**努力（effort）**有所重視。當個人或公司收到各界人士的**幫忙、關心、邀請**或**捐贈（donation）**時，可以寄送感謝函，信中應提及寫信者想感謝的具體事項，並明確表示謝意（gratitude）。寄送感謝函是種**商業禮儀（etiquette）**，有助於企業間維持良好關係。

10	Congratulation Letters（恭賀信）
	在有些特殊場合，會寄發恭賀信給其他**公司**，例如祝賀對方有新分店（new branch）開張。恭賀信也會寄給**個人**，例如慶祝對方升遷（promotion）。亦可藉由恭賀信，向公司或個人表示你**期望未來如何與他們合作**。信件內容應著重**慶賀對方的成就（achievement）**與喜事，用字（wording）應力求**真誠親切**，展現寫信者是真心替對方開心。

11–12	Complaint and Suggestion Letters（客訴與建言信）
	當對於一家公司的行為不滿意（unsatisfied）時，可以寄發客訴信，藉此**指出對方的商品或服務發生哪些問題**，並對此**要求解決方法（solution）或補償（compensation）**。客訴信亦有助收件的公司注意到自身缺失。建言信則是提供想法，**建議對方公司有何可以改進（improve）**之處，語氣會比客訴信正面（positive）許多。

13	Apology Letters（致歉信）
	生意很難一帆風順，錯誤所在多有。當業務往來或提供服務時發生錯誤，以致造成客戶**不便（inconvenience）或損失（loss）**，就可透過致歉信**承認（acknowledge）**錯誤並**請求原諒（forgiveness）**，這對於維持企業互信非常重要。致歉信應**及時發出**，說明錯誤原因並表達歉意，而**不應羅織藉口（excuse）**，以免影響公司商譽。

14–15	Cover Letters & Resumes/CVs（求職信和簡歷／履歷表）
	求職信和簡歷／履歷表是**求職者（applicant）謀求職缺（opening）**時的常用文書。求職信會**大略介紹**自身背景和能力，需行文清楚、態度自信，以吸引未來雇主（employer）注意。簡歷／履歷表則會**列舉教育程度、工作經歷和技能（skill）**等細節，各個項目（item）要以清楚的方式排列，讓審閱者能迅速判斷求職者是否勝任該職位（position）。

16	Emails（電子郵件）
	現今多數商務溝通（business communication）都是透過電子郵件，為發送訊息**快速、有效率（efficient）**的方式，可以寄發邀請、道歉等上述各項內容。然而，雖然電子郵件比一般郵件便捷，依然**須遵守商業書信的許多規則**，例如應加上書信該有的稱謂和結尾敬辭等，並避免使用網路聊天時常用的首字母縮寫詞（acronym）或簡化之字詞。
17	Memos（便函）
	便函是公司內部用來**布達（announce）重要事項**的文件，例如公司新政策（policy）、活動（activity）、培訓（training）日期等，用途廣泛，且因為便函的文體**較一般商用書信簡單**，能**節省溝通所需時間**，提升業務進行效率。但是便函也需具備**發文者、收件者、日期、主旨**等書信要素。
Appendix **附錄**	Letters of Inquiry（詢價信）
	指潛在顧客看到宣傳或促銷活動後，或有意購買商品／服務時，用來**詢問商品或服務價格的信**。詢價信主要目的是詢問每單位產品的價格，信中的常見問題除了商品單價外，也可包括折扣有無、產品運送細節等，以利寫信者後續可以依對方回覆，考量是否向對方下單採購。
	Letters of Quotation（報價信）
	指在收到詢價信後，**進行報價或後續溝通的回覆信**。報價信中的報價可以大致分為「**穩固報價**」（firm offer）或「**非穩固報價**」（non-firm offer），前者表示承諾以固定價格出售產品或提供服務，後者則代表報價的相關條件仍待確認，可能改變。
	Order Letters（訂貨信）
	為向對方公司**訂購商品或服務的信**，可以透過電子郵件、書信、電話或傳真等各種形式寄發，收到後需要留意寫信者是否提供所有需要的資訊。訂貨信也常和**訂單表格（order form）**一起寄出，有時候則是訂貨信本身就充當訂單。
	Letters of Resignation（離職信）
	為員工**有意提出辭職（resign）時寫給公司的信**，信中一般不需說明離職後的計畫或工作，應著重清楚**說明離職意願**，並寫出離職日期，也可交代需要的過渡工作相關內容。離職信可能會由原公司留存在員工檔案裡，所以應謹慎書寫，不可因即將離職而口無遮攔。
	Reference/Recommendation Letters（推薦信）
	寫信者寄給被推薦人（正在求職者）未來的雇主的信件，意在**幫助其取得下一份工作**。完整的推薦信除了說明被推薦人的過去職務、薪資、工作起訖時間外，還會敘述被推薦者以往良好的工作表現、個性、技能等正面職場特質，**顯示其能勝任未來職位**。

Lesson 2 Exercises

1 In the boxes below are the different types of business letters covered in this book. Match each one to its description.

(sales letters) (invitation letters) (thank-you letters) (congratulation letters)

(complaint letters) (suggestion letters) (apology letters) (cover letters)

(resumes) (emails) (memos)

Type of Letter	Description
❶ [ ]	Used to let others know that their time and effort were valued.
❷ [ ]	Used to admit errors and ask for forgiveness.
❸ [ ]	Used to introduce oneself when applying for a new job.
❹ [ ]	Used to explain one's goods and services to a potential customer.
❺ [ ]	Used very often in business communication today because they are fast and efficient in sending messages.
❻ [ ]	Used to express one's unhappiness with a company's goods or services.
❼ [ ]	Used to detail one's experience and skills when applying for a new job.
❽ [ ]	Used to express one's pleasure to someone on the occasion of success or good fortune.
❾ [ ]	Used to share one's ideas on how a company might improve.
❿ [ ]	Used to notify people within the same company of something important, such as a new company policy, event, or training day.
⓫ [ ]	Used to request that someone attend a company event.

Lesson 3 商業書信的結構與格式 Structure and Format of Business Letters

關鍵字 Key Words

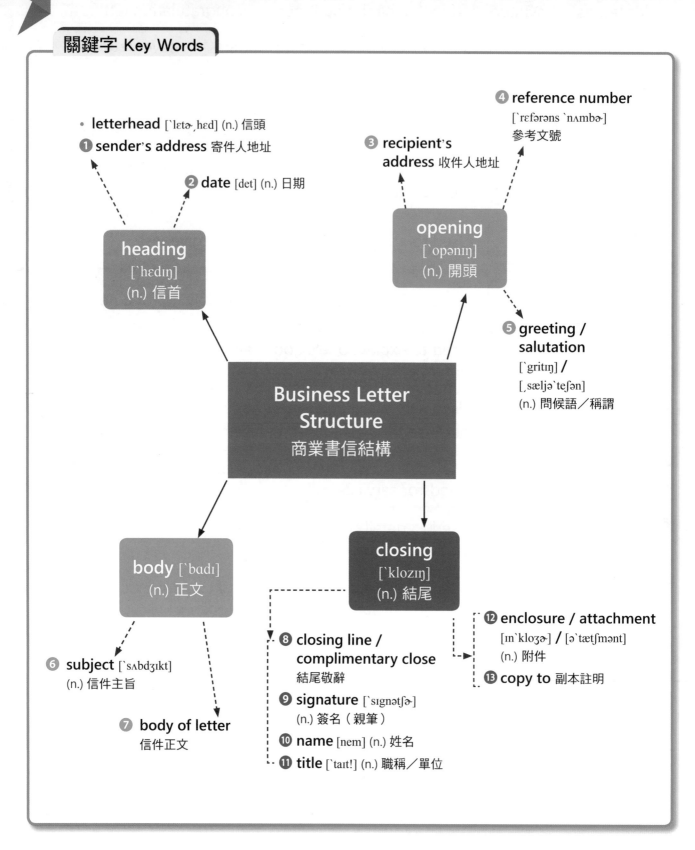

• letterhead [ˋlɛtɚˏhɛd] (n.) 信頭

❶ sender's address 寄件人地址

❷ date [det] (n.) 日期

❸ recipient's address 收件人地址

❹ reference number [ˋrɛfərəns ˋnʌmbɚ] 參考文號

heading [ˋhɛdɪŋ] (n.) 信首

opening [ˋopənɪŋ] (n.) 開頭

❺ greeting / salutation [ˋgritɪŋ] / [ˏsæljəˋteʃən] (n.) 問候語／稱謂

Business Letter Structure
商業書信結構

body [ˋbɑdɪ] (n.) 正文

closing [ˋklozɪŋ] (n.) 結尾

❻ subject [ˋsʌbdʒɪkt] (n.) 信件主旨

❼ body of letter 信件正文

❽ closing line / complimentary close 結尾敬辭

❾ signature [ˋsɪgnətʃɚ] (n.) 簽名（親筆）

❿ name [nem] (n.) 姓名

⓫ title [ˋtaɪtl] (n.) 職稱／單位

⓬ enclosure / attachment [ɪnˋklozɚ] / [əˋtætʃmənt] (n.) 附件

⓭ copy to 副本註明

1 基本商業書信結構 Basic Business Letter Structure

信首 **Heading**

❶ James Brothers Publishing
675 Walter Street
New York, NY 10002
U.S.A.

❷ September 15, 2023

開頭 **Opening**

❸ Mary Wang
Waiyu Education Group
12F, No. 42, Sec. 2, Jinshan S. Rd,
Da'an Dist, Taipei City 10603
Taiwan (R.O.C.)

❹ Ref. 091222

❺ Dear Ms. Wang:

❻ Re: Catalog request

正文 **Body**

❼ Thank you for your letter requesting the latest edition of our catalog. Please find one enclosed with this letter.

We have also recently launched an online order platform. You can now buy from us online at www.jamesbrothers.com/shop.

If you would like to receive samples of any of our books, please let us know.

❽ Yours sincerely,

結尾 **Closing**

❾ David James

❿ ⓫ David James, Director

⓬ Enc. (1)

⓭ cc: Chris Chen

19

❶

Quality Cosmetics, Inc.
302 Beauty Lane, Suite 5
San Bruno, CA 94066
(650) 656-7000
act@cos.com
[1 blank line]
October 12, 2023 ❷

CERTIFIED MAIL ❸
PERSONAL ❹
[1 blank line]
Permissions Department
Harbinger Publishing
309 Ditmas Ave
Brooklyn, NY 11218-4901 ❺
[1 blank line]
Attention Mr. Donald Williams ❻
[1 blank line]
Re: Your letter dated October 9, 2023 ❼
[1 blank line]
Dear Permissions Department: ❽
[1 blank line]
Subject: Illustration: Girl Applying Lipstick ❾
[1 blank line]
May I use one of your illustrations in my in-house report titled "Third Quarter Growth in the Cosmetics Industry"? The illustration is called "Girl Applying Lipstick." ❿
[1 blank line]
Thanks for your time and attention. Please contact me at your earliest convenience at (415) 748-9852.
[1 blank line]

> 本封書信採**「改良齊頭式」**格式書寫，因此寄件人住址、日期、結尾敬辭和簽名等部分需從**中間稍右的地方起頭**。其餘部分和「齊頭式」相同，從左方邊界起頭。
>
> 詳見本課第2節「Format（商業書信的格式）」說明。

Regards, ⓫
[1 blank line]
Irina Safarova ⓬
[1 blank line]
Irina Safarova ⓭
Analyst, Quality Cosmetics ⓮
[1 blank line]
IS/jd ⓯
[1 blank line]

Enc: catalog ⓰
[1 blank line]
cc: Flora Lopez ⓱
[1 blank line]
P.S. ⓲

①　SENDER'S ADDRESS 寄件人住址 ★
- 如果信紙上印有信頭（letterhead），就不需要再打上這些資料。信頭就是公司專用信紙上，印有公司名稱與商標的地方。寫商務書信時，最好使用已經印好信頭的公司專用信紙，看起來比白紙要專業。

②　DATE 日期 ★
- 美式的日期寫法：月—日—年（例如 October 12, 2023）
- 英式的日期寫法：日—月—年（例如 12 October 2023）

③　SPECIAL MAILING NOTATIONS 郵寄方式註記
- CERTIFIED MAIL 掛號信件
- SPECIAL DELIVERY 限時專送
- AIR MAIL 航空信件

④　ON-ARRIVAL NOTATIONS 內部信件種類註記
- PERSONAL 私人信件
- CONFIDENTIAL 機密文件
- PRIVATE AND CONFIDENTIAL 私人機密文件
- STRICTLY CONFIDENTIAL 極機密文件

⑧　GREETING / SALUTATION 問候語／稱謂 ★
- Dear Sir:
- Dear Sir or Madam:
- Dear Ms. XXX:
- Dear [Full Name]:
- To Whom It May Concern:
- Ladies and Gentlemen:

⑨　SUBJECT 信件主旨

⑪　CLOSING LINE 結尾敬辭 ★

⑬　NAME (typed) 姓名（打字）★

⑮　IDENTIFICATION INITIALS
of the writer and typist 鑑別符號
當寫信人和打字者不是同一個人時使用，各取其姓名首字母縮寫。寫信人的姓名縮寫用大寫放在前面，打字者的姓名縮寫用小寫置於後，格式如下：
- IS/jd
- IS:jd

（指寫信人是 Irina Safarova，打字者是 Joe Davis）

⑤　RECIPIENT'S ADDRESS 收件人及地址 ★
常見內容包含如下：
- name of person addressed
  收件人名稱
- title of person addressed
  收件人職位名稱
- name of organization 公司單位名稱
- street number and name 號碼與街名
- city, state, and postal code
  城市、州、郵遞區號
- country of destination
  寄送國家名稱（應單獨一行）

⑥　ATTENTION 致（指定的受信人）
如果收件人地址上已寫明（見第 5 點），就不用加寫這一行。此外，Attention 的對象應與信封上的收件人相同。

⑦　REFERENCE 信件參考文號
將信件分類和編碼，以便日後參照。例如註記是求職信、發票信或是回覆某信等。

⑩　BODY OF LETTER 信件正文 ★
(first paragraph)（第一段）

⑫　SIGNATURE (handwritten) 親筆手寫簽名 ★

⑭　TITLE 單位或職位名稱

⑯　ENCLOSURE/ATTACHMENT 附件
（常用縮寫：Enc. 或 Encl.）

⑰　COPY TO 副本註明（說明另寄副件給某人）
- cc 是指 carbon copy
- 也可作 pc，指 for photocopy

⑱　POSTSCRIPT 附注
商業書信應避免使用。

1 Structure（紙本商業書信的結構）

翻開本課開頭的書信範例，複雜的結構元素是不是令你一時眼花撩亂呢？現代商務溝通已邁向電子化，**電子郵件**往往取代紙本書信的角色（**有關電子郵件格式與結構說明，請見 Lesson 16 電子郵件**）。然而，學會看懂並寫作**傳統紙本書信**依然重要，畢竟未來職場需求難以預料，多學會一種技能，等於多了一項武器、一分競爭力。

以下將詳細介紹紙本書信的結構元素；各元素在信中依序排列如下：

1 **Letterhead / Sender's Address**（信頭／寄件人地址）：公司通常會使用印有**信頭**的信紙，即印在信紙上端的特殊文字區塊，內容包括**公司名稱、地址及聯絡電話**（請見下方圖示）。如果信紙沒有印信頭，就必須在頁首**手動**（manually）輸入寄件人地址。

信頭**不須**列出寄件人姓名或職銜，因為相關資訊會出現在信尾，只需寫出**公司名稱、門牌號碼、街道名、城市名、郵遞區號**（post code）**與國家**，而地址的每行後方不須加逗號。

2 **Date**（寫信日期）：商業書信的內容往往**具有時效性**（time-sensitive），因此請務必註明寫信的**日期**。填寫日期時，不能只用數字表示（如：05/12/22），以免引起混淆。由於世界各地書寫日期的方式不盡相同，所以**要將月分完整**拼寫出來，**年分也要完整寫出**。

美式用法中，日期按照「月、日、年」順序書寫，但在其他英語系國家，書寫順序大多是「日、月、年」，有些人則認為以「年、月、日」的順序書寫最清楚，但是此種格式不常使用。

排列法順序	❌ 不能只用數字	✓ 年分／月分完整寫出
美式（月／日／年）	3/15/2023	March 15, 2023
英式（日／月／年）	15/3/2023	15 March 2023
按 年／月／日	2023/3/15	2023 March 15

3 **Receiver's Address**（收件人地址）：接著，要寫上收件人的姓名、公司名稱、門牌號碼、街道名、城市名、郵遞區號與國家。跟寫寄件人地址一樣，收件人地址的每一行後方都不用加逗號。

4 **Reference Number**（參考文號，非必須）：**參考文號**通常是**一組英文字母或數字**的組合。商業書信中未必一定需列出參考文號，但若有這項標注，有助於後續文件**歸檔**（filing）以及追蹤雙方對話內容。參考文號通常會寫成「**Reference**」或「**Ref.**」，後方列出號碼。回覆對方的信件時，應使用第一封信裡提供的參考文號。以下為幾種參考文號的範例：

- Ref. No. 126587
- File number 126587
- Reference number AB698

5 **Greeting & Salutation**（問候語和稱謂）：**問候語**通常以 **Dear** 開頭，後面放收件人的姓氏與稱謂。**稱謂**就是寫信者稱呼收件人的方式，包含以下三個部分：

Title（收件人的頭銜）

❶ 務必把收件人的頭銜寫對。

❷ 不同專業人士可能有不同的頭銜，醫生和博士的頭銜是 Dr.；大學教授可能是 Dr.（博士）或是 Professor（教授）；法官、政府官員和高級職員的頭銜一定要先查清楚。

❸ 寫信給不具醫師、博士或教授等頭銜的**女士**時，要用 **Ms.**（女士），除非對方明確要求你使用 Mrs.（夫人）或 Miss（小姐）。

Name（收件人的姓名）

❶ 除非你跟對方已經熟識到**可以互稱名字**的地步，否則就以「**頭銜＋姓氏**」的方式稱呼對方，如 Dear Dr. Howard。

❷ 如果**不知道對方的姓名**，可以寫出收件人的**職銜**，例如 Dear Sales Manager（親愛的業務經理）。

❸ 如果你**不知道對方的姓名**，但**知道對方的性別**，就可以寫 **Dear Sir**（親愛的先生）或 **Dear Madam**（親愛的女士）。

❹ 如果你連對方的**性別也不知道**，就寫 Ladies and Gentlemen 或 Dear Sir or Madam（親愛的先生／女士），或使用 To Whom It May Concern（敬啟者）。

❺ 如果跟對方**很熟識**，可以直接寫對方的**名字**，例如 Dear Jessica。

❻ 若不清楚收件人的**慣用稱謂**，可寫出收件人**全名**，如 Dear Jordan Green。

Punctuation（標點符號）

❶ 最常見的就是在名字後面加一個**冒號**（colon），例如「Dear Ms. White:」。

❷ 也可以在名字後加上**逗號**（comma），例如「Dear Ms. White,」（傳統上，逗號常用於較不正式的信件或私人信件。根據美國普渡大學的 Purdue OWL 寫作建議，商業書信之稱謂後方標點符號應用冒號，不可使用逗號）。

❸ 但是也可以**完全不加標點符號**，例如「Dear Professor Bard」。

6 **Subject Line**（主旨，非必須）：信件「主旨」的目的是告知閱信者這封信的**主題**，長度只需簡短幾個字即可，有以下幾種寫法：

- Re: Our meeting last week（關於：上週的會議）
- Subject: Our meeting last week（主旨：上週的會議）
- Our meeting last week（上週的會議）

7 **Body**（正文）：正文是信件最主要的部分，通常由**段落組成**，其長度取決於你有多少資訊要傳達給對方。正文應該要**簡潔扼要**，**內容要有組織**，方便讀者找到需要的資訊。建議的段落安排可見以下說明：

First Paragraph（第一段）

在第一段裡，清楚說明寫作這封信的**目的**，如：

- With reference to our conversation of August 3, （就我們八月三日的對話……）
- I am seeking a position in your Data Management Department.
  （本人欲應徵貴公司的資料管理部門工作。）

如果你的信會很長，可以在第一段把信件的內容條列出來，常用的開頭用語如：

- With reference to your letter/email/fax of (date) . . .
  （就您於……月……日的來信／電郵／傳真）
- Thank you for your letter/email/fax/catalog/etc.
  （謝謝您的來信／電郵／傳真／目錄等）
- Regarding our meeting on Thursday . . . （有關我們星期四的會議……）

Middle Paragraphs（中間的段落）

中間的段落應該用來**詳細說明主題**，並給予**重要的細節或指引**。段落盡量簡短，每段只處理一個小主題。如果有重要資訊，不妨用**項目符號**或**數字**編成清單。此外，務必保持內容**簡潔**，讀者會希望你的信簡短扼要。

Conclusion / Final Paragraph（結論／最後一段）

結論的內容取決於信中傳達的資訊。你可以在結論裡**提出推薦**、**總結想法**，或**表示願意提供幫助**。如果是求職信，最好在結尾加上**如何**（how）、**何時**（when）、**哪裡**（where）可以聯絡到你。

商業書信最後一段常用的說法有：

- Please don't hesitate to contact us again if you have any questions or concerns.
  如果您有任何疑問，歡迎再次向我們洽詢。
- Please let me know if I can be of more assistance.
  如果還有什麼我可以幫上忙的地方，請通知我。
- If you need further help, please contact us again.
  如果您還需要進一步協助，請再與我們聯絡。
- We look forward to (our next meeting / working with you).
  我們誠心期盼〔下一次的會面／合作〕。

8 **Closing Line / Complimentary Close**（結尾敬辭）：結尾敬辭有常見的專業、制式用法，也有較親切、個人化的用語，可依據信件的整體語氣來選用。結尾敬辭**只有第一個字的首字母要大寫**，後方則要用**逗號**，不可使用句號。

商業書信常見結尾敬辭	較個人化的結尾敬辭
• Yours truly, • Respectfully (yours), • Cordially (yours), • (Yours) Sincerely, • Sincerely yours, • (Yours) Faithfully,* • Faithfully yours,	• Love, • With love, • Best wishes/regards, • Warmest/Kindest regards, • Your devoted friend, • Cheers, • As always,

* 在英式用法中，**(Yours) Faithfully** 常用作**不確定收信人姓名**時的結尾敬辭，此時收信人稱謂常為 Dear Sir 或 Dear Madam；若**確定收件人姓名**，則會用 **sincerely** 取代 faithfully。

9 **Signature**（簽名）：商務書信都要簽名，而且最好用高級的筆簽。比起大量印刷的商業信函，附上親筆簽名的商務書信感覺起來更有溫度。親筆簽名下方需打上**寫信者的名字**和**公司職稱**，如果不是很長就寫成一行，而名字和職稱太長則應分成兩行：

- Jackie Smart, President ← 不是很長 → 寫成一行
- Reginald K. Dahl ← 太長 → 寫成兩行
  Marketing Director

如果是電子郵件，要在郵件**最下方**輸入**寫信者的名字**，並附上一個「.sig」的**簽名檔**。本書將在 Lesson 16 詳細說明如何寫作商務電子郵件。

10 **Enclosure**（附件，非必須）：附件就是**隨信附上的文件**，可能是簡章、訂單、目錄、報告或其他的文件。你應該在**正文的第一段**就告訴對方你隨信附上了附件，然後在**頁面底端簽名的下方再提一次**。你在第一段可以採用這些說法：

- We are enclosing . . . 隨信附上……
- We enclose . . . 隨信附上……
- Enclosed is . . . 隨信附上……
- Please find enclosed . . . 請見附件中的……

頁尾寫法	範例
Enclosure 完整地打出來，括號寫出附件數目	Enclosures (3)
用 Enclosure 的縮寫	Enc. (3)
列出全部附件名稱	Enclosures (1) Invoice 1029; (2) Return slip; (3) Customer satisfaction survey

2 **Format**（商業書信的格式）

　　每家公司都會自訂一套商業書信的寫作格式，因此員工應該按照自家公司偏好的格式來撰寫商業信函。一般公司常用的商業書信格式有三種，分別如下：

❶ 齊頭式（block style）
廣受歡迎

❷ 縮排式（indented style）
逐漸式微

❸ 改良齊頭式（modified block style）**亦屬常見**

James Brothers Publishing
675 Walter Street
New York, NY 10002
U.S.A.

September 15, 2023

Mary Wang
Waiyu Education Group
12F, No. 42, Sec. 2, Jinshan S. Rd,
Da'an Dist, Taipei City 10603
Taiwan (R.O.C.)

Ref. 091222

Dear Ms. Wang:

Re: Catalog request

Thank you for your letter requesting the latest edition of our catalog. Please find one enclosed with this letter.

We have also recently launched an online order platform. You can now buy from us online at **www.jamesbrothers.com/shop.**

If you would like to receive samples of any of our books, please let us know.

Yours sincerely,

David James

David James, Director

Enc. (1)

cc: Chris Chen

1 **Block Style**（齊頭式）：齊頭式是簡便的商務書信格式，信中的每個部分（即每項基本要素）都是**從頁面的左方邊界開始行文**，各個基本要素和段落之間，則以**空行**的方式隔開。齊頭式很簡單，因此非常受到歡迎，是現代商業書信裡採用最廣的格式。

齊頭式主要格式的詳細說明如下：

- **段落齊頭**：在齊頭式中，文件或信中的每個部分都從**左邊的邊界**起頭。
- **不同的段落之間要空行**：不同的部分（比如說不同的段落，或商務書信中的地址），則以**空行**的方式隔開：

❶ 收信人地址和日期之間：空一行或空三行
❷ 「問候語／稱謂」與信件內文的第一段之間：空一行
❸ 信件內文的段落之間：空一行
❹ 大小標題與隨後的段落之間：不空行

　　一般來説撰寫電子郵件時，段落格式安排也建議採用**齊頭式**，也就是**段落首行不需縮排、各段落以空行隔開**。若有需強調的內容，如**項目符號／編號清單**或**引述內容**，可考慮**適時縮排**。當然，若公司對於電子郵件有特定內部規範，遵守公司規定即可。

James Brothers Publishing
675 Walter Street
New York, NY 10002
U.S.A.

1 blank line

September 15, 2023

1 blank line

❶ 齊頭式信件的各段文字，都是從左邊的邊界起頭，句首不需任何空格或縮排，讓信件文字開始位置整齊劃一。

Mary Wang
Waiyu Education Group
12F, No. 42, Sec. 2, Jinshan S. Rd,
Da'an Dist, Taipei City 10603
Taiwan (R.O.C.)

1 blank line

Ref. 091222

1 blank line

Dear Ms. Wang:

1 blank line

❷ 齊頭式信件中，各部分和正文當中的各段落須用空行隔開，以利讀者閱讀。

Re: Catalog request

1 blank line

Thank you for your letter requesting the latest edition of our catalog. Please find one enclosed with this letter.

1 blank line

We have also recently launched an online order platform. You can now buy from us online at www.jamesbrothers.com/shop.

1 blank line

If you would like to receive samples of any of our books, please let us know.

1 blank line

Yours sincerely,

David James

3 blank lines

1 blank line

David James, Director

1 blank line

Enc. (1)

1 blank line

cc: Chris Chen

2 **Indented Style**（縮排式）：縮排式較齊頭式複雜。在正文部分，每個新段落的開頭都會**向內縮排約 1.5 公分**，縮排方式是**按下鍵盤上的「Tab」鍵**。除了段落開頭要縮排外，信裡的部分區塊應從**頁面中線稍右的位置起頭**，這些部分包括：

- 寄件人地址（sender's address）
- 日期（date）
- 結尾敬辭（complimentary close）
- 簽名（signature）

一般認為，縮排式比齊頭式更顯得傳統老式，如今已逐漸式微，**較少人採用**。

縮排式信件範例

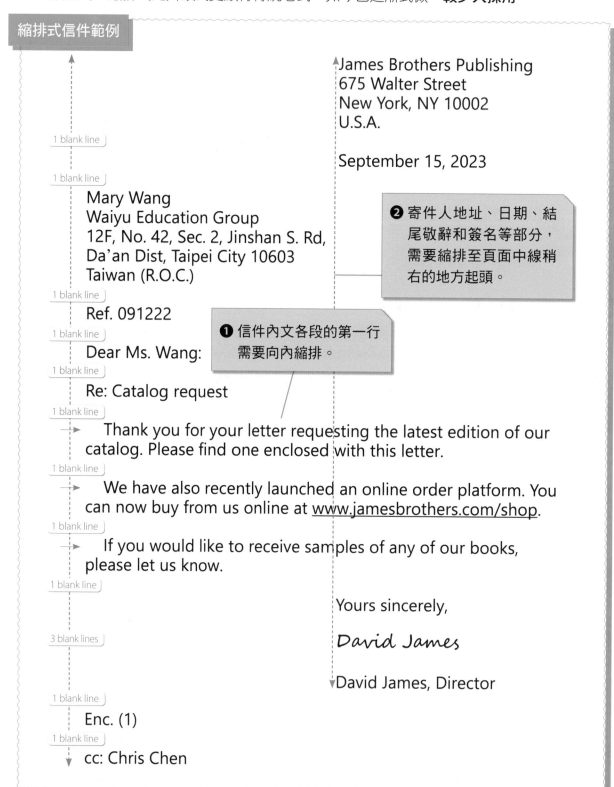

James Brothers Publishing
675 Walter Street
New York, NY 10002
U.S.A.

September 15, 2023

1 blank line

1 blank line

Mary Wang
Waiyu Education Group
12F, No. 42, Sec. 2, Jinshan S. Rd,
Da'an Dist, Taipei City 10603
Taiwan (R.O.C.)

❷ 寄件人地址、日期、結尾敬辭和簽名等部分，需要縮排至頁面中線稍右的地方起頭。

1 blank line

Ref. 091222

1 blank line

❶ 信件內文各段的第一行需要向內縮排。

Dear Ms. Wang:

1 blank line

Re: Catalog request

1 blank line

Thank you for your letter requesting the latest edition of our catalog. Please find one enclosed with this letter.

1 blank line

We have also recently launched an online order platform. You can now buy from us online at www.jamesbrothers.com/shop.

1 blank line

If you would like to receive samples of any of our books, please let us know.

1 blank line

Yours sincerely,

3 blank lines

David James

David James, Director

1 blank line

Enc. (1)

1 blank line

cc: Chris Chen

3 **Modified Block Style**（改良齊頭式）：改良齊頭式結合了**縮排式**與**齊頭式**的要素，其中寄件人地址、日期、結尾敬辭以及簽名等區塊起頭的位置和縮排式一致，然而**正文段落的首行卻不會縮排**，即和齊頭式的正文排列方式相同。改良齊頭式和齊頭式一樣，信件版面排列清楚、整齊，也是商業書信時常採用的格式。

改良齊頭式信件範例

❶ 信件正文從左邊的邊界起頭，不須縮排，和「齊頭式」相同。

James Brothers Publishing
675 Walter Street
New York, NY 10002
U.S.A.

September 15, 2023

1 blank line

Mary Wang
Waiyu Education Group
12F, No. 42, Sec. 2, Jinshan S. Rd,
Da'an Dist, Taipei City 10603
Taiwan (R.O.C.)

❷ 寄件人地址、日期、結尾敬辭和簽名等部分，需要縮排至頁面中線稍右的地方起頭，和「縮排式」相同。

1 blank line

Ref. 091222

1 blank line

Dear Ms. Wang:

1 blank line

Re: Catalog request

1 blank line

Thank you for your letter requesting the latest edition of our catalog. Please find one enclosed with this letter.

1 blank line

We have also recently launched an online order platform. You can now buy from us online at www.jamesbrothers.com/shop.

1 blank line

If you would like to receive samples of any of our books, please let us know.

1 blank line

Yours sincerely,

David James

3 blank line

David James, Director

1 blank line

Enc. (1)

1 blank line

cc: Chris Chen

1. Label the parts of the following letter with the terms provided in the boxes below.

signature   date   receiver's address   closing line

reference number   subject line   body   sender's address   greeting

Pet Paradise
2 Roosevelt St.
Bronx, NY 10462
U.S.A.

❶ ....

September 14, 2023

❷ ....

Haru Tanaka
Sales Manager
Nippon Kitty Dinner Co.
270-1212, Horikiri
Katsushika-ku
Tokyo, Japan

❸ ....

Ref. 091422

❹ ....

Dear Mr. Tanaka:

❺ ....

Catalog request

❻ ....

I am interested in stocking some of your cat food products in our New York stores. Would it be possible for you to send me a catalogue of your current product list?

❼ ....

Thank you for your help.

Yours sincerely,

❽ ....

Leah Conti

❾ ....

Leah Conti
Purchase Manager, Pet Paradise

Lesson 4

商業書信的寫作原則
Principles of Writing Business Letters

關鍵字 Key Words

The Eight Cs 「8C」原則

✔️

❌

1	**clear** [klɪr] (a.) 清楚明確的	← - - - →	**complex** [ˋkɑmplɛks] (a.) 複雜的
2	**concise** [kənˋsaɪs] (a.) 言簡意賅的	← - - - →	**repetitive** [rɪˋpɛtətɪv] (a.) 重複的
3	**correct** [kəˋrɛkt] (a.) 正確無誤的	← - - - →	**incorrect** [͵ɪnkəˋrɛkt] (a.) 不正確的
4	**courteous** [ˋkɝtɪəs] (a.) 客氣有禮的	← - - - →	**rude** [rud] (a.) 無禮的
5	**considerate** [kənˋsɪdərɪt] (a.) 體貼周到的	← - - - →	**inconsiderate** [͵ɪnkənˋsɪdərət] (a.) 不體貼的
6	**concrete** [kɑnˋkrit] / [ˋkɑnkrit] (a.) 言之有物的	← - - - →	**abstract** [ˋæbstrækt] (a.) 抽象的
7	**complete** [kəmˋplit] (a.) 詳實完整的	← - - - →	**incomplete** [͵ɪnkəmˋplit] (a.) 不完整的
8	**cohesive** [koˋhisɪv] (a.) 流暢連貫的	← - - - →	**fragmented** [ˋfrægməntɪd] (a.) 破碎凌亂的

1 The Eight Cs（「8C」原則）

　　第一次寫商業信函時，不免會覺得這項任務相當具挑戰性，因為許多地方都有可能會出錯，但是只要遵守幾項基本寫作原則，就能確保對方可以讀懂信中希望傳達的訊息，也能夠獲得慎重回覆處理。

　　每封商業信函都應務求能**有效達成寫信目的（purpose）**，並使字裡行間的**語氣恰當得體**，同時展現出**對於讀信者的尊重**。為了達成上述目標，寫信時需掌握商業寫作的「**8C**」原則。「8C」原則分別為以下幾點，請在寫作時格外留意：

「8C」原則	
1 清楚明確 Clear	5 體貼周到 Considerate
2 言簡意賅 Concise	6 言之有物 Concrete
3 正確無誤 Correct	7 詳實完整 Complete
4 客氣有禮 Courteous	8 流暢連貫 Cohesive

1 **Clear**（清楚明確）：清楚易懂（clarity）是商業寫作中非常重要的原則。信中每一句話，都應該寫得讓讀者能一看便懂。話雖如此，一封信想要寫得清楚明白，並不是那麼容易，因為**有許多因素會導致信件的語意模糊不清**，例如句子太長、句型太過複雜，或者由於寫信者思緒跳躍，使得內容前後邏輯不通。有時，信中充斥過多**專業術語（jargon）**，或是讀信者不了解事情的來龍去脈，抑或信中用字具有多重字義等，都可能造成信件晦澀難懂。

> **為確保對方能讀懂信件內容，動筆時得做到以下幾點：**
>
> ❶ 簡要說明事情相關的**前因後果（context）**。
>
> ❷ 若使用**首字母縮寫詞（acronym）**，必須解釋清楚。
>
> ❸ 使用**淺顯易懂（plain）的英文**表達，並盡量避免專業術語。
>
> ❹ 運用**項目符號或清單（bullet points or lists）**，條列出重要資訊。
>
> ❺ 句子**簡短直接**，不拐彎抹角。
>
> ❻ 將龐大、複雜的概念想法，細分成一個個**簡短、清楚的小重點**。

請參考以下範例說明：

❶ 提供信件主題相關的背景資訊。

❷ 提及首字母縮寫詞時則需有說明。

❸ 文句淺顯易懂並
❹ 使用項目符號的清單列出重點資訊。

❺❻ 句型簡潔、清楚，每句表達簡短清楚的重點概念。

❶ The conference will take place in the ❷ Midtown Chamber of Commerce (MCOC) on May 5, at 10 a.m. ❸ The purpose of the conference is to help local businesses thrive. Topics covered will include:
· How to build a strong local business.
· How to make the most of your business network.
· The Middtown economy.
· What MCOC can do for you.
❹

❺❻ We hope you can attend. If so, please let us know using the attached form.

2 **Concise**（言簡意賅）：商務人士通常日理萬機，每天的來信眾多，處理每封信的時間卻非常有限，因此切勿把一切跟主題有關的內容，全都不假思索地塞進信裡。要是信函過於冗長，對方得費心抽絲剝繭，梳理出（sort out）重要相關資訊，勢必很快就會心生厭煩。然而，信函也需講求清楚明確，所以**不可簡潔過度**，**疏漏掉重要資訊**。正確做法是**把資訊分成數小塊**，讓讀者可以一次掌握一個主題。做法如下：

❶ 把多餘的**冗詞贅字去掉**（trim），如：

- 用 **costs**（花費）→ 代替 **costs the sum of**（花費……金額）
- 用 **complete details**（完整的細節）
  → 代替 **full and complete details**（完整全面的細節）

❷ 避免 **I think**（我認為）或 **I feel**（我覺得）等**填充詞**（filler），這類用語占了空間，卻無法提供任何重要資訊。

> **商業書信簡潔扼要的寫作要點：**
> ❶ 開門見山，**迅速切入正題**。
> ❷ 僅保留**重要資訊**。
> ❸ 刪去**冗詞贅字**。
> ❹ 同一件事說一次即可，**避免重複**。

❶ 信件開頭直接切入重點。

❷ 僅保留重要的相關細節資訊。

❸ 須刪減未提供新資訊的冗句。

❹ 非必要的形容詞、副詞或冗長片語可適時刪去。

> Dear Mr. Smith:
>
> ❶ I am writing to report a problem with your last shipment of smart TVs (product order 24EX6).
>
> ❷ Several of the TVs were damaged and did not turn on when tested several times. ❸ ~~We tried several times to turn them on but they remained broken.~~
> ❹ I ~~really~~ hope we can ~~work together to~~ find a quick ~~and simple~~ solution to this ~~terrible~~ problem.

3 **Correct**（正確無誤）：務必檢查信裡資訊是否正確，包括**具體的數字**（如**訂單編號**〔order number〕）以及所有其他細節。信中提供的資訊若有誤，可能會衍生嚴重後果，而要是信函錯誤屢屢發生，恐使雙方商業關係生變或破裂。檢查**文法與拼字**也很重要：商業信函若出現此類低級錯誤，**會顯得寫信者粗心大意**（careless），使得對方失去信任，並可能進而損害彼此的業務往來，因此在寄出信件前，一定要反覆檢查。

> **確保信件內容正確無誤的要點：**
>
> ❶ 檢查信中所有名稱、日期、事實與數字是否無誤。
>
> ❷ 檢查**拼字**及**文法**正確。
>
> ❸ 檢查行文**語氣**（tone）是否恰當。
>
> ❹ 檢查書信**格式**（formatting）正確。
>
> ❺ 檢查信紙是否有信頭。如果沒有，則須**手動輸入**寄件人地址。
>
> ❻ 檢查**信封上的寄件人地址**是否正確，**信封**是否乾淨整潔。

4 **Courteous**（客氣有禮）：**禮貌**（courtesy）不只體現在使用 please（請）、thank you（謝謝）等話語，更要確保信件語氣始終**保持客氣有禮**，並且積極**站在讀信者的立場思考**。客氣十足的商業信函通常會獲得同樣客氣的回信，禮尚往來下，友好關係得以建立，業務進展也會更加順利。

即使需在信裡提出**客訴**（complaint），或拒絕對方**提議**（offer），語氣仍須保持禮節。在信中出言不遜不僅有損企業形象，還可能致使客戶流失。就算是負面情緒，也可以表達得婉轉有禮。

> **商業信件裡展現禮貌的要點：**
>
> ❶ **盡快回覆**對方來信。
>
> ❷ **誠實回應**對方的問題。
>
> ❸ 提供對方需要的一切**資訊**。
>
> ❹ 使用正確**稱謂**（title）來稱呼對方，例如 Dr.（博士）或 Ms.（女士）。
>
> ❺ 信尾要使用**結尾敬辭**（closing line）。
>
> ❻ 不使用**指責式的**（accusing）語氣。
>
> ❼ 不使用**侮辱性質**（insulting）的語言。
>
> ❽ 有事請求對方協助或幫忙時，使用**問句取代祈使句或直述句**。

❶ 以下為**符合禮貌**的寫作例句：

誠實回答目前未能滿足對方需求，並交代後續處理方式。

> I'm sorry but I don't have the details you requested at the moment. However, I will let you know as soon as I do. 很抱歉，我目前不清楚您所要求的細節資訊。然而，我了解之後會盡快向您告知。

清楚說明對方需要的所有資訊。

> To access this discount, please type the code 15OFFAYC into the "Discount Code" box on our online order form. 若欲取得折扣，請在線上訂購表單的「折扣碼」欄位中輸入代碼「15OFFAYC」。

寫作者透過問句傳達請求，聽起來較為客氣、有禮貌。

> Would you be willing to have an interview with me so that we can discuss my fit for the position? 您是否願意與我進行面談，以討論我與該職位的契合度？

❷ 以下為**有失禮貌的寫作方式，須避免出現**：

在標有底線的文字中，寫作者提出不必要的指責並侮辱對方，無益於溝通，寫作中應加以刪除。

> My last order arrived late <u>and it is clearly your fault. You are the worst person I have ever done business with</u> . . . 我的訂單貨物延遲抵達，<u>這顯然是你的錯。你是我往來過最糟的人員</u>……

使用祈使句直接表達請求，可能會讓讀者有唐突的感受，為較不禮貌的寫法。

> Do have an interview with me so that we can discuss my fit for the position. 務必要與我進行面談，以討論我與該職位的契合度。

⑤　Considerate（體貼周到）：得體的商業信件會將重點放在**讀信者的需求**，設身處地體諒對方**的處境，並提供協助**。商業信件的目的是要促成讀信者以積極態度回應，因此不可只關注自家公司需求，而關閉對話管道。

欲在商業信函裡展現體貼周到，寫作要點如下：

❶ 考量讀信者**身分**，他們的**角色**（role）、**背景**（background）等。

❷ 清楚讓對方知道你有考慮到他們的需求。

❸ 使用以 **you**（您）為中心的句子。

❹ 感謝對方撥冗協助。

❺ 提供對方採取行動所需的一切細節資訊。

❻ 以對方可以使用的形式提供資訊。

❼ 如期提供這些資訊給對方。

I understand that ❶ as sales manager ❷ ❸ you are very busy at this time of year, so ❹ thank you for taking the time out of your busy schedule to deal with this. ❺ ❻ I have enclosed a list of the orders we have yet to receive, along with their PO numbers, and the relevant dates . . .

6　**Concrete**（言之有物）：提供給讀信者的資訊必須**具體明確**（solid），而非**含糊其詞**（vague），並避免使用**抽象**（abstract）詞彙或專業術語，而是提供實際情況、數字給對方。具體作法包括：

❶　**日期精確**：若提及日期，讀信者會需要得知精確的日子，而不是模糊的應付：

❌ 不要說	✅ 要說
I will send the money **sometime next week**. 我將於下週付款。	I will send the money **on May 23**. 我將於5月23日付款。

❷　**避免籠統的（fuzzy）語詞**：使用例如 problem/issue（問題）、situation（狀況）等**概括式的單字**時，需避免單獨出現而無具體說明，以免讀者不清楚所指涉的情事為何，或者可以盡量**避免這類籠統用字**，盡量具體描述討論主題。

❌ 不要說	✅ 要說
I am writing to apologize for the **situation** we discussed on the phone. 本次來信，意在為我們之前在電話討論的情況致歉。	I am writing to apologize for the **late order of smart TVs** that we discussed on the phone. 本次來信，意在為我們之前在電話討論過的智慧型電視訂單延遲致歉。

確保信件言之有物的寫作要點：

❶ 提供具體**事實**、**數字**與**日期**等。

❷ 如果無法提供這些資訊，需**清楚說明原因**。

❸ 讓閱信者知道你**何時會**提供上述資訊。

❹ 避免使用含糊的語詞，而要使用**具體的**（specific）語句。

❺ 使用**強而有力、明確的動詞**來描述動作。

❶ 提供確切的數字和時間、日期資訊，並
❺ 使用直接且明確的動詞（如 order）。

❷對於尚未能告知的資訊（如 shipping costs 運費），提供無法告知的理由。

❸❹以具體明確的語句，說明何時可以告知上述未知資訊。

❺
❶ I ordered two hundred pairs of leather shoes (item # 5646) on March 4. ❷ I am still waiting for a reply from our delivery partners on the shipping costs for these items. ❹ I hope to have these details by the end of next week.

7 **Complete**（詳實完整）：商業信函裡應提供足夠資訊，以利讀信者了解事情的**來龍去脈**（**the full picture**）。假如對方無法掌握整體情況，便無法正確回應，因此寫信時要仔細考量對方讀信時可能會有的問題，也要將對方已知、未知的資訊都考慮進去。

專業、內容完整的商業信件可以補全讀信者資訊上的**缺口**（**gap**）。若信件內容不完整，時間就會浪費在信件往返、確認所需資訊上，徒增雙方困擾。

確保信件內容完整的寫作要點：
❶ 回答對方**先前提問**的問題。
❷ 考量對方**已知的**資訊。
❸ 考量對方**還需要知道**什麼資訊。
❹ 提供對方**採取行動**所需的細節資訊。

❶ 回答對方先前的提問（職位相關資訊）。

❷ ❸ 判斷對方已知資訊，推想對方可能還會想知道哪些資訊。

❹ 提供對方後續動作所需要的細節資訊。

Thank you for your interest in the position of office manager. ❶ In answer to your questions: the position will begin on July 4, and the salary range is between NT$30,000 and NT$40,000 based on experience. ❷ ❸ For your reference, I have also enclosed a list of the job's key responsibilities. To apply for the position, ❹ please send us a resume along with two letters of reference.

8 **Cohesive**（流暢連貫）：**連貫**（**cohesion**）代表各個部分銜接得恰到好處，渾然一體。有連貫性的信函中，各個段落會排列得**條理分明、邏輯清楚**（**clearly and logically**），而且整體行文流暢，資訊皆**按明確的順序排列**（例如**以最重要程度安排**），使閱信者可以**循序漸進**（**go step by step**）從頭讀到尾，而不會有任何閱讀障礙。

若信件篇幅較長，則可使用**小標題**（**header**），來讓結構更加清晰，並有助於讀信者迅速跳到相關資訊來閱讀。

具連貫性信件的寫作要點：

❶ 考量行文的**起承轉合**（flow）；信件的開頭、正文以及結尾都需明確清楚。

❷ 考量訊息的**結構**（structure），要確保各個部分**編排井然有序**（in the right order）。

❸ 確保信中的**小標題**可以輕易辨識。

❹ 確保小標題與下方內容**對應正確**。

❺ 考量對方能否**迅速找到**想要的資訊。

❶ ❷ Thank you for inquiring about our shipping methods and rates.

❸ ❹ ❺ Our shipping methods
❶ ❷ We use Flymail International Express services for all international orders (delivery time: 5 business days). Customers can choose a priority option (2 business days) for an extra fee.

❸ ❹ ❺ Shipping rates
Shipping rates depend on the size and weight of each order. Please see the chart enclosed for more details.

❶ ❷ I hope this information has answered your questions. If you have any more questions, please feel free to contact me directly on (908) 978-4567.

❶ ❷ 清楚的開頭、中間段落和結尾。資訊鋪陳具有邏輯性。

❸ ❹ ❺ 使用方便辨識的小標題，並且和下方資訊正確對應，有助讀信者快速掌握想要的資訊。

小結 Summary

❶ 商業書信需著重在如何達到寫信的目的、字裡行間的語氣保持恰當得體，並且展現對讀信者的尊重。

❷ 為了達到上述目標，寫信者應遵循商業寫作的「8C」原則。

❸ **Clear**（清楚明確）、**Concise**（言簡意賅）且 **Cohensive**（流暢連貫）的商業信函，能確保信件受到對方理解且鄭重以對。

❹ **Courteous**（客氣有禮）、**Considerate**（體貼周到）且 **Concrete**（言之有物）的信函會給人留下好印象、建立彼此信任感並促使對方積極處理回應。

❺ 需確保信件內容 **Complete**（詳實完整）、**Correct**（正確無誤），這將有助業務進展更順利。

Lesson 5 商業書信寫作技巧 Tips for Writing Business Letters

關鍵字 Key Words

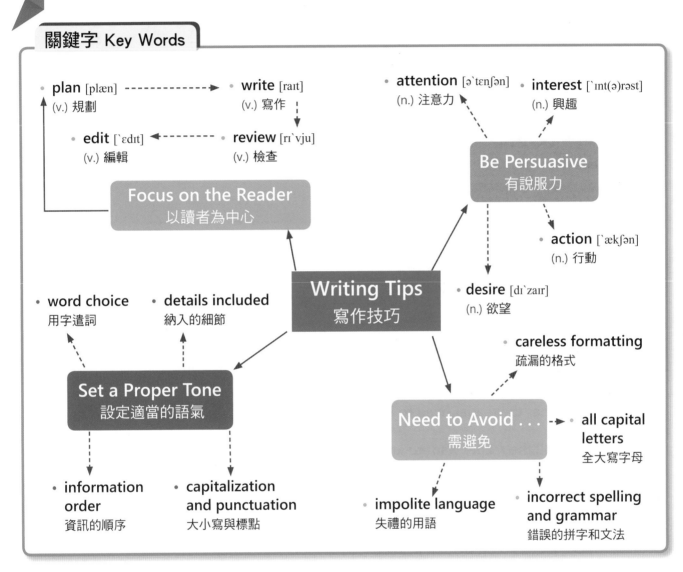

上一課介紹了商業書信寫作的「8C」原則，這些原則有助我們撰寫各類商業信函時，能有效達成理想目標。除了時時牢記這八大原則外，接下來本課將介紹如何組織商業書信，並提供保持行文恰當、語氣合宜的技巧。

1 Focus on the Reader（以讀者為中心）

最重要的寫作技巧，就是要**以讀者（閱信者）為中心（reader-focused）**、從讀者的立場著手寫信。這個觀念在 Lesson 1 時已有初步提及，本課將會進一步探討其內涵和實作方式。

「以讀者為中心」來寫作，是考量到商業書信的讀者都是忙碌的商業人士，他們會根據信件來推進工作和業務。如果信件內容盡量做到以讀者為中心，就能很有效地促使讀者採取我們所期望的行動，例如決定下單、提供優惠，甚至是達成交易等。

「以讀者為中心」的理念，在下列撰寫商業書信的三大階段裡，都需時時放在心上：

Step 1 內容規劃（planning）

Step 2 信件撰寫（writing）

Step 3 檢查與編輯（reviewing and editing）

現在，就讓我們依序詳細討論每個階段要注意的要點。

1 **Planning**（**內容規劃**）：動筆寫信前，不妨先透過一連串的問題，來決定寫作方向。回答完這些問題後，寫信者可以更了解讀者是誰、他們的需求為何、又會想知道何種資訊。這將幫助你決定在信件中要寫入（或者省略）哪些內容，還能確保在寫信過程能**聚焦重點**（**keeps its focus**）。

開始寫信前，可以試著回答下列基本問題：

❶ Who will read the letter?	這封信的讀者是誰？
❷ What is the reader's role in the company?	讀者在公司是什麼職位？
❸ What does the reader know about the subject?	讀者對信件主題了解多少？
❹ What does the reader need to know?	讀者需要知道什麼資訊？
❺ What will the reader want to know?	讀者會想要知道什麼資訊？
❻ Will the reader be expecting the letter?	讀者是否預期讀到這封信？
❼ What will the reader do with the letter (make a decision based on it, keep it as a record, etc.)?	讀者會怎麼運用這封信（例如依此做出某項決定、留作紀錄等）？
❽ How can you give the reader information they want and need quickly?	如何將讀者想要、所需的資訊迅速傳達給他們？

以上這些問題僅提供建議參考，但每封商業信件的情境不盡相同，所以在設想與讀者有關的問題時，可能需要更具體一些。寫信前可以仔細思考：讀者閱讀信件時，會有什麼樣的疑慮？然後**盡量完整地回答這些問題**。萬事起頭難，但透過預想這些問題，能讓撰寫商業信函時有踏實的第一步。

2 **Writing**（信件撰寫）：回答完自行設想的關鍵問題後，接著就開始實際寫信了。想想需要納入信中的詳細資訊有哪些，其中對讀者最有用的資訊又是哪些，然後按其優先順序列舉出來。以下幾個方法有助於做到這點：

❶ Start With the Purpose（開宗明義說明目的）

讀者會想要盡快知道來信的重點，所以在信件的**第一段**，就要直截了當地告訴讀者**信件的目的和主旨**。越早切入正題，讀者就能越早掌握所需資訊並進入狀況，也更能輕鬆理解信件後幾段提供的各項細節。

❷ Use Headers to Highlight Main Points（使用標題顯現段落重點）

標題（header）的功能是提綱挈領，向讀者呈現**信件的「骨架」**（skeleton）。並非每封商業書信都會安排小標題，篇幅偏短的信函中尤其少用，但如果書信篇幅很長且資訊眾多，標題便能有效輔助讀者抓住重點。讀者一般很難從冗長的書信中，精準查找所需的詳情，因此若能借助標題，將長篇大論切割成各個小段落，讀者就能大致掃讀過信件後，根據標題切入，找到需要的資訊。

❸ Use Bulleted and Numbered Lists to Present Details
（使用項目符號與數字編號列出細節資訊）

項目符號（bullet point）與**編號式清單**（numbered list）跟標題一樣，並不是每封商業書信都會用到。然而，條列清單有助讀者一目了然看出重點或細節資訊。假如你有幾項重要的構想要報告或討論，使用**清單條列**出來會是不錯的做法，例如欲呈現以下內容時，就很適合列點說明：

1. Important decisions made at a meeting（會議中的各項重要決定）
2. Important upgrades to a product（產品的數項重要更新）
3. Problems with a project, or solutions to a problem
   （針對企劃的各項問題和問題的解決方案）

若是欲呈現的資訊**有特定順序**，則可用**數字編號**（numerical symbol）來協助條列。

有關如何運用上述寫作技巧，請見下頁範例信及說明。

New Message

From: jeanie@fineprintsmasden.com

To: calvin.james@psconsulting.com

Subject: New Local Printing Service Now Open for Business

❶ 第一句就開宗明義說明信件目的。

Dear Mr. James,

❶ I am writing to inform you about our new printing business—Marsden Fine Prints—that has recently opened in the area. I believe our services will be of use to you.

❷ 使用多個小標題，幫助讀者迅速抓住重點。

What we do ❷

We can provide you with all your printing needs, including:

- booklets
- business cards
- banners
- manuals
- posters
- T-shirts
- flyers
- signs

❸ 使用項目符號清單將細項列出，有助讀者一目了然。

Our services are reasonably priced, high-quality, and fast. In most cases we can offer same-day printing. Also, we pride ourselves on our excellent customer service. We will always do our upmost to fulfil your printing needs.

Our prices

A full list of our prices can be found on our website: www.fineprintsmarsden.com/prices.

Special offer for local business owners

For the next six months we are offering a 20% discount to all local business owners who use our services. Come and visit us in-store and bring along your business card. We will add you to our list of special customers.

Where to find us

Our store is located at 24 Oak Road, Marsden. (map)

We look forward to meeting you and providing you with our high-quality printing service.

Kind regards,

Jeanie Bond, Manager

③ Reviewing and Editing（檢查與編輯）：信件寫作完成後，請多次檢查，確保內容正確無誤。若能確實執行檢查與編輯，信中各項錯誤可望無所遁形。

檢查時可參考下列步驟進行：

❶ 確認文中**姓名**、**事／物名稱**與**數字**皆正確無誤。

❷ 檢視信件**架構**（structure）是否合理、所有**重要資訊**是否容易查找。

❸ 回顧寫作最初**自行設定的問題**，確認是否都有涵蓋到。

❹ 檢視書信**格式**是否正確、**語氣**是否適當。

❺ 查看有無**拼字**、**文法**錯誤。

❻ 若時間許可，可以將信件暫時擱置，一段時間後再重新檢查。

以上有些問題看似繁瑣，卻對信件給人的觀感影響甚大。暫且不論內容，如果信中格式、拼字或文法等錯誤連篇，整體就會顯得馬虎草率、粗心大意。商業書信通常要求**專業**、**嚴謹的敬業態度**，所以透過檢查和編輯來避免錯誤就是達到此目標的第一步。

2 **Set a Proper Tone**（設定適當的語氣）

語氣（tone）會決定文章**帶給讀者的感受**，同時反映出寫信者**對讀者的態度**。寫信的語氣可以正式拘謹、也可以隨興輕鬆；可以親切友善，也可以就事論事；可以幽默風趣，也可以莊重嚴肅。作者要運用何種語氣表達，取決於**書信的主題**以及**讀者對象**，不過一般來說，嚴肅、專業的語氣幾乎適用於各類型商業信函。

會影響書信「語氣」的各項因素如下：

① **Word Choice**（遣詞用字）：下列兩個句子說明了相同的資訊，用字遣詞卻不同。

❶ 使用簡單用字和句型直接說明重點。

❶ Today's activities have been canceled because of the storm. 今日活動因暴風雨而取消。

❷ 用語繞口艱澀，句子長度拖長，使讀者不易掌握重點訊息。

❷ Due to unforeseen weather conditions, the previously scheduled activities are hereby postponed until a later date.
鑒於預料之外的天候狀況，原定活動特此順延至他日舉行。

兩個句子的語氣都很正式，但是正式的程度有明顯高低。第一句的用字直截了當，第二句則使用了繞口、艱澀的語詞，其實是正式到矯枉過正了，畢竟句子的目的只是為了提供有用的資訊。寫作商業信函並不一定必須使用過於一板一眼的語氣。對讀者來說，太過正經八百和太過輕浮隨興的語氣，同樣都很不可取。

2　**Details Included**（納入的細節）：若想讓書信維持較**專業、就事論事**的語氣，信中需以**客觀的事實陳述**為主，避免寫入無關信件主旨和目的的細節，這也是為了配合 Lesson 4 談到「8C 原則」當中的 concise（言簡意賅）。若寫入**個人主觀感受或意見**，有時可能會使語氣變得**較為親切**，但有時可能會造成**過於隨興**（casual）。例如，請見以下兩段客訴信的摘錄；寫作主旨皆是投訴住房狀況，但納入的細節有所差異：

❌ ❶ 寫作者納入與**信件主旨無關的細節**（如時差問題、花紋聯想），未充分考量讀者需求，語氣顯得**散漫、隨便**。

> ❶ I had bad jet lag and couldn't sleep for three nights in a row. What's more, the floral pattern on the bed sheets reminded me of my grandmother's curtains back home.
> 當時我嚴重時差，連續三晚都睡不著覺。而且床單上的花紋圖案，使我想起我家裡奶奶的窗簾。

✅ ❷ 寫作者**提供的細節緊扣住房問題**，包括床鋪過硬、使人身體痠痛等，清楚讓讀者知道問題所在，**語氣專業、就事論事**。

> ❷ I was disappointed with the poor room situation. The bed was extremely hard, making it difficult to sleep comfortably. I woke up with aches and pains, and it negatively affected my stay at your hotel.
> 我對於房況不佳的狀況非常失望。床鋪十分硬，讓人很難舒適安睡。我起床後就各處痠痛，使我在貴飯店的住房經驗大打折扣。

可以注意到，第二段只陳述了必要事實，所以語氣比第一段還要客觀、直白。

3　**Information Order**（資訊的排列順序）：若信件是**以最重要的資訊開頭**，會使信件語氣顯得**直接**、不拐彎抹角，也更具溝通效率。若是以較不相關的資訊開頭，而**將重要資訊置於後方**，那麼信件讀起來會較不易看到重點，也會顯示出寫信者**較無考慮到讀者讀信時的需求**，這是**違反「8C 原則」中的 considerate**（體貼周到）。

❌ ❶ 以讀信者未要求得知的無關資訊開頭，❷ 卻把讀信者提出的問題放到最後才回答，未能分辨事項輕重緩急，使語氣顯得散漫、失去專業感。

> Dear Mr. Smith:
>
> ❶ I would like to inform you that we are currently offering free shipping for any orders over $2,000 up until the end of September. Please let me know if you would like to take advantage of this opportunity.
>
> ❷ Also, in answer to your previous question, your recent order should arrive by the 17th of this month. The tracking number is 2435 3456 3245.

✅ **❶** 開門見山切入主旨，迅速回應讀信者先前提出的問題，**❷** 之後才轉而提到較不緊急的主題，顯示寫作者具備判斷力，使信件語氣顯得直接、專業。

Dear Mr. Smith:

❶ In answer to your question, your order should arrive by the 17th of this month. Should you want to track the order on the shipper's website, the tracking number is 2435 3456 3245.

❷ Also, we are currently offering free shipping for any orders over $2,000 up until the end of September. Please let me know if you would like to take advantage of this opportunity.

4　**Capitalization and Punctuation**（大小寫和標點符號）：若使用**全大寫字母**（**all capital letters**）來書寫（例如：PLEASE FILL OUT THIS FORM〔請填寫表格〕），會讓人覺得是在**對讀信者大聲喝斥**，因此信件語氣會顯得火爆急躁。同理，使用**驚嘆號（!）**的句子，語氣也會顯得激動或不耐煩，一樣不太適用於正式商業書信。

❌ **❶** 使用全大寫行文 **❷** 並使用驚嘆號，使語氣變得像在吼叫且不耐煩。

❶ FILL OUT THIS FORM CORRECTLY **❷**! DO NOT USE COLORED PENS OR PENCILS. DO NOT WRITE OUTSIDE THE INDICATED BOXES. DO NOT TEAR OR REMOVE PAGES FROM THE FORM.

✅ 大小寫正常，未使用驚嘆號，語氣較中立和緩。

Fill out this form correctly. Do not use colored pens or pencils. Do not write outside the indicated boxes. Do not tear or remove pages from the form.

接著讓我們從下一頁的範例中，討論以上各項重點如何應用在實際的商業書寫作上。

45

Discussion: Is Tina's Letter Good or Bad?

Titan Safety Gear
2600 S Hoover St, Los Angeles, CA 90007, USA

May 12, 2023

Ryan Sweet
Splash! Rafting Tours
23 Dunkeld Rd
Aberfeldy
PH15 2AQ
UK

Dear Mr. Sweat:

Re: <u>Discount request</u>

Thanks you for your letter. We work hard to give everyone the best prices. As a result, we just had our best year ever.

After speaking with our kind sales director, I can offer you 15% off your next order!!!

To claim this, I invite you to UTILIZE THE SPECIAL ORDER FORM ENCLOSED.

Also, the discount only applies if you order 20 or more items.

Yours truly,

Tina Nowak

Tina Nowak, Salesperson

這封信件是新人業務員 Tina Nowak 針對客戶詢問所寫的回覆信。你覺得這封信寫得如何？請根據本課 43-45 頁的原則，討論以下問題：

❶ **Word Choice**（遣詞用字）：仔細閱讀信中的用字，足夠通順好懂嗎？有沒有哪些太繞口的字可以用更直白的說法取代？

❷ **Details Included**（納入的細節）：信中納入的資訊對讀者來說都是必要、重要的嗎？是否有資訊可以省略？又有哪些資訊應該納入、卻沒有寫進去？

❸ **Information Order**（資訊的排列順序）：信中各段資訊的順序安排合理嗎？你覺得 Tina 的段落安排有什麼考量？如果是你，安排方式會和 Tina 一樣嗎？

❹ **Capitalization and Punctuation**（大小寫和標點符號）：信中大小寫和標點符號的使用合適嗎？你會給 Tina 什麼建議？

問題討論完畢後，請自行或和同學一起對這封信進行 p. 43 提到的 **reviewing and editing**（檢查與編輯）動作。

3 **Write Persuasively: AIDA**（增進寫作說服力：AIDA 法則）

　　有時，寫信的目的是為了**說服（persuade）讀者採取行動**，例如推銷信跟求職信就是屬於這類信函。我們可以使用**「AIDA 法則」**，幫助寫出具有說服力的商業信函。AIDA 是 **Attention（注意力）**、**Interest（興趣）**、**Desire（欲望）**、**Action（行動）**四個要素的字首縮寫。以下將詳細討論每個要素的內容：

1　**Attention**（注意力）：說服他人的第一步，就是要引起對方注意力。要做到這一點，可以透過**強而有力的開場白（opening statement）**，或者**針對讀者需求而設計的問題**，促使讀者關心、在乎這封信件，並想繼續讀下去。

　　「格式」（formatting）也是引起讀者注意力的有效方式：標題用**粗體（boldface）**表示，輔以**項目符號條列（bulleted list）**，就可讓人清楚了解信中資訊的重要性，並更感到切身相關。

　　以下為吸引讀者注意的幾種方法範例：

❶ 透過強而有力的開場白，讓讀者受到吸引，願意往下閱讀。

❶ Save Up to 20% on Delivery Today!
今天就享運費最高 8 折優惠吧！

❷ 針對讀者需求做出提問，抓住讀者的注意。

❷ Do you want to say goodbye to your back pain?
想要和你的背痛問題說再見嗎？

❸ 改變文字格式，以醒目的粗體和顏色呈現標題，讓讀者眼睛一亮。

❸ **Limited Time Special Offers**
限時特別優惠

2 **Interest**（興趣）：引起讀者的注意後，就要盡快激發讀者興趣，為此必須用有效率的方式提供相關資訊，而前文提到的**項目符號清單**就是個好方法。此外，也可以用**「設問法」**（questioning）來引起讀者興趣：

❶ 以設問法引起興趣

以「設問法」讓讀者思考是否有相關需求，有助引發讀者閱讀興趣。

> **❶** Do you know that many delivery services charge their customers too much?
> 您知道許多快遞公司的收費都太高了嗎？
>
> **❷** How often do you get back pain?
> 您的背痛多常發作一次？
>
> **❸** Isn't it about time to upgrade your computer system?
> 是時候升級您的電腦系統了吧？

❷ 提供問題答案

請確保提出的問題與己方提供的產品或服務有相關，然後**給出問題的答案**。要提供事實資訊，但不要一下子給太多，語氣也要輕鬆愉悅，以免導致讀者面對大量、枯燥的文字，覺得意興闌珊、不想閱讀。

以下為針對上列三點提問的回答範例：

針對前文向讀者提出的問題，後方要以具體、語氣輕鬆的方式給出問題的答覆。回答時也可**給出確切的事實或數據**，以增加可信度。

> **❶** Our research shows that delivery companies often charge 10% to 20% above the market rate.
> 我們的研究顯示，快遞業者時常收取高於市場行情一至二成的費用。
>
> **❷** Back pain is a common problem, but it can be easily fixed with the right tools.
> 背痛是常見的毛病，但只要用對工具，就能輕易治好。
>
> **❸** Most computer systems need upgrading after five years.
> 多數電腦系統經過五年後會需要更新。

3　**Desire**（欲望）：寫作時請著重你所提供的產品或服務，將**會給讀者帶來何種好處**，這樣讀者心中自然就會對其產生欲望。**說故事**（story）給讀者聽是很好的方式，講述你的產品或服務曾經對他人或類似企業創造何種效益，但須切記：**敘述要簡短、且與讀者切身相關**。接著，請說明**你如何能以同樣方式幫助對方**，一定要寫得清楚明瞭，也要避免使用晦澀難懂的專業術語。

❶ 使用直白簡單的用語描述自家服務，避免用難懂的專業術語來過度包裝。

❶ Saving money on delivery means you can invest more money in marketing your products.
節省運費意味貴公司可以將更多資金投資在產品的行銷。

❷ 表示其他消費者對自家產品相當滿意，暗示產品也能對讀信者產生效益。

❷ Nine out of ten doctors recommend our back massage machine.
九成的醫師都推薦我們的背部按摩機。

❸ 說故事給讀者聽，告知提供的服務已對他人**提供具體成效**。

❸ This system was recently installed at ABC Company, and their sales increased by 15% in just one month.
ABC公司最近安裝這套系統，一個月內銷售量就增加了15%。

4　**Action**（行動）：最後，就是說服讀者**付諸行動**（take action）。這個行動可能是購買你的產品、聯繫你去面試、造訪你的網站等。想要達到這個目的，信中就要給予讀者**明確的指示**。亦可**營造急迫感**（urgency），告知讀者若未採取行動將有何損失。

❶ 給予讀者明確指示，方便讀者直接進行下一步動作。

❶ Contact me for a quote at (123) 456-7899.
請致電 (123) 456-7899 與我聯繫並索取報價。

❷ 營造迫切感，向讀者說明若不盡速行動可能會有何種損失（存貨將賣完）。

❷ These models will soon be out of stock. So it's best to order as soon as possible.
這款存貨即將售罄，欲購從速，以免向隅。

❸ 給予明確行動指示，並告知行動「**免費**」，讓讀者更願意照做。

❸ Fill in the online form to book a free consultation with one of our system engineers.
填寫線上表單，與我們的系統工程師預約免費諮詢吧。

1 Fill in the blanks in the following business letter using one of the options provided.

Tools 4 U

234 Maiden Ave.
Boston MA 02199
Tel: 617-535-2801

April 12, 2023

Malcolm McFry
Tyson Motor Repair
1405 Christie Way
Boston MA 02110

Dear Mr. McFry:

- I am writing to inform you that your payment for order number 45523 is more than three months late.
- I hope you are doing well since we last spoke at the conference in New York last year.

❶ ....

.... We sent you a reminder on March 12 requesting payment for your order of 10 cordless wrenches. But we have still not heard from you.

If there was a problem with your order, we are happy to discuss this with you. If this is not the case, however, then we must request that you transfer the full amount of $2,234 into our account by April 30. ❷ ....

I have enclosed copies of the original invoice along with the first payment reminder. Please don't hesitate to contact me on 617-535-2801 ext. 2 if you have any questions. I hope this situation can be resolved quickly and professionally.

Yours sincerely,

Raymond Chang

Raymond Chang
Operations Manager, Tools 4 U

- In fact, I think your behavior is REALLY RUDE!!! And I will refer this to our lawyers if you keep being so unprofessional.
- If we do not receive the due payment on time, we will be forced to refer this matter to our lawyers.

Enc. (2)

2 According to the AIDA method, put the sentences below in the correct categories. The first one has been done for you.

> **Topic 1: Italian Ingredients**
> - To request a pack of free samples, call us on 555-345-245.
> - Do you struggle to find authentic Italian ingredients? We stock ingredients straight from Italy at very low prices.
> - Diners will love the taste of our high-quality ingredients, making your restaurant the talk of the town.
> - Bring the Flavors of Italy into Your Restaurant Today!
>
> **Topic 2: Skin Lotion**
> - Our customers consistently rate our products as being more effective than our competitors'.
> - Do you dream of having smoother, softer skin? Our new lotion can make this dream a reality.
> - Get Younger-Looking Skin in Just 4 Weeks!
> - To see a list of our products or place an order, visit our website today!

	1. Italian Ingredients	2. Skin Lotion
Attention	① Bring the Flavors of Italy into Your Restaurant Today!	②
Interest	③	④
Desire	⑤	⑥
Action	⑦	⑧

Lesson **6**　推銷信
Sales Letters

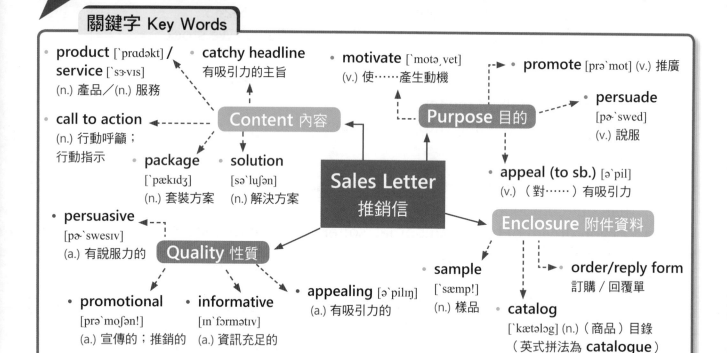

- **product** [`prɑdəkt] /
  service [`sɝvɪs]
  (n.) 產品／(n.) 服務
- **catchy headline**
  有吸引力的主旨
- **motivate** [`motə͵vet]
  (v.) 使……產生動機
- **promote** [prə`mot] (v.) 推廣
- **call to action**
  (n.) 行動呼籲；
  行動指示
- **Content** 內容
- **Purpose** 目的
- **persuade**
  [pɚ`swed]
  (v.) 說服
- **package**
  [`pækɪdʒ]
  (n.) 套裝方案
- **solution**
  [sə`luʃən]
  (n.) 解決方案
- **Sales Letter**
  推銷信
- **appeal (to sb.)** [ə`pil]
  (v.) （對……）有吸引力
- **persuasive**
  [pɚ`swesɪv]
  (a.) 有說服力的
- **Quality** 性質
- **Enclosure** 附件資料
- **sample**
  [`sæmp!]
  (n.) 樣品
- **order/reply form**
  訂購／回覆單
- **promotional**
  [prə`moʃən!]
  (a.) 宣傳的；推銷的
- **informative**
  [ɪn`fɔrmətɪv]
  (a.) 資訊充足的
- **appealing** [ə`pilɪŋ]
  (a.) 有吸引力的
- **catalog**
  [`kætəlɔg] (n.) （商品）目錄
  （英式拼法為 **catalogue**）

1 **What Are Sales Letters?**（推銷信是什麼？）

　　推銷信（sales letter）的目的有很多種，有可能是為了**建立商業關係**，也可能是用來**宣傳公司或推廣（promote）產品**，或者**討論某項服務**或其他**商業機會（opportunity）**，可透過一般郵寄或電子郵件寄發。推銷信有助說服消費者選擇某件商品或服務，內容**比起廣告**（advertisement）來說會更加**個人化（personal）**，也就代表可以更有效地鼓勵讀者採取行動。

2 **How to Write**（如何撰寫推銷信）

　　撰寫推銷信有幾項關鍵要點需要考慮，包括信件的**主旨與標題（headline）**、**目的（purpose）**以及發信**對象（audience）**，另外也應該向對方說明**為什麼應該選擇信中推廣的產品或服務**。

1 **Catchy Headline**（有吸引力的主旨）：撰寫推銷信時，建議**一開始**就透過醒目、有吸引力的**主旨句（subject line）或標題抓住讀者的目光**，以期讀者願意繼續閱讀。若開頭無趣，讀者可能根本不願往下閱讀。

　　推銷信的開頭句應**簡潔有力**，若有提供特殊優惠或吸引人的賣點（selling point），建議開頭就讓讀者知道，使讀者覺得手中的信件**值得再花時間讀下去**。以下為有效的推銷信主旨／標題範例：

> Beautiful Wedding Flowers . . . 30% Off!
> 婚禮用美麗花禮，7折優惠中！
> Professional Business Cards Printed in Minutes,
> Delivered the Next Day
> 專業商務名片速印，隔日可到貨

2 Purpose（目的）：推銷信主要有三種基本目的：

推銷信的目的	推銷信要提供的資訊
❶ 引起對方對產品的興趣	包含**足夠的產品資訊**，引起對方的興趣，促使採取行動。但不提供過多詳細的資訊，以免對方當下就斷定不需要你的產品，或因信太長而不想閱讀。只要留下聯絡資訊，讓顧客跟業務代表聯絡。
❷ 直接銷售產品	提供**產品詳細完整的資訊**，因為這封信就是一個完整的銷售活動，需要跟對方說明怎麼下訂單。
❸ 說服對方造訪商店、網站、商品展場	寫出**所有能夠吸引人的產品資訊**，同時**用詞要有說服力**，但不需要提供訂貨或聯絡資訊。

3 Audience（寫信對象）：成功的推銷信能將每句話說到讀信者的心坎裡，打動（appeal to）對方內心的需求（needs）和願望（wishes）。因此撰寫推銷信時，一定要從讀者的角度著眼，了解對方對於產品或服務可能會產生的疑問，並在信中加以解答。

❶ 推銷信通常不會只單獨寄送給一個人，而是大量發送給很多人，雖是如此，稱呼和信封上也要**直接寫出對方的名字**，讓信件感覺是與讀者直接對話。因此開頭招呼語勿用 **Dear Sir or Madam**（親愛的先生女士），或 **To Whom It May Concern**（敬啟者）這種制式的開場白，容易導致失敗。

❷ 信件資訊應**簡單易讀**，段落應清楚簡短，重要細節則要加以**強調，加上醒目的標題**。

❸ 推銷信須點出讀者**應做出的行動**，清楚寫出明確的「**行動呼籲**」（call to action，即呼籲對方該如何行動的陳述）。

4 **Reason for Customers to Buy**（消費者購買的原因）：推銷信必須清楚讓讀者知道信中推廣的產品能帶來什麼好處，並了解產品或服務的價值所在。高明的推銷信會激發讀者的行動力。

說服讀信者購買商品、使用服務的理由應要充分有力。可於信中適時**補充額外資訊**，例如提供**資料傳單**或**產品目錄（catalog）**，這些資料都有助讀者對該產品或服務更有感覺，也能藉此得到更多細節和有用資訊。

3 **AIDA**（運用 AIDA 原則）

我們在 Lesson 5 介紹過 AIDA 原則，可幫助讓寫作更具有說服力，它也很適合套用到推銷信的撰寫上，其運用原則與方式說明如下：

AIDA 要素	段落安排	說明
Attention 注意力	第一段	必須要能引起「**注意力**」。開頭第一句尤為重要，可以用**問句**、引人注目的**事實**或**數字**來**吸引**（draw in）讀者關注。
Interest 興趣	第二、 第三段	要能引起對方的「**興趣**」。可以說明為什麼這項商品或服務有其需求。了解消費者會受到什麼因素**驅動**（motivate），是此處的關鍵。
Desire 欲望	第四、 第五段	要創造「**欲望**」。方法有很多，例如引述其他顧客的好評。另外，向對方保證公司會提供產品退款，則能讓對方產生信任感，而提供免費**樣品**（sample）也相當有效。
Action 行動	最後一段	必須促使讀者採取「**行動**」。此處要具體說明對方應該如何行動，而不應使對方不知所措。例如，可請讀者造訪網站或撥打電話，或可附上**訂購單**或**回覆單**（order or reply forms）。

當然，以上只是提供大方向，並不需要拘泥遵守。推銷信的篇幅不限於六段。最重要的是，撰寫推銷信時必須考慮到讀者，以讀者的觀點（perspective）來思考。

① **推廣新商家的信件 A Letter Promoting a New Business**

The Great Outdoors

876 Davis Avenue, Vancouver BC V6O 483, Canada
Tel: 604-555-9874　email: tgo@gotmail.com

September 14, 2023

Rupert Helm
Metro Vancouver Nature Club
1345 Arlington Road
Burnaby BC V3J 900

> **❶ Attention（注意力）**：首段以新店開張的資訊吸引讀者注意。

> **❷ Interest（興趣）**：接著說明產品優勢，引起興趣。

Dear Mr. Helm:

I am pleased to **inform**[1] you that The Great Outdoors is now open for business at 876 Davis Avenue, Vancouver.

We think our wide range of outdoor gear will be **of great interest**[2] to the members of your club. Our products are designed **with** the local climate **in mind**[3]. We have **a good choice of**[4] waterproof items ideal for rainy weather. In addition, we have a large **variety**[5] of tents and camping gear.

Our staff is well trained and eager to help buyers find exactly what they need. Please find enclosed a partial list of our current **stock**[6]. Feel free to drop by and see what else we are **carrying**[7] in our store before the products you want end up in someone else's cart!

> **❹ Action（行動）**：最後呼籲讀者來店購買商品。

> **❸ Desire（欲望）**：以附件提供產品清單，引發購買欲望。

Yours truly,

Alan Greenman

Alan Greenman
Executive Vice President of Sales
The Great Outdoors

Enclosure 1

Key Terms 核心字彙片語

1 **inform** [ɪn`fɔrm] (v.) 告知
2 **of (great/no) interest (to sb.)** 使……（很／不）感興趣
3 **with (sth.) in mind** 考量到……
4 **a good/wide choice of (sth.)** 各式……可供選擇
5 **variety** [və`raɪətɪ] (n.) 各種；多樣化
6 **stock** [stɑk] (n.) 存貨；庫存
7 **carry** [`kærɪ] (v.) （商店）販售（某物）

55

Galaxy Solutions

2789 Rudolph Street, Kuala Lumpur 53980, Malaysia

Phone: +60 03-876-7634　email: galaxy@asiamail.com

November 10, 2023

Jessica Hsu
Horizon Insurance Ltd.
Ark Tower
9475 Century Road
Kuala Lumpur 52084
Malaysia

❶ Attention（注意力）：開場透過一串問句吸引讀者關注。

Dear Ms. Hsu:

Is your current **server**[1] working for you? Is your office **software**[2] helping your staff work faster? Does your network assist you in making sales? If you answered "no" to these questions, it's time for a change.

How Can Galaxy Solutions Help You?

❷ Interest（興趣）：強調產品可帶來的幫助，引起讀者興趣。

We Help You Grow

We have solutions for all your needs. Our wide range of **packages**[3] are designed to be highly **flexible**[4]. So no matter what size your **operation**[5] is or what problems you face, we can help. With Galaxy Solutions, you can adjust any package to suit your needs.

❸ Desire（欲望）：說明產品可依需求調整且有專家引導，使用便利，激起購買欲望。

We Save You Time

Let our experts guide you to the most efficient way to operate. We can connect your **entire**[6] office with the latest apps and other software, letting you focus on your **core**[7] business.

How Do I Learn More about Galaxy Solutions?

Contact our Sales Team: visit our website www.galaxysolutions.com
Why wait? Act now! _____

❹ Action（行動）：邀請讀者聯絡業務人員。

Sincerely,

Randall Parker

Randall Parker, Marketing Director

Key Terms 核心字彙片語

1 **server** [`sɝvɚ] (n.) 伺服器
2 **software** [`sɔft͵wɛr] (n.) 軟體
3 **package** [`pækɪdʒ] (n.) 套裝方案
4 **flexible** [`flɛksəbl̩] (a.) 有彈性的
5 **operation** [͵ɑpə`reʃən] (n.) 營運
6 **entire** [ɪn`taɪr] (a.) 整個的
7 **core** [kor] (n.) 核心

3　推銷服務的信件　A Letter Promoting a Service

Trinity Cargo

Topshelf Industrial Centre, Tsuen Wan, Hong Kong
Phone: +852 3302-5236　email: lucille@trinitymail.com

April 23, 2023

Jasmine Chang
J's Fashion
1458 Lindsay Avenue
Hong Kong

Dear Ms. Chang:

I am excited to let you know about a new service that we are now offering. We have begun to **partner**[1] with some new **carriers**[2]. This will allow us to **deliver**[3] goods much faster than before. With our new Global Express service, most **shipments**[4] can go **from door to door**[5] in just one night.

For more details, such as a list of the countries we deliver to, please visit our website. We deliver to most countries around the world. And as ever, our prices **remain**[6] low.

We look forward to helping you meet your customers' needs with our new Global Express **option**[7]. As you are one of our most valued **clients**[8], we would like to **extend**[9] this special offer to you. For May and June, please enjoy Global Express at a 15% discount.

Best regards,

Lucille Ma

Lucille Ma, Manager
Trinity Cargo

❶ **Attention**（注意力）：開頭說明推出新服務，引起讀者注意。

❷ **Interest**（興趣）：說明新產品有別以往的優勢，引發繼續閱讀的興趣。

❸ **Action**（行動）：呼籲讀者前往網站，另也於信末邀請讀使用折扣。

❹ **Desire**（欲望）：提供限時折扣，激發讀者使用服務的欲望。

Key Terms 核心字彙片語

1 partner [ˋpɑrtnɚ]
(v.) 和……搭檔合作（＋ with）

2 carrier [ˋkærɪɚ] (n.) 運輸業者

3 deliver [dɪˋlɪvɚ] (v.) 運送

4 shipment [ˋʃɪpmənt]
(n.) 運輸（的貨品）

5 from door to door
[frɑm dor tu dor] 從路程開始到結束
（此處指貨品從寄貨者送到收貨者）

6 remain [rɪˋmen] (v.) 保持……

7 option [ˋɑpʃən] (n.) 選項

8 client [ˋklaɪənt] (n.) 客戶

9 extend [ɪkˋstɛnd] (v.) 提供；給予

57

1 | 介紹自己或自己的公司 Introducing Yourself or Your Business

① I would like to tell you more about my business . . . 　我想跟您多介紹一下本公司……

② Please allow me to introduce our new product . . . 　請容我為您介紹我們的新產品……

③ I would like to take this opportunity to tell you . . . 　希望利用這個機會告訴您……

④ I am excited to let you know about . . . 　很高興讓您知道……

2 | 抓住注意力、引起興趣、激起欲望 Grabbing Attention, Stimulating Interest, and Creating Desire

① Why is it that business owners are always complaining about how hard it is to find qualified staff? 為什麼公司老闆總是在抱怨很難找到適任的員工？

② The _____ [name of product] will change your life by . . .

〔產品名〕將會透過……，來改變您的生活。

③ The _____ [name of product] has been used with great success for more than _____ [length of time] . . .

〔產品名〕在過去〔一段時間〕來不斷受到用戶好評……

④ We think you'll love _____ [name of product] —but we understand that you might not. That's why we offer a complete refund if you aren't happy with the _____ [name of product]. 我們相信您會愛上〔產品名〕——但我們也了解也許您未必滿意，因此如果您對〔產品名〕不滿意，我們將提供全額退款。

3 | 呼籲讀信者採取行動 Calls to Action

① Why wait? Act now! 　還等什麼呢？現在馬上行動！

② Don't let this fantastic offer expire. 　不要錯過這個好康。

③ Visit our website today. 　現在就上我們的網站。

④ Don't delay! 　動作要快！

4 | 說明特價與折扣 Announcing Sales and Discounts

① We would like to extend the following offer to you . . . 　我們想提供您以下優惠……

② We are pleased to offer you our new customer discount . . .

我們很高興為您提供新客戶折扣……

③ It's time again for our annual sale . . . 　又到了我們年度特賣活動……

④ This is a limited-time offer . . . 　這是限時優惠……

Lesson 6 Exercises

1 Read the sales letter below. Fill in the blanks using the sentences and headers in the box.

> - Each piece is simple and functional, but also beautiful.
> - **How we can help you**
> - You can find images of our furniture and details about our prices on our website.
> - **Our items**
> - Wouldn't you like your office to be a brighter, more modern space?

Fjord Office Furniture

1026 Adams St
North Chicago, IL 60064

November 10, 2023

James Miller
Swan Solutions
1538 Victoria Ave
North Chicago, IL 60064

Dear Mr. Miller:

Does your office furniture look old fashioned? **❶** ....

.... If so, please read on.

❷ (header) ....
Fjord Office Furniture offers a wide range of comfortable, stylish office furniture for the modern workplace. All our items are designed in the Northern European style.
❸ ....

❹ (header) ....

- office chairs
- filing cabinets
- plant pots

- desks
- lamps
- and much more . . .

- bookshelves
- decorative art

Learn more about our furniture and prices

❺ ....

.... Pay us a visit at www.fjordfurniature.com and let us bring your office to life!

Yours sincerely,

Fredrik Hansen

Fredrik Hansen

Director of Sales, Fjord Office Furniture

Lesson 7

商務邀請函與回覆邀請
Business Invitations and Responses to Business Invitations

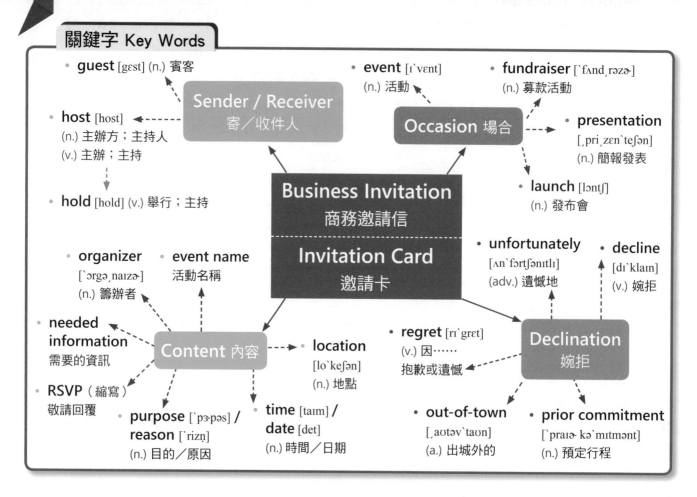

關鍵字 Key Words

- **guest** [gɛst] (n.) 賓客

- **host** [host] (n.) 主辦方；主持人 (v.) 主辦；主持

- **hold** [hold] (v.) 舉行；主持

Sender / Receiver 寄／收件人

- **organizer** [ˋɔrgəˏnaɪzɚ] (n.) 籌辦者

- **event name** 活動名稱

- **needed information** 需要的資訊

- **RSVP** （縮寫） 敬請回覆

Content 內容

- **purpose** [ˋpɝpəs] / **reason** [ˋrizn̩] (n.) 目的／原因

Business Invitation 商務邀請信

Invitation Card 邀請卡

- **location** [loˋkeʃən] (n.) 地點

- **time** [taɪm] / **date** [det] (n.) 時間／日期

- **event** [ɪˋvɛnt] (n.) 活動

Occasion 場合

- **regret** [rɪˋgrɛt] (v.) 因…… 抱歉或遺憾

- **fundraiser** [ˋfʌndˏrezɚ] (n.) 募款活動

- **presentation** [ˏprizɛnˋteʃən] (n.) 簡報發表

- **launch** [lɔntʃ] (n.) 發布會

- **unfortunately** [ʌnˋfɔrtʃənɪtlɪ] (adv.) 遺憾地

- **decline** [dɪˋklaɪn] (v.) 婉拒

Declination 婉拒

- **out-of-town** [ˏaʊtəvˋtaʊn] (a.) 出城外的

- **prior commitment** [ˋpraɪɚ kəˋmɪtmənt] (n.) 預定行程

1 What Is a Business Invitation?（商務邀請信是什麼？）

　　商務邀請信（business invitation）是**商業活動**（business event）的邀請函。由於多數商業活動屬正式性質，所以通常會寄發正式邀請。這類邀請函可能會以**公司信紙**撰寫，而在特別重要或正式的場合，則可能使用傳統**邀請卡**（invitation card）。

2 How to Write a Business Invitation?（如何撰寫商務邀請信？）

　　使用公司信紙寄出的正式邀請信，應包含以下內容：

1 **Who?**（活動主辦人／單位為何？）

　　無論活動主辦方是你的公司、其他團體或個人，都一定要**列出主辦人／單位的名稱**。

2 **What?**（活動性質為何？）

　　須說明活動內容，例如為**產品發表會**（product launch）、**募款活動**（fundraiser）、**簡報說明會**（presentation）等活動，並請寫出會讓受邀者對活動有興趣的細節資訊。

3 **Where?**（活動地點在哪裡？）

告知活動舉行場地的確切地址。如果要提供交通指引，須另以附件獨立放置，不應直接寫在邀請信上。

4 **When?**（活動時間為何？）

須告知活動的日期和時間。

5 **Why?**（活動舉辦的原因？為什麼對方受到邀約？）

須說明**活動舉辦的緣由**，如展示新產品、迎接新主管等，同時也要說明**為什麼邀請對方**，例如表達對方是公司重視的客戶等。

6 **How and by When?**（回應邀約的方式與時限？）

在邀請函末尾處，應告知**回覆期限和方式**，例如透過電話、信件、電子郵件或其他管道。此時可使用「**RSVP**」一詞（法文「répondez s'il vous plaît」的縮寫，意思是「請回覆」），用法可見下方例句：

- **RSVP** by phone or email by January 11th.
  請在 1 月 11 日前以電話或電子郵件回覆。

7 **Personal Touch**（帶點人情味）

邀請信的稱謂應**個別寫出受邀對象個人**，而避免使用 **Dear Sir or Madam**（親愛的先生／女士）等籠統稱謂，最好也能親筆為邀請信署名。

8 **Other Needed Information**（其他必要的交通、服裝等資訊）

設身處地思考：受邀者要如何前來參加活動？如需提供**停車**（parking）、**飯店**或**其他資訊**，應該單獨放在附件中。如活動有**服裝規定**（dress code），就在邀請函中說明，也要告知客人**能否攜伴參加**。另外，賓客抵達活動時所必須知道的所有資訊，也都要一併告知。

3 Traditional Invitation Cards（以傳統邀請卡書寫正式邀請信）

寫在卡片上的邀請函，通常比使用公司信紙的邀請函簡短。撰寫傳統邀請卡需遵守以下步驟：

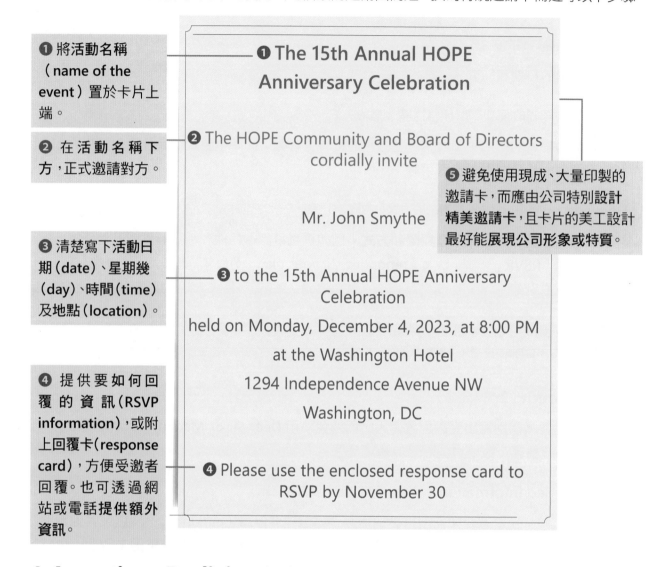

❶ 將活動名稱（name of the event）置於卡片上端。

❷ 在活動名稱下方，正式邀請對方。

❸ 清楚寫下活動日期（date）、星期幾（day）、時間（time）及地點（location）。

❹ 提供要如何回覆的資訊（RSVP information），或附上回覆卡（response card），方便受邀者回覆。也可透過網站或電話提供額外資訊。

❶ The 15th Annual HOPE Anniversary Celebration

❷ The HOPE Community and Board of Directors cordially invite

Mr. John Smythe

❸ to the 15th Annual HOPE Anniversary Celebration
held on Monday, December 4, 2023, at 8:00 PM
at the Washington Hotel
1294 Independence Avenue NW
Washington, DC

❹ Please use the enclosed response card to RSVP by November 30

❺ 避免使用現成、大量印製的邀請卡，而應由公司特別設計精美邀請卡，且卡片的美工設計最好能展現公司形象或特質。

4 Accepting / Declining（如何接受／婉謝正式邀請？）

❶ 雖然商務邀請函有時會附上電子郵件地址或電話，方便對方回覆，但是一般的做法還是要在接到邀請的**一至三日內**，寄一封**正式的回覆信**，表明接受邀請的意願。如果邀請函附有**回覆卡（response card）**，可以**直接把回覆卡寄回**，就不需要再寫一封回覆信。

❷ 婉謝（decline）正式邀請時，應說明自己無法參加的原因，以符合禮節。一般來說，可以接受的原因包括**已有其他預定行程**，或將**在外地（out-of-town）**遠行。說明理由時不需要深入交代細節，也**不要以生病為藉口（excuse）**，以免主人禮貌上要進一步詢問你的健康狀況。

❸ 可以在回信表達遺憾不克參加時，多加上祝福的話，例如：

• **Wishing you every success with (the event).** 預祝〔該活動〕圓滿成功。

邀請信範例 Invitation Letter

Audrey Kim Hair Salons

228 West 31st Street
New York, NY 10006

June 24th, 2023

Margaret Howard
Apartment 4B
34-40 79th Street
Jackson Heights, NY 11372

Dear Ms. Howard:

You are one of our most **valued**[1] customers. So, we would like to invite you to a private **preview**[2] of our new Nakamichi hair care **products line**[3]. This line includes shampoos, conditioners, and tonics. Audrey Kim is proud to be among the very first salons in the United States to offer Nakamichi products.

The event will be held at our main location at 228 West 31st Street in Manhattan on Friday, July 15th. It begins at 7:00 pm and ends at 11:00 pm. A map is enclosed with **directions**[4] to our salon.

A salesperson from Nakamichi will be **on hand**[5] to discuss the products and answer any questions.

Please RSVP to Jenny DiAngelo at (212) 618-9947 or by email at jennyd@audreykim.com by July 8th.

We look forward to seeing you at the **showing**[6] and sharing our new line with you.

Sincerely yours,

Bethany Wade

Bethany Wade, Assistant Manager
Audrey Kim Hair Salons

Enc. (1)

Key Terms 核心字彙片語

1 **valued** [ˈvæljud] (a.) 貴重的
2 **preview** [ˈpriˌvju] (n.) 預展
3 **product line** [ˈprɑdʌkt laɪn] (n.) 產品線
　（同家廠商推出的一系列類似產品或服務）
4 **directions** [dəˈrɛkʃənz] (n.)〔複〕（交通）路線指引
5 **on hand** [ɑn hænd]（因特定目的）在場的
6 **showing** [ˈʃoɪŋ] (n.) 展覽

② 接受邀請的信件 Acceptance Letter

Samuel Potts

Mailander Strasse 4,
Frankfurt am Main, 60598

23 October 2022

Blumenschein, Inc.
Adickesallee 3, 94855
Frankfurt am Main, Germany

Dear Mr. Blumenschein:

Re: New Knife **Collection**[1] Showing

Thank you for your kind invitation. It is **with pleasure**[2] that I accept your invitation to the showing on Friday, 5 November.

Yours sincerely,

Samuel Potts

Samuel Potts

> **Key Terms 核心字彙片語**
>
> 1 collection [kə`lɛkʃən] (n.) 收集物
> 2 with pleasure [wɪð `plɛʒɚ] 非常樂意

③ 婉拒邀請的信件 Declining a Formal Invitation

✉ New message — ⤢ ✕

From: meg1227@dotmail.com
To: jennyd@audreykim.com
Subject: Re: New Hair Products Line Preview

Dear Ms. DiAngelo,

Thank you very much for your kind invitation to the preview of your new line of hair care products. Unfortunately, **due to**[1] a **prior**[2] **commitment**[3], I will be **unable**[4] to attend. I wish you the best of luck with the new line.

Yours truly,

Margaret Howard

> **Key Terms 核心字彙片語**
>
> 1 due to [dju tu] 由於……
> 2 prior [`praɪɚ] (a.) 先前的
> 3 commitment [kə`mɪtmənt] (n.) 必須處理的事情
> 4 unable [ʌn`eb!] (a.) 不能夠的

4 邀請卡 Invitation Cards

The 15th Annual[1] Premier Holdings Charity[2] Dinner

❦ ─── ⟐ ─── ❦

The Premier Holdings **Board of Directors**[3] proudly invites

Mr. and Mrs. Desmond Morris

to the 15th Annual Premier Holdings Charity Dinner

held Sunday, June 25th, 2023 at 7:30 p.m.

at the Lorelei Hotel
2745 Melrose Avenue
Los Angeles, CA

Please use the enclosed response card to RSVP by June 8th.

The Wedding of Samantha Potts and Karl Blumenschein

Mr. and Mrs. Samuel Potts request the pleasure of Edward Gabler's **company**[4] to celebrate the wedding of their daughter Samantha to Karl Blumenschein

on Thursday, 6 July at 14:00 at Saint Matthew's Church,

Mailander Strasse 4, Frankfurt am Main.

One **additional**[5] guest is welcome.

Please RSVP by email to Samuel or Judi Potts
at spotts26@deutschemail.com no later than June 30th.

Key Terms 核心字彙片語

1 **annual** [`ænjʊəl] (a.) 年度的

2 **charity** [`tʃærətɪ] (n.) 慈善（事業）

3 **board of directors** [bord ʌv dəˋrɛktɚz] (n.) 董事會

4 **company** [`kʌmpənɪ] (n.) 陪伴

5 **additional** [əˋdɪʃən!] (a.) 額外的

The 15th Annual HOPE Celebration

Monday, December 4, 2023

Name:_____

Guest Name:_____

□ Will attend

□ Will not attend

這裡有一行「**Guest Name**」（來賓姓名），表示受邀者還可以帶一位伴侶出席。

有時回覆卡並不會要求寫出伴侶姓名，但是在勾選是否出席的地方，會有一欄「**plus one**」（再加一位），意指受邀者可再帶一名伴侶參加。

常用句型及用語 Common Sentence Patterns and Phrases

1 發出正式邀請 Making a Formal Invitation

① As you are one of our most valued customers, we would like to invite you to . . . 因為您是我們極為重視的顧客，我們想邀請您……

② The Premier Holdings Board of Directors proudly invites _____ [name] to . . . 卓越控股公司董事會敬邀〔人名〕參加……

③ Mr. and Mrs. _____ [name] request the pleasure of _____ [name's] company to celebrate . . .
〔人名〕夫婦敬邀〔人名〕賞光，一同慶祝……

④ We would be delighted if you could attend the launch of . . .
如果您能蒞臨……的發表會，我們將不勝喜悅。

2 接受正式邀請 Accepting a Formal Invitation

① Thank you for your invitation to the launch of . . . I would be delighted to attend. 感謝您邀請本人參加……的上市發表會，我很樂意出席。

② Thank you for your invitation to Samantha's wedding. We will be very pleased to attend. 謝謝您邀請我們參加莎曼莎的婚禮，我們將非常樂於出席。

③ Thank you for your invitation to . . . I am happy to confirm my attendance.
謝謝您邀請本人參加……在此非常高興與您確認我將出席。

3 婉謝正式邀請 Declining a Formal Invitation

① Thank you very much for your kind invitation to . . . 非常感謝您好意邀請……

② Unfortunately, due to a prior commitment, I will be unable to attend.
可惜我預先有其他安排，這次不克參加。

③ I wish you the best of luck with . . . 預祝您……一切順利。

④ It is with regret that I must decline your invitation to . . .
很遺憾，我必須婉拒您的邀請……

1 Complete the following invitation letter inviting a customer to a special preview of a new range of painting products from Italy.

The event will be held at 13 Baldwin Road, Leeds on May 2. After a short introduction, attendees will have the opportunity to test the products themselves. If attending, the invitee should RSVP to Kelly Chen at k.chen@brushtrokeart.co.uk by April 25.

Dear Ms. Price:

We at Brushstroke Art Supplies would like to invite you to **❶** ....

from Leonardo, one of Italy's finest producers of paints and brushes. We at Brushstroke Art Supplies are very pleased to be partnering with Leonardo to offer these high-quality products to our UK customers.

Our special preview event will be held at our main store **❷** ....

The event will run from 4 p.m. to 6 p.m. and will begin with a short product introduction from one of Leonardo's representatives. **❸** ....

The Leonardo representative will be happy to answer any questions.

If you would like to attend, please RSVP to **❹** ....

We look forward to seeing you at the event.

Sincerely,

Kelly Chen

Kelly Chen, Manager, Brushstroke Art Supplies

---

2 Complete the following invitation card with the phrases from the box.

- at the Pinetree Hotel
- proudly invite
- to RSVP by October 21
- to the Fjord Office Furniture One Year Anniversary Party
- at 8:00 p.m.

Fjord Office Furniture
One Year Anniversary Party

The Fjord Office Furniture Owners

1 ....

James Miller

2 ....

held Saturday, October 31, 2023 **3** ....

4 ....

1926 Honore Road
North Chicago, IL

Please use the enclosed response card **5** ....

---

3 You are invited to a company opening by Ms. Patel, the owner. Complete this short letter politely accepting the invitation.

The invitation included a "plus one." Inform Ms. Patel that you will be bringing a guest with you. The invitation did not mention a dress code. Ask Ms. Patel if there is any dress code she would prefer you to follow.

Scent Magazine
67 Mill Road, London, NW92 8NM

12 March 2023

Padma Patel
Perfume by Padma
90 Green Lane
London
NW29 4TL

Dear Ms. Patel:

Re: Invitation to Company Opening

❶ ....
I look forward to learning more about your business and sampling some of your products.

As the invitation included a plus one, **❷** ....
Also, may I ask, **❸** .... ?

❹ ....

Kind regards,

Mark Tomson

Mark Tomson
Reporter, Scent Magazine

4 **You are invited to a company's anniversary dinner by the CEO, Mr. Grey.**

You won't be attending the event because you'll be out of town on that date. Even so, you still want to congratulate him on the important milestone and wish him success with the event.

New Message
From: kt.jones@lightningelectronics.com
To: vincent.grey@flashforward.com
Subject: Invitation to Our Anniversary Dinner

Dear Mr. Grey,

Thank you for ❶ ....
However, it is with regret that I have to decline the invitation as ❷ ....
....

Even though I am unable to attend, I would nonetheless like to ❸ ....
.... and wish
you many more successful years in the future. I hope ❹ ....
....

Thank you once again for the invitation, and my apologies for being unable to attend.

Kind regards,

KT Jones
Owner, Lightning Electronics

Lesson 8　撰寫給具特定對象的感謝信
Thank-You Letters With a Specific Audience

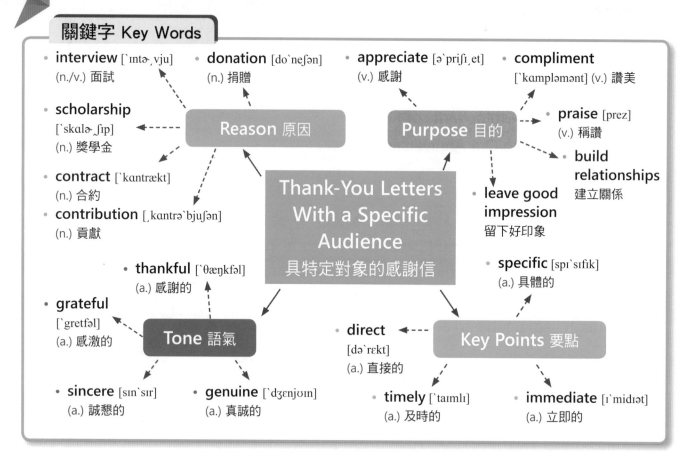

關鍵字 Key Words

- **interview** [`ɪntɚˌvju] (n./v.) 面試
- **scholarship** [`skɑlɚˌʃɪp] (n.) 獎學金
- **contract** [`kɑntrækt] (n.) 合約
- **contribution** [ˌkɑntrə`bjuʃən] (n.) 貢獻
- **donation** [do`neʃən] (n.) 捐贈
- **appreciate** [ə`priʃɪˌet] (v.) 感謝
- **compliment** [`kɑmpləmənt] (v.) 讚美
- **praise** [prez] (v.) 稱讚
- **build relationships** 建立關係
- **leave good impression** 留下好印象
- **specific** [spɪ`sɪfɪk] (a.) 具體的

Reason 原因

Purpose 目的

Thank-You Letters With a Specific Audience
具特定對象的感謝信

- **thankful** [`θæŋkfəl] (a.) 感謝的
- **grateful** [`gretfəl] (a.) 感激的
- **sincere** [sɪn`sɪr] (a.) 誠懇的
- **genuine** [`dʒɛnjoɪn] (a.) 真誠的

Tone 語氣

- **direct** [də`rɛkt] (a.) 直接的

Key Points 要點

- **timely** [`taɪmlɪ] (a.) 及時的
- **immediate** [ɪ`midɪət] (a.) 立即的

1　What Is a Thank-You Letter? （感謝信是什麼？）

「感謝信」是為了向對方表達**感謝之意（gratitude）**的信函，寄信的對象可以是私下寄給特定的企業、團體或個人，也可以公開供不特定的公眾、社區居民、顧客群等閱覽。本課將先介紹具特定發信對象的感謝信，並於下一課（Lesson 9）介紹如何寫感謝信給不特定對象。

有時你是**作為個人**寄感謝信，有時則可能需**代表所屬企業或團體**感謝對方。兩者立場的不同，可以透過信中使用的主詞來分辨：若使用的主詞是「**we**」（我們）而不是「**I**」（我），就表示這封感謝信是以整個企業／團體的名義而寫，而非從個人出發。

在商界或學術界生涯中，需要寄送感謝信的原因很多，寄出感謝信的原因可能是要答謝對方贈送的**禮物（gift）**、**提供的服務（service）**，或者對方帶給你值得感謝的**體驗（experience）**。以下舉例幾種寄送感謝信的時機：

代表……	感謝緣由	說明
Individual 個人	**Job interview**（求職面試）	求職**面試結束後**，可寫封感謝信給**面試官**（interviewer）。
	Job offer（職缺機會）	接到工作的錄取通知後，可寫封感謝信給**招聘經理**（hiring manager）。
	Reference / Recommendation（推薦信）	對於幫你寫商務推薦信的人，應寫封感謝信。
	Scholarship（獎學金）	可寫封感謝信給提供獎學金給你的機構。
Corporation/ Organization 企業／組織	**New board member**（新任委員會成員）	寫感謝信給同意成為商務**諮詢委員會**（advisory board）成員的人士。在他們擔任諮詢成員期間，也建議可以定期寫感謝信向他們致謝。
	New contract（新合約）	在與別家公司簽完新的合約後，理應寫封感謝信給對方。
	Help in a tough situation（處境艱難時的協助）	如果有人在公司陷入緊急情況（emergency）時給予協助，公司可能會以私人感謝函向對方致謝。
	Personal favor（個人出力幫忙）	如果有人對公司提供協助，像是同意免費提供諮詢等，禮貌上要寄送感謝信給對方。
個人或企業／ 組織	**Excellent service**（優質服務）	當一家企業為你提供了**非常優質的服務或產品**，你可能會想要寫封感謝信，例如可以寫封感謝信給去過的餐廳，讚美（commend/ compliment / praise）當天的侍者服務周到，或是也可以寫信感謝曾替你緊急維修物品的維修業者，甚至也可以寫給曾經特別為你創作作品的藝術家。
	Donation（捐贈）	若特定人士或企業對於你的公司行號給予餽贈，或是捐款給你支持的組織機構，可寫封感謝信致謝。

個人或企業需要寫感謝信致謝的原因尚有各式各樣，並不侷限於以上列舉的例子。

2 **Tips for Thank-You Letters**（感謝信要怎麼寫？）

　　感謝信的語氣應該**親切**、**友好**而**專業**，而信中內容應該**具體明確**，信件應**及時傳達**，且行文需**直截了當**：

1 Specific（具體明確）

感謝信的主題應著重於**明確的餽贈**、**特定的服務**或具體的經歷上，並在信中解釋這項餽贈、服務或經歷的重要性（importance），以及對自己的影響為何。感謝信的內容不應含糊不清，對讀信者的讚美也**不宜流於空泛**（general）或**逢迎誇大**（flattering）。

2 Timely（及時傳達）

信件寄出的時間點（timing）也很重要，應該在**想要致謝的事件發生後不久**，就寄出感謝信給對方。寄送感謝信的最佳時機為**事件發生後的幾天內**，或者**最多數週內**。

3 Direct（直截了當）

感謝信**不宜長篇鋪陳**，而是要在開頭的**第一或第二句話就立即**（immediately）**向對方致謝**，接著詳加說明為何來信感謝，並於結尾時換另一種說法（expression）重申感謝之情。

　　感謝信有不同的寄送方式。許多人常會在求職面試完，或在收到推薦信後，透過**電子郵件**寄發感謝信給對方。不過，有些情況則非常適合寄送**紙本（paper）感謝信**或**卡片**，例如獲得捐贈後、歡迎董事會新成員加入時，或是感謝新客戶時。

1 感謝面試官 Thanking a Job Interviewer

Dear Ms. Kwan:

Subject: Thank you for meeting with me

Thank you for **meeting with**[1] me today to **discuss**[2] the office manager position. I **appreciated**[3] the chance to learn more about the job and the company. It was also very useful to speak with the other members of the office team and hear about their daily **tasks**[4]. Now, I'm even more excited to bring the skills from my **recent**[5] training program to the office manager role.

Please contact me if you need any more information. Thanks again for meeting with me. I look forward to hearing from you.

Sincerely,

Darla Watts

Darla Watts

Key Terms 核心字彙片語

1 **meet with (sb.)** [mit wɪð] 和……見面
2 **discuss** [dɪˋskʌs] (v.) 討論
3 **appreciate** [əˋpriʃɪˌet] (v.) 感謝
4 **task** [tæsk] (n.) 任務；工作
5 **recent** [ˋrisn̩t] (a.) 近期的

Global Scholars Projects

1624 East 73rd Street
New York, NY 10021

June 1, 2023

Albert Grouse
Grouse Designs
100 Winding Creek
Dobson NC 27017-8589

Dear Mr. Grouse:

Thank you so much for your $1,500 **donation**[1] to the Global Scholars Project. Generous gifts like yours help us enormously in **advancing**[2] our important **mission**[3].

Your donation will help us buy school books and backpacks for 100 students in Central Asia next year. It will also help us build 10 new school buildings and five health clinics. Your **contribution**[4] will **impact**[5] hundreds of families!

One of these families is the Akhbetov family of Tajikistan. Because of your donation, eight-year-old Timur Akhbetov will get a backpack, paper, pencils, and books for the coming school year. His family could not **afford**[6] these **supplies**[7]. Now they can!

Thank you once again for this donation and for your continued support. Your gift will help students' dreams come true.

Many thanks,

Susanna Charles

Susanna Charles

Key Terms 核心字彙片語

1 **donation** [do`neʃən] (n.) 捐款；捐贈
2 **advance** [əd`væns] (v.) 推進
3 **mission** [`mɪʃən] (n.) 任務；使命
4 **contribution** [ˌkɑntrə`bjuʃən] (n.) 貢獻
5 **impact** [ɪm`pækt] (v.) 影響
6 **afford** [ə`ford] (v.) 負擔
7 **supply** [sə`plaɪ] (n.) 用品；供給品

3 感謝對方業者的服務 Thanking a Business for Their Service

Flora Event Planning
3115 Park Road NW
Washington, DC 20010

August 31, 2023

Stellar **Plumbing**[1]
2616 V Street
Arlington, VA 20301

Attention: Client Services Manager

Dear Sir or Madam:

I am writing to say thank you for the actions of the Stellar Plumbing team last week. Your workers helped save an important event for my business. A **pipe**[2] burst in our ballroom during one of our most important events of the year. Thanks to the quick work of the Stellar Plumbing team, the problem was **solved**[3] and our event was able to continue. I want to thank manager David Crane **in particular**[4]. He was very kind and **helpful**[5] during our crisis.

I want to **commend**[6] the work of the team and to thank them once again for arriving so quickly. I will definitely call you for any future plumbing needs and I will **recommend**[7] Stellar Plumbing's services!

Thanks again for saving our event.

Sincerely,

Iris Root

Iris Root
Principal, Flora Event Planning

Key Terms 核心字彙片語

1 **plumbing** [ˋplʌmɪŋ] (n.) 水管工程

2 **pipe** [paɪp] (n.) 管線；水管

3 **solve** [sɑlv] (v.) 解決

4 **in particular** [ɪn pɚˋtɪkjələ] 尤其

5 **helpful** [ˋhɛlpfəl] (a.) 有幫助的

6 **commend** [kəˋmɛnd] (v.) 稱讚

7 **recommend** [͵rɛkəˋmɛnd] (v.) 推薦

Photo Journeys
4223 16th Street NW
Washington, DC 20010

September 5, 2023

Milton Daniels
88 Chevy Chase Boulevard
Bethesda, MD 20817

Dear Milt:

Thank you so much for agreeing to be part of the Photo Journeys **board**[1]. As you know, this is a new challenge for me. I need all the advice I can get. I know you have a busy schedule, so I really appreciate you **making time**[2] to advise me on this **project**[3]. I truly hope, with your advice and the **input**[4] of the rest of the board, to build a business we can all be proud of.

Thank you for your **investment**[5] in me.

Sincerely,

Matt Peterson

Matt Peterson
President, Photo Journeys

Key Terms 核心字彙片語

1 **board** [bord] (n.) 董事會；委員會
2 **make time** [mek taɪm] 空出時間
3 **project** [ˋprɑdʒɛkt] (n.) 專案；工程
4 **input** [ˋɪn͵pʊt] (n.) 投入
5 **investment** [ɪnˋvɛstmənt] (n.)（時間、精力）投入；（金錢）投資

1　表達感謝之意的用語 Expressing Thanks

① <u>Thanks for</u> meeting with me today.　謝謝您今天和我見面。

② <u>Thanks to</u> the quick work of the team, we were able to continue.
由於團隊的動作迅速，我們才得以繼續進行。

③ <u>Thank you so much for</u> your advice.　非常感謝您的建議。

④ We at Eckington Steel <u>want to thank you for</u> your business.
我們埃金頓鋼鐵廠衷心感謝您的惠顧。

⑤ <u>I'd like to express my thanks for</u> your donation.　我想就您的捐款一事表示感謝。

⑥ <u>We are very grateful for</u> your feedback.　我們非常感謝您的意見回饋。

⑦ <u>I want to share my gratitude for</u> your trust.　我想感謝您對我的信任。

2　描述服務或經歷的影響的用語 Describing the Impact of a Service or Experience

① <u>It was very useful to</u> learn more about the job and the company.
能夠更了解這份工作的內容與公司概況，對我受用匪淺。

② Our meeting helped me understand my new responsibilities.
這次見面讓我明白了自己的新職責。

③ Your donation <u>will help us</u> build a new clinic.
您的捐款將幫助我們興建一間新診所。

④ Your contribution <u>will impact</u> hundreds of families!　您的貢獻將造福數百個家庭！

⑤ <u>Because of</u> your quick response, <u>we were able to</u> continue with our event.
由於您們反應迅速，我們的活動才得以繼續進行。

⑥ Your letter of reference helped me get my dream job.
您的推薦信幫我找到了我夢寐以求的工作。

⑦ The flowers you provided for our party created an elegant atmosphere.
您為我們的宴會準備的鮮花，營造出高雅迷人的氛圍。

⑧ <u>Without</u> your advice, our business <u>would not be as</u> productive.
若非有您的建議，本公司無法達成如此成效。

1 Choose three of the sentences in the box below to complete the thank-you letter.

- I have worked at my current job for five years.
- I will be sure to use your services for any future events we throw.
- The event was a big success.
- I have some ideas about how things could have run more smoothly.
- Please also pass along my special thanks to Martin Douglas.

Shelter for All
88 Mayflower Road
Washington, DC 20395

January 31, 2023

Tina Gray
Flora Event Planning
3115 Park Road NW
Washington, DC 20010

Dear Ms. Gray:

I am writing to thank you for all your hard work on our fundraising event last week. Thanks to you and your staff, everything ran smoothly. ❶ ....
....

❷ ....
He did an excellent job hosting the charity auction. Because of him, we raised a lot of money for our cause.

I am very glad we chose Flora to run this event. ❸ ....
....

Thank you again for your great work.

Sincerely,

Rhonda Tan

Rhonda Tan
Director, Shelter for All

Lesson 9

企業撰寫給未具特定對象的感謝信及公開謝函
Corporate Thank-You Letters With an Unspecified Audience and Public Thank-You Messages

關鍵字 Key Words

- **press release** [prɛs rɪ`lis]
  (n.) 新聞稿
- **form letter** [fɔrm `lɛtɚ]
  (n.) 制式信件
- **newspaper**
  [`njuz͵pepɚ]
  (n.) 報紙
- **corporate**
  [`kɔrpərɪt]
  (a.) 公司的
- **public** [`pʌblɪk]
  (a.) 公開的
- **automatic**
  [͵ɔtə`mætɪk] (a.) 自動的
- **mass** [mæs]
  (a.) 大批的
- **Quality** 性質
- **unspecified**
  [ʌn`spɛsə͵faɪd]
  (a.) 未特定的
- **Form** 形式
- **social media**
  [`soʃəl `midɪə]
  (n.) 社群媒體

Thank-You Letters With an Unspecified Audience and Public Thank-You Messages
未具特定對象的感謝信及公開謝函

- **receive an order**
  收到訂單
- **hit a milestone**
  達到里程碑
- **Reason** 原因
- **take part in an event**
  參與活動
- **express thanks**
  表達感謝
- **earn trust**
  贏得信任
- **customer**
  [`kʌstəmɚ]
  (n.) 顧客
- **participant**
  [pɑr`tɪsəpənt]
  (n.) 參與者
- **Audience** 對象
- **donor** [`donɚ]
  (n.) 捐贈者
- **community**
  [kə`mjunətɪ]
  (n.) 社區

1 Thanking an Unspecified Audience（感謝不特定的對象）

　　企業常也需要撰寫感謝信以對**不特定的個人或群體**致謝，這種信件除了以**大宗（mass）**、**制式信函（form letter）**的方式，以**不公開**的媒介（電子郵件、紙本書信等）寄給大量收件人外，也常見於發布在**社群媒體（social media）**，或是以**新聞稿（press release）**的方式刊載在報章媒體上，作為**公開謝函**，對公眾、顧客群或其他不特定對象統一表示謝意。以下為幾種企業可能撰寫感謝信給非特定對象的時機。

感謝緣由	說明
Hitting a milestone（達到特定的里程碑）	公司在達到重要的目標後，可能會公開感謝顧客對他們的支持。
Choosing a certain type of business（選擇特定類型企業）	例如，小型企業可能會為了感謝顧客選擇自家公司，而非中大型企業，而公開向顧客致謝。
After a difficult time（度過艱困期）	公司有時會經歷艱辛的（tough）低潮時期。對於在艱困期間依然不離不棄的顧客，公司理應公開向他們致謝。
Thanking a community（感謝社區民眾）	有時社區民眾會受邀對當地企業進行評比，其中一例便是地方報紙每年彙整的「最佳」業者名單（"best-of" list）。頂尖排名的企業，可能會想要公開感謝顧客的忠實支持。
Large donation（大筆捐款）	公司若獲贈不具名的大筆捐款，可能希望公開感謝捐贈者。
Participation in an event（參與活動）	繁忙的活動過後，公司可能會想公開感謝參與者（participant）的蒞臨。
Placing an order（感謝顧客下單）	公司可能在顧客下單後，設定由系統自動（automatically）寄出感謝函給顧客。這類感謝信通常都很簡短，而且寄給所有顧客的內容完全相同，寄出方式可能是跟著顧客的訂單一併寄出，或以電子郵件發送。

2 How to Write（如何寫作給不特定對象的感謝信／訊息）

具／不具特定對象的感謝信，在寫作上有幾項重要差異，但也有許多共同處。寫給不特定對象的**大宗、制式感謝函**，內容可能非常簡短，篇幅或許只有一、兩句話，並且只針對某個**特定行動**表示感謝，例如顧客送出訂單後，常會收到制式的感謝訊息。

其他具／不具特定對象的感謝信的異同處有以下幾點：

1 所有的感謝函都應**內容具體（specific）、及時發出（timely）**且行文**直截了當（direct）**。

2 首先，寫信者應清楚說明**致謝的原因**，然後描述對方的善舉**對己方有何正面影響（impact）**。通常公司在公開發布的感謝函中，會說明公司與讀信者之間的關係，或者陳述希望將來如何和讀信者往來互動，而寫給特定個人或團體的感謝函就不一定需要。

3 無論是否寫給特定對象，感謝信的語氣都應該**親切、友善**且**專業**。一般來說，大宗感謝信和公開謝函是**以企業的名義**寄出，因此信中自稱應該使用「**we**」（我們／本公司），而不用「**I**」（我）。

Examples

 1 地方報紙上致當地居民的公開感謝函 Publicly Posted Thank-You Letter to a Community in a Local Newspaper

THANK YOU, BROWNSVILLE

We at Fast Times Car Repair want to thank the people of Brownsville for making us your number one choice for **auto**[1] repairs! We know you have many options **when it comes to**[2] auto repair. So we are proud to have **earned**[3] your trust. Fast Times Car Repair has served this community for 15 years. With your continued support, we hope to keep this town's **automobiles**[1] running **smoothly**[4] for many years to come.

We are grateful for your business, this year and every year!

Key Terms 核心字彙片語

1 **auto** [`ɔto] (n.) 汽車
（**automobile** [`ɔtəmə͵bɪl] 的簡稱）
2 **when it comes to . . .**
[hwɛn ɪt kʌmz tu] 說到……
3 **earn** [ɝn] (v.) 贏得
4 **smoothly** [`smuðlɪ] (adv.) 平穩地

 2 感謝參加者出席活動的公開感謝函 Publicly Posted Thank-You Letter Thanking Participants in an Event

July 3, 2023

Press release

From: Big Baskets Bike Shop CEO Shireen Wheeler

Thank you to all 2023 Big Baskets 10 km participants

Big Baskets Bike Shop wants to **express**[1] our thanks to all who took part in our 10 km bike **race**[2] this year! In 2023, we welcomed almost twice as many people as last year. We were happy to see everyone who joined for a second time. And we were **honored**[3] to meet all the new **cyclists**[4] racing for the first time. We hope to see even more friendly faces next year!

We didn't do this alone, of course. Thank you to local businesses Sweetie Donuts and the Soda Shack for providing food and drink. And thank you to Squeaky's Bike Repair for helping everyone ride safely. Once again, thank you to the community of Jackson Falls! This is not only a bike race but also a chance to become better **neighbors**[5]. Thank you for **taking part**[6].

See you next year!

Key Terms 核心字彙片語

1 **express** [ɪk`sprɛs] (v.) 表達
2 **race** [res] (n.) 比賽
3 **honored** [`ɑnəd] (a.) 備受榮幸的
4 **cyclist** [`saɪk!ɪst] (n.) 單車騎士
5 **neighbor** [`nebə] (n.) 鄰居
6 **take part (in)** [tek pɑrt] 參與

Dear Valued Customer:

Thank you for choosing Taylor's **Cosmetics**[1] for your **beauty**[2] needs. Enclosed are your goods as ordered. We hope they meet your **satisfaction**[3].

At Taylor's we always want to provide the best goods and services for our customers. If you have time, please visit our website and **fill out**[4] a customer opinion form.

Thank you once again for your order.

Sincerely,

The Taylor's Cosmetics Team

Key Terms 核心字彙片語

1 **cosmetics** [kɑz`mɛtɪks] (n.) 〔複〕化妝品
2 **beauty** [`bjutɪ] (n.) 美麗
3 **satisfaction** [͵sætɪs`fækʃən] (n.) 滿意
4 **fill out** [fɪl aʊt] 填寫

1 表達感謝之意 Expressing Thanks

① Thank you to the community of Jackson Falls.　感謝傑克森瀑布市的居民。

② We know you have many choices, and we thank you for choosing us.
我們知道您的選擇眾多，所以很感謝您選擇了本公司。

③ Thanks for helping us get here.　感謝您幫助本公司達到如今的成就。

④ Thank you for making us your top choice.　感謝您優先選擇本公司。

⑤ We appreciate your support during this difficult year.
我們很感激您在這艱難的一年裡，對本公司的支持。

⑥ Thank you all so much for your participation.　非常感謝各位的參與。

⑦ We want to express our gratitude for your support.
我們想對您的支持，表達由衷感謝。

**2 描述寫信者與閱信者之間的關係
Describing the Relationship Between Writer and Reader**

① We are proud to do business in this town.　我們很榮幸能在本鎮提供服務。

② Fast Times has served this community for 15 years.
「迅時代」已經在地深耕15年。

③ We hope to keep this town's automobiles running for years to come.
我們希望將來繼續在本鎮確保各位的愛車行車順暢。

④ Thanks for helping us each become better neighbors.
感謝您讓我們彼此成為更好的鄰居。

⑤ We couldn't have done it without you.　沒有您的支持，我們就沒有今天的成就。

⑥ We will work hard to be your number one choice every year.
我們會努力成為您每年的首選。

⑦ Your support keeps us in business.　您的支持讓本公司得以持續經營。

1. Copy the following paragraphs into the body of the mass thank-you letter in the correct order.

> For your information, our 2023 summer sale begins on 1 May. Many of our goods will have a discount of 20% or more.

> Please visit our website for more details about our sale. Thank you once again for your order.

> Thank you for choosing Chef's Kiss Cookware for your purchase. Your goods are enclosed. We hope they meet your satisfaction.

Chef's Kiss Cookware
88 Grange Road
Exeter
EX22 2KN

1 April 2023

935 Highfield Road
Watford
WD33 3QU

Dear Valued Customer:

1 ....

....

2 ....

....

3 ....

....

Sincerely,

Chef's Kiss Cookware

2 Here is a publicly posted thank-you letter from Chef Mike's Fine Food to everyone who supported them in their first year of business. Follow the instructions in the box to complete the letter.

❶ Identify your company and the purpose of your letter.

❷ Thank three other local businesses (Millie's Bakery, Bart's Interior Design, and Kitchen Planet) for their help in your business's success.

❸ Promise to continue providing your popular dishes at affordable prices.

❹ Thank everyone again for their support.

❶ ....

.... Starting a new business is always difficult, and new businesses cannot survive without the support of the local community. We knew our first year would be a challenge, but with your support, it has been a great success. ❷ ....

....

....

With your continued support, we hope that our second year will be even better than our first. ❸ ....

.... We will also be introducing some new and exciting items to our menu, which we are very excited for you all to try.

❹ ....

Yours sincerely,

The Chef Mike's Fine Food Team

Now, **work with a partner** to compose a public thank-you letter of your own. Here is the scenario:

You are the owner of a bookshop. You just had a successful event where several authors read aloud from their works, answered questions from fans, and signed copies of their books. You want to write a thank you letter to everyone who supported the event.

Lesson 10 恭賀信 Congratulation Letters

關鍵字 Key Words

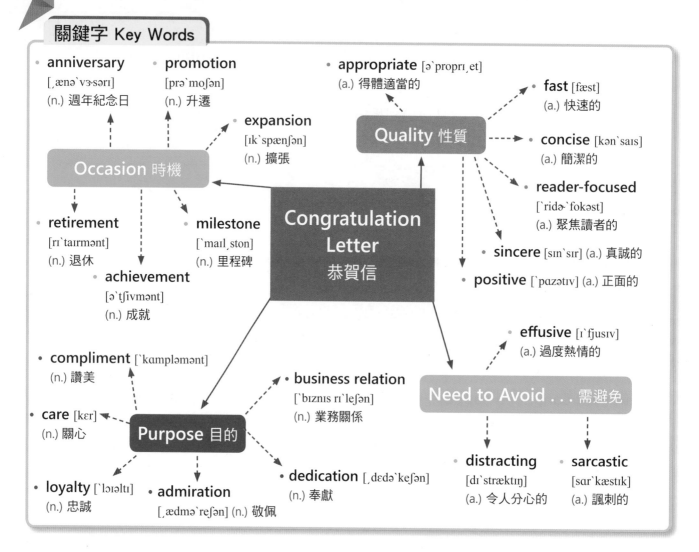

- **anniversary** [ˌænəˈvɝsərɪ] (n.) 週年紀念日
- **promotion** [prəˈmoʃən] (n.) 升遷
- **expansion** [ɪkˈspænʃən] (n.) 擴張
- **appropriate** [əˈproprɪˌet] (a.) 得體適當的
- **fast** [fæst] (a.) 快速的
- **concise** [kənˈsaɪs] (a.) 簡潔的
- **reader-focused** [ˈridəˈfokəst] (a.) 聚焦讀者的
- **sincere** [sɪnˈsɪr] (a.) 真誠的
- **positive** [ˈpɑzətɪv] (a.) 正面的

Quality 性質

Occasion 時機

- **retirement** [rɪˈtaɪrmənt] (n.) 退休
- **milestone** [ˈmaɪlˌston] (n.) 里程碑
- **achievement** [əˈtʃivmənt] (n.) 成就

Congratulation Letter 恭賀信

- **effusive** [ɪˈfjusɪv] (a.) 過度熱情的

Need to Avoid . . . 需避免

- **compliment** [ˈkɑmpləmənt] (n.) 讚美
- **care** [kɛr] (n.) 關心
- **business relation** [ˈbɪznɪs rɪˈleʃən] (n.) 業務關係
- **loyalty** [ˈlɔɪəltɪ] (n.) 忠誠
- **admiration** [ˌædməˈreʃən] (n.) 敬佩
- **dedication** [ˌdɛdəˈkeʃən] (n.) 奉獻
- **distracting** [dɪˈstræktɪŋ] (a.) 令人分心的
- **sarcastic** [sɑrˈkæstɪk] (a.) 諷刺的

Purpose 目的

1 What Is a Congratulation Letter?（什麼是恭賀信？）

　　「恭賀信」（congratulation letter）目的在於肯定個人在職涯中、或公司行號**達成重要里程碑（milestone）**，寄發的對象可以是自家公司的員工，或者寄給其他公司。

　　寄送恭賀信有助於建立正向的業務交流關係（business relation），例如老闆寄發恭賀信給員工，可以展現出對部屬的關心（care），有助**促進員工的忠誠度（loyalty）**；而發送恭賀信給其他公司，則可以**展現敬佩（admiration）**，使收信人對發信者的印象加分，有助增加雙方公司未來業務往來的機會。

撰寫恭賀信時應留意以下重點：

1 **Offer Congratulations**（表達祝賀）：表達祝賀的話語應該出現在**信件開頭**，而且語氣要**正式而誠懇（sincere）**。

2️⃣ Give Details（說明相關細節）：信中須**具體說明祝賀事由**，並可以回顧對方達成這項成就（achievement）的歷程（例如其所扮演的角色、付出等）。同時，也要向對方**表明自己充分理解**為何該項成就對於讀信者，以及公司具有重要意義。

3️⃣ Who the Sender Is（務必清楚註明發信者）：必須讓讀信者清楚知道發送這封恭賀信的人是誰，因此信中須提及**發信者的公司名稱、職銜、聯絡方式**。如此一來，讀信者才能確切知道未來可以向誰接洽（get in touch）業務。

2 **When to Write**（寄發恭賀信的時機）

可以發送恭賀信的時機很多，而常見的恭賀事由有以下幾種：

- 升遷（promotion）
- 完成艱鉅的工作專案（project）
- 達成個人目標（personal goal）
  （如個人業績紀錄）
- （結婚／任職／組織成立等）週年慶
  （anniversary）

- 新事業（new business）開張
- 事業版圖擴大（expansion）
- 獲頒獎項（award）
- 退休（retirement）

3 **How to Write**（如何撰寫恭賀信）

恭賀信應該**清楚而誠懇**，內容旨在獻上誠摯祝福，而不能讓對方有任何負面感受。
為了確保恭賀信達到上述目標，寫作時請遵循以下要點：

1️⃣ **Appropriate**（得體合宜）	提筆之前，須確定對方收到信時**不會覺得困擾（troubled）**。有時候，對方可能不希望外人論及自己的成就或事件，或者他們其實對於該件事情（例如退休）感到憂喜參半。	
2️⃣ **Act fast**（即時傳達）	恭賀信要在值得道賀的喜事發生後，就**盡快**寄出。	
3️⃣ **Positive**（保持正面）	信中只須寫下**讚美（praise）**之詞，任何負面評論或壞消息都不應該出現在文中。	
4️⃣ **Concise**（簡潔）	恭賀信務求**清楚、簡短**，過度的讚美反而會顯得**虛情假意（insincere）**。	
5️⃣ **Reader-Focused**（將焦點放在對方）	信中不需要提到有關寫信者自身的正面消息，**以免轉移（distract）恭賀的重點**。另外，也要避免暗指對方的喜事亦會對你帶來好處，以免讓信件讀起來有失誠懇。	
6️⃣ **Watch Your Tone**（注意語氣）	信中的用字和句型講求**簡單、正面**。若使用**充滿溢美之詞的（effusive）**長句，恐怕會讓信件讀起來**帶有諷刺（sarcastic）**。	

祝賀升遷 Congratulations on a Promotion

Chen Baking Supplies

70 Chenggong Road, North District, Tainan 704, Taiwan

January 30, 2023

Lina Fischer
Schmidt Manufacturing, Inc.
Fugger Strasse 89
Potsdam
Brandenburg 14471
Germany

Dear Ms. Fischer:

This is just a short note to offer our best wishes on your promotion to sales manager this month.

Having worked with you for a long time, we know **firsthand**[1] how **capable**[2] you are. We have always felt **in safe hands**[3] when dealing with you. I am very happy that your hard work is being **rewarded**[4]. All of us here at Chen Baking Supplies wish you every success in your new role.

We also look forward to working with the person who is **taking over**[5] your old role. If there is anything we can do on our **end**[6] to help with the **transition**[7], please let us know.

Kind regards,

Jane Chen

Jane Chen
Owner, Chen Baking Supplies

Key Terms 核心字彙片語

1 **firsthand** [ˋfɝstˋhænd] (adv./a.)
第一手地（的）

2 **capable** [ˋkepəb!] (a.) 有能力的

3 **in safe hands** [ɪn sef hændz]
令人覺得安心可靠

4 **reward** [rɪˋwɔrd] (v./n.) 回報

5 **take over** [tek ˋovɚ] 接任

6 **end** [ɛnd] (n.) 方面；部分

7 **transition** [trænˋzɪʃən] (n.) 過渡（期）

② 祝賀事業擴展 Congratulations on a Business Expansion

Prosperity Entertainment Devices

28 Fung Yi Street
Ma Tau Kok, Kowloon
Hong Kong
Tel: 852-36821820　Fax: 852-36821820

23 May 2023

Robert McBan
Zips and Zaps
4 Mount Macarthur Blvd.
Sydney, NSW 4723
Australia

Dear Mr. McBan:

We were very happy to hear that Zips and Zaps has opened two new stores this year. Everyone here would like to wish you many **congratulations**[1].

We too began as a small company. So we know how much hard work it takes to grow a business. You must be very proud to have achieved so much in such a short time. In our **dealings**[2] so far, it has been clear that you are a person of great **passion**[3]. And your strong **leadership**[4] is **certainly**[5] a **key**[6] **factor**[7] in you achieving this milestone.

Please accept once again our sincere **compliments**[8] and warm wishes for the future. If we can assist you in any way during this busy time, please let me know.

Sincerely,

Sally Leung

Sally Leung
Head of Client Relations
Prosperity Entertainment
Devices

Key Terms 核心字彙片語

1 **congratulation** [kənˌgrætʃəˈleʃən] (n.) 祝賀（詞）
2 **dealing** [ˈdilɪŋ] (n.) （商業）往來
3 **passion** [ˈpæʃən] (n.) 熱情
4 **leadership** [ˈlidɚʃɪp] (n.) 領導（能力）
5 **certainly** [ˈsɝtənlɪ] (adv.) 絕對地
6 **key** [ki] (a.) 關鍵的
7 **factor** [ˈfæktɚ] (n.) 因素
8 **compliment** [ˈkɑmpləmənt] (n.) 讚美

Ruby Textiles, Inc.

39 Abdul Rehman Street
Mumbai 400003
India
Ph: +91 22-24935374 Fax: +91 22-24935375

22 July 2023

Divya Manda
Ruby Textiles, Inc.
39 Abdul Rehman Street
Mumbai 400003
India

Dear Ms. Manda:

Many congratulations on your fifth year with Ruby Textiles. **On behalf of**[1] the company, I would like to thank you for your hard work during this time.

In recent years, our company has gone **from strength to strength**[2]. And I know that this is **in no small part**[3] **down to**[4] you. You are very hardworking and have a strong business **sense**[5]. I have often been **impressed**[6] with your **dedication**[7] and **shrewd**[8] decision making. We would certainly not be so successful without your efforts.

I hope that you will remain with us for many years to come. Your **talent**[9] and loyalty are highly valued. I offer you my best wishes for your future success.

Yours truly,

Advik Birla

Advik Birla
President, Ruby Textiles

Key Terms 核心字彙片語

1 **on behalf of** [ɑn bɪˋhæf ʌv] 謹代表……

2 **from strength to strength** [frɑm strɛŋθ tu strɛŋθ] 日益茁壯;蒸蒸日上

3 **in no small part** [ɪn no smɔl pɑrt] 在不小程度上

4 **(be) down to (sb.)** [daʊn tu]〔英式用法〕（某事是）仰賴、歸功於（某人）

5 **sense** [sɛns] (n.) 判斷力

6 **impress** [ɪmˋprɛs] (v.) 使……印象深刻

7 **dedication** [ˌdɛdəˋkeʃən] (n.) 奉獻

8 **shrewd** [ʃrud] (a.) 精明的

9 **talent** [ˋtælənt] (n.) 才能

祝賀開業 Congratulations on an Opening

Prince's Print Services

960 Nootka Street, Vancouver
British Columbia V5M 3M5

March 15, 2023

Liam Steel
Steel Accounting
988 Nootka Street
Vancouver
British Columbia

Dear Mr. Steel:

Many congratulations on the opening of your new business. We at Prince's Print Services welcome you to the area. We wish you great success.

We have been in need of a good accounting **firm**[1] in this area for some time. There are many here who will **benefit**[2] from your services. In fact, I print a **monthly**[3] **newsletter**[4] for the area's small businesses. I would be happy to do a **profile**[5] of you and your business for next month's **issue**[6]. It would be a good way to introduce yourself to the **community**[7]. If that is something you would like to do, feel free to give me a call on 778-227-3682.

Further[8], if you need any printing services, I provide them at a discount for businesses who are in their first year.

Our store is just a short distance south of yours on Nootka Street.

If there is anything else I can do to help you **settle in**[9], please let me know.

Kind regards,

Roger Prince

Roger Prince
Owner, Prince's Print Services

Key Terms 核心字彙片語

1 **firm** [fɝm] (n.) 公司
2 **benefit** [ˋbɛnəfɪt] (v.) 得益
3 **monthly** [ˋmʌnθlɪ] (a.) 每月的
4 **newsletter** [ˋnjuzˏlɛtɚ] (n.) 通訊
5 **profile** [ˋprofaɪl] (n.) 傳略；人物簡介
6 **issue** [ˋɪʃʊ] (n.) （報刊的）期
7 **community** [kəˋmjunətɪ] (n.) 社區；社群
8 **further** [ˋfɝðɚ] (adv.) 另外
9 **settle in** [ˋsɛt! ɪn] 安頓下來

Tiny Flower Gardening

32 Crown Street
London
SW17 2BL
Tel: 020 7946 0103
Fax: 020 7946 0104

11 November 2023

Lina Lee
Tiny Flower Gardening
32 Crown Street
London
SW17 2BL

Dear Lina:

I wanted to wish you congratulations on your retirement. After so many years of hard work for us, you will be deeply missed.

Your role in **marketing**[1] has been **vital**[2] in helping our company grow to its current success. Your strong **work ethic**[3] has always set an excellent example for your **coworkers**[4]. And your bright smile and humor always made the office a happier place.

I know that you are now looking forward to spending time with your family and traveling the world with your husband, Roy. I wish you all the best and hope you find plenty of joy in your retired life. If anyone **deserves**[5] it, it's you!

I will also be sure to send you an **invitation**[6] to our **yearly**[7] dinner. That way we can all have a chance to **catch up**[8] soon.

All the best wishes for the future,

Anthony White

Anthony White, Executive Director
Tiny Flower Gardening

Key Terms 核心字彙片語

1 **marketing** [`mɑrkɪtɪŋ] (n.) 行銷
2 **vital** [`vaɪt!] (a.) 極重要的
3 **work ethic** [wɝk `ɛθɪk] (n.) 工作態度；職業道德
4 **coworker** [`ko͵wɝkɚ] (n.) 同事
5 **deserve** [dɪ`zɝv] (v.) 值得
6 **invitation** [͵ɪnvə`teʃən] (n.) 邀請
7 **yearly** [`jɪrlɪ] (a.) 每年一度的
8 **catch up** [kætʃ ʌp] 聊聊近況；敘舊

1　表達祝賀 Offering Congratulations

① It is my great pleasure to congratulate you on your retirement.

我非常榮幸恭喜你榮退。

② Many congratulations on your recent promotion.　非常恭喜你近期升遷。

③ Please accept the congratulations of all of us at Ruby Textiles on the opening of your new branch store.

請容我們「紅寶石紡織」全體員工祝福您新分店開幕順利。

④ We at Tiny Flower Gardening were delighted to hear about your achievement.

聽聞您的成就，我們「小花園藝」感到非常開心。

⑤ We would like to offer you our warmest congratulations on your huge success.　我們想致上最熱烈的祝賀，恭喜您大獲成功。

⑥ We are delighted to hear that you won the national design contest.

聽到您贏得全國設計競賽，我們感到開心。

2　給予未來祝福 Offering Good Wishes

① We wish you every success in your new role / the future.

祝福你在新崗位上／在未來順利成功。

② I offer you my best wishes for the future / your future success / your retirement.　為你的未來／你未來的成功／你的退休，我獻上最好的祝福。

③ Please accept our warmest wishes for the future / your future success / your retirement.　為你的未來／你未來的成功／你的退休，請容我們獻上最溫暖的祝福。

④ All the best wishes for the future / your future projects / your retirement.

為你的未來／你未來的計畫／你的退休，在此獻上最真摯的祝福。

⑤ Your future success is very well deserved.　你在未來定將鴻圖大展。

1 Here is a letter sent by Nit to congratulate his business acquaintance Divya on her promotion. Choose three of the sentences in the box below to complete the congratulation letter.

- I hope you find this new challenge rewarding.
- I would like to inform you about our new range of products.
- Many congratulations on your recent promotion to director of sales.
- I have always appreciated your hard work and dedication.
- I'm afraid there was a problem with your last shipment.

Deluxe
P.O. Box 876, Bangkok
10200 Thailand
Ph: 66-2-8465354
Fax: 66-2- 8465355

April 3, 2023

Divya Manda
Ruby Textiles, Inc.
39 Abdul Rehman Street
Mumbai 400003
India

Dear Ms. Manda:

❶ ....

We here at Deluxe were delighted to hear the news.

❷ ....

Thanks to you, our companies have been able to maintain a long and successful relationship.

❸ ....

And I wish you every success for the future.

Yours truly,

Nit Kaouthai

Nit Kaouthai, Manager, Deluxe Clothing

2 Now complete the following congratulation letter from a company owner to an employee on his anniversary with the company. Use the information in the box to help you.

- **Employee:** Nit Kaouthai
- **Occasion:** tenth anniversary
- **Traits:** strong leadership, continued focus
- **Owner's hope:** stay with the company for many more years

Deluxe
P.O. Box 876, Bangkok
10200 Thailand
Ph: 66-2-8465354
Fax: 66-2- 8465355

Nit Kaouthai
Deluxe
P.O. Box 876
Bangkok 10200
Thailand

Dear ❶ .... :

❷ ....
On behalf of the company, I would like to thank you sincerely for your many years of hard work.

❸ ....
Your work over the past decade has helped our company grow from strength to strength.

❹ .... And I wish you every success for the future.

Yours truly,

Hathai Anuman

Hathai Anuman, Owner, Deluxe Clothing

3 Complete the following congratulation letter for a new business opening.

The letter is from Mille May, owner of Millie's Bakery, to Michael Powell, the owner of Chef Mike's Fine Food. Use the instructions in the letter to help you.

Millie's Bakery

2740 Circle Drive, Houston, TX, 77032

December 1, 2022

Michael Powell
Chef Mike's Fine Food
1160 Lime Street
Houston, TX
77021

❶ [Greeting/Salutation] ....

❷ [The letter's purpose]

....

....

Your talents as a chef are well-known in the local area. I am sure your business will be a great success.

❸ [Offer to help with promoting the business]

....

....

Millie's Bakery has a large social media following of local food lovers, and I would be happy to help you get the word out.

❹ [Wish the owner luck]

....

....

❺ [Closing line] ....

❻ [Sender's name] ....

....

Owner, Millie's Bakery

Now, **work with a partner** to compose a congratulation letter of your own for a new business opening. Here is some necessary information.

- **Sender:** Bartholomew Lee (Bart's Interior Design)
- **Receiver:** Kenneth Champion (Kitchen Planet)
- **Points to cover:** Congratulate the owner on the new business. Compliment the owner/the business. Wish the owner success.

Lesson 11 客訴信、建言信撰寫 Complaint and Suggestion Letters

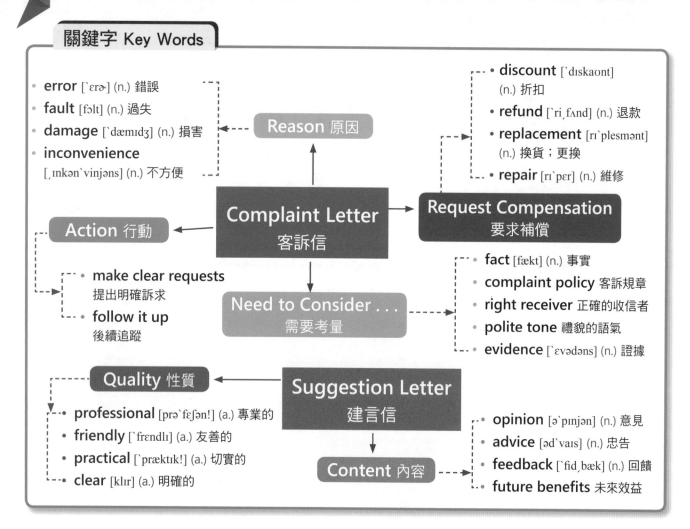

關鍵字 Key Words

- **error** [`ɛrə] (n.) 錯誤
- **fault** [fɔlt] (n.) 過失
- **damage** [`dæmɪdʒ] (n.) 損害
- **inconvenience** [͵ɪnkən`vinjəns] (n.) 不方便

Reason 原因

- **discount** [`dɪskaʊnt] (n.) 折扣
- **refund** [`ri͵fʌnd] (n.) 退款
- **replacement** [rɪ`plesmənt] (n.) 換貨;更換
- **repair** [rɪ`pɛr] (n.) 維修

Complaint Letter 客訴信

Request Compensation 要求補償

Action 行動

- **make clear requests** 提出明確訴求
- **follow it up** 後續追蹤

Need to Consider . . . 需要考量

- **fact** [fækt] (n.) 事實
- **complaint policy** 客訴規章
- **right receiver** 正確的收信者
- **polite tone** 禮貌的語氣
- **evidence** [`ɛvədəns] (n.) 證據

Quality 性質

- **professional** [prə`fɛʃən!] (a.) 專業的
- **friendly** [`frɛndlɪ] (a.) 友善的
- **practical** [`præktɪk!] (a.) 切實的
- **clear** [klɪr] (a.) 明確的

Suggestion Letter 建言信

Content 內容

- **opinion** [ə`pɪnjən] (n.) 意見
- **advice** [əd`vaɪs] (n.) 忠告
- **feedback** [`fid͵bæk] (n.) 回饋
- **future benefits** 未來效益

1-1　What Is a Complaint Letter?（客訴信是什麼？）

　　「客訴信」是顧客為了表達心中不滿，因而寫給對方公司的信件。顧客在信中會說明自己**不滿的原因**，以及公司可以做出**哪些措施來彌補錯誤（repair errors）或解決問題（solve problems）**。如果一家公司表現不佳，公司的顧客寫封客訴信給對方，是合情合理的做法，因為客訴信能讓公司認知到自身疏失（fault）所在，同時為這次錯誤留下正式紀錄；如果顧客要針對此事採取進一步行動，客訴信就能派上用場。

1-2　How to Write（客訴信該怎麼寫？）

　　即使顧客寫信時有滿腹牢騷，也**不宜在客訴信裡口出惡言（insult）**。客訴信的語氣反而應該要**彬彬有禮、通情達理**，同時也要**清楚明確、據理力爭**。寫信者不應該以激怒公司或是以侮辱收信人為目的，畢竟做錯事情的可能並非收信人。

　　為了讓客訴信能達成**正面結果**，寫信時應嘗試做到以下幾點：

1️⃣ **Check Facts**（確認事實經過）：充分了解事件全貌，確保提出的客訴**有理有據（reasonable）**。

2️⃣ **Check Complaints Policies**（查看對方公司的**客訴規章**）：許多公司對於客訴的處理，都會遵循具體的規範，顧客可以特別留意，以便雙方能節省許多時間。

3️⃣ **Write to the Right Person**（寫給正確對象）：客訴信若能**具體寫出收件人姓名**，將能發揮更大的影響力。如果不確定該寫給誰，不要猶豫，可將信件同時寫給多個對象。

4️⃣ **Be Precise**（內容講求明確）：務必清楚說明客訴內容，例如可在信中提供**姓名（name）**、**日期（date）**、**訂單編號（order number）**等資訊。然而，須避免給出不必要的小細節，讓客訴信直截了當、切中要點。

5️⃣ **Be Polite**（保持禮貌）：無論發生什麼事，都應該**維持專業、就事論事的口吻（tone）**。若客訴信以侮辱公司為目，一般都不會受到重視。有禮且講理的客訴信有更高機會被看見，並獲得積極回覆。

6️⃣ **Send Evidence**（寄出證據）：應隨信附上與客訴相關的**正式文書副本**，使客訴案件更受重視。

7️⃣ **Make Clear Requests**（做出明確訴求）：應要求對方**在合理時間內（例如兩週內）答覆**，亦可建議對方給予合理的**補償（compensation）**，如下次購物時提供**折扣（discount）**、為產品**退款（refund）**、提供**換貨（replacement）**或**修理（repair）**等。

8️⃣ **Follow It Up**（後續追蹤）：如果沒有及時收到對方答覆，就應該以更加強硬的語氣再次寫信給該公司，或者也可以將客訴信寄給公司的其他高層人士。

2-1　**What Is a Suggestion Letter?**（建言信是什麼？）

　　在與一家公司往來時，顧客可能會發現該公司在特定方面，服務上有應該加強的地方。這種情況下，顧客不妨寫封建言信給對方公司。在這類信函中，寫信的顧客會針對該公司應如何改進，提出**意見（opinion）**與**忠告（advice）**，以期將來顧客可以享有更佳的服務體驗。

2-2　**How to Write**（建言信該怎麼寫？）

　　為使建言信得到重視，寫信時應做到以下幾點：

1️⃣ **Use Professional and Friendly Tone**（語氣要保持專業、客氣友善）：這將確保該公司會**以開放的心胸（with an open mind）**接納建言。若以命令的口氣頤指氣使，結果未必能夠如願以償。

2️⃣ **Thank the Reader**（感謝收信者給予提供建言的機會）：並不是每家公司都樂於聽取他人的建言，所以感謝對方願意花時間閱讀建言信，是建言信的重點。

3️⃣ **Think Practically**（提出切實可行的意見）：請確定信中建言切實可行。不妨站在該公司的立場思考看看：你的建議是否可能輕易地**付諸實行（put into practice）**？

4️⃣ **Be Clear**（敘述要明確）：務必具體說明**可以改進的部分**、以及**需要改進的原因**，並將你的想法用簡單明瞭的語言詳盡說明。

5️⃣ **Focus on Benefits**（著重未來效益）：**信中需具體說明**這些建言會如何為公司帶來**正面影響**。若有其他公司也採取了和建言相同的做法，也可以提出來，有助提高說服力。

1 訂單的客訴信 A Complaint Letter About an Order

Spark Electronics

326 Jurong East Street 31
Singapore 600326
Tel: 65 65 646163 Fax: 65 65 646164

March 15, 2023

Attn: Mr. Matthew Lau
Sales Manager
Prosperity Entertainment Devices
28 Fung Yi Street
Ma Tau Kok, Kowloon
Hong Kong

Ref: **PO**[1] 040127

Dear Mr. Lau:

I am sorry to have to write to tell you that our order of March 1, PO 040127, was not delivered correctly.

Our order was for 200 smart speakers (item number CP08) and 200 smart TVs (item number G01). They arrived yesterday on time. However, we received only 20 speakers and 20 TVs. I have **enclosed**[2] a copy of our purchase order and the paid **invoice**[3] **for your reference**[4].

Smart speakers and TVs are very popular items in our store. This error has meant that we will not be able to **meet our customers' demands**[5]. I hope you can send the correct number of items as soon as possible. A **partial**[6] **refund**[7] for the **inconvenience**[8] this error has caused would also be appreciated. I hope that there can be no more mistakes with our orders in future.

Sincerely,

James Chew

James Chew, Purchasing Manager
Spark Electronics

Enc. (2)

Key Terms 核心字彙片語

1 **PO = purchase order** (n.) 訂購單
2 **enclose** [ɪn`kloz] (v.) 隨信附上
3 **invoice** [`ɪnvɔɪs] (n.) 請款帳單；發貨單；發票
4 **for your reference** 供你參考
5 **meet (one's) demands** 達成⋯⋯的要求
6 **partial** [`pɑrʃəl] (a.) 部分的
7 **refund** [`ri͵fʌnd] (n.) 退款
8 **inconvenience** [͵ɪnkən`vinjəns] (n.) 不方便

2 產品損壞的客訴信 A Complaint Letter About Damage

Deluxe
P.O. Box 876, Bangkok
10200 Thailand
Ph: 66-2-8465354
Fax: 66-2- 8465355

May 3, 2023

Attention: Divya Manda
Ruby Textiles, Inc.
39 Abdul Rehman Street
Mumbai 400003
India

Reference: PO 12L15

Dear Ms. Manda:

It is with **regret**[1] that I **inform**[2] you of some serious problems with your delivery of two boxes of leather slippers, PO 12L15.

When I opened the boxes today, the slippers inside were damaged due to **rot**[3]. Though my staff and I tried to clean them, they remained too damaged to be **put on sale**[4]. I do not know what caused the slippers to arrive in this condition. Perhaps there was a problem in the way they were stored or something happened during delivery.

I have always been happy with the **quality**[5] of your goods in the past, but I am afraid I will have to ask for a refund or **replacement**[6] for this order.

Please **contact**[7] me as soon as possible at 66-2-8465354, ext. 2.

Best wishes,

Nit Kaouthai

Nit Kaouthai, Manager, Deluxe Clothing

Key Terms 核心字彙片語

1 **regret** [rɪ`grɛt] (n./v.) 遺憾

2 **inform** [ɪn`fɔrm] (v.) 通知

3 **rot** [rɑt] (n.) 腐蝕；長霉

4 **put (sth.) on sale** 將⋯⋯推出販售

5 **quality** [`kwɑlətɪ] (n.) 品質

6 **replacement** [rɪ`plesmənt] (n.) 更換

7 **contact** [`kɑntækt] / [kən`tækt] (v.) 聯繫

Saturn Systems

1176 N. Ventura Avenue, Oak View, CA 93022, USA
Tel: +1 719 392-9068 Fax: +1 719 392-9069

September 15, 2023

Yoichi Fujita
Tech PCO
18-20 Nihonbashi Koami-cho
Chuo-ku
Tokyo 103-0016
Japan

Dear Mr. Fujita:

Thank you for inviting me to be a speaker at the recent data systems conference. The hotel you **arranged**[1] for me was great. And the driver who drove me to and from the conference center was polite and on time. **If you don't mind,**[2] however, I do have a small suggestion for you.

I noticed that many of the talks had small audiences. This was because many guests did not know the event **schedule**[3]. As a result, they missed key talks. I know the schedule had been sent out to guests in an email. But may I suggest that in the future you also provide the schedule in paper form at the center itself? You could also post it on the event's website so people can **access**[4] it easily on their phones. This is how things have been done at other events I have been to. Doing so helps everyone avoid being disappointed.

Thank you once again for the chance to **present**[5] at the event and to provide you with this **feedback**[6].

Kind regards,

Kevin Miller

Kevin Miller, CEO
Saturn Systems

Key Terms 核心字彙片語

1 **arrange** [əˋrɛndʒ] (v.) 安排
2 **If you don't mind, . . .** 如果你不介意……
3 **schedule** [ˋskɛdʒʊl] (n.) 時程表
4 **access** [ˋæksɛs] (v.) 取用
5 **present** [prɪˋzɛnt] (v.) 發表
6 **feedback** [ˋfidˏbæk] (n.) 回饋

常用句型及用語 Common Sentence Patterns and Phrases

1 提出客訴時的用語 Making a Complaint

① <u>I am sorry to inform you that</u> the room I stayed in was not properly cleaned.
我很抱歉要告知你們，我住的房間並未經妥善清潔。

② <u>I regret to inform you that</u> I did not receive my order.
我很遺憾通知你，我並未收到我的訂單商品。

③ <u>It pains me to report that</u> your server was not helpful when I visited.
我很難過要告知你們：我到貴店時並未得到你們服務生妥善服務。

④ <u>Unfortunately, there is a problem with</u> the products I received from you.
很遺憾，我從你們那邊收到的產品有問題。

2 請求解決辦法或換貨 Asking for a Resolution or Replacement

① I hope you can <u>deal with this issue</u> as soon as possible.
我希望您能儘快處理好這個問題。

② I hope you can <u>resolve this problem</u> without delay.
我希望您能立即解決這個問題。

③ Some measure of compensation <u>would be appreciated</u>.
如能有些補償措施，將不勝感激。

④ <u>I am afraid I will have to ask for</u> a refund or replacement for this order.
這張訂單我可能必須要請求你們退款或換貨。

3 提供建議 Offering a Suggestion

① <u>I have a small suggestion about</u> the music played at your store.
關於貴店播放的音樂，我有個小小的建議。

② <u>May I offer some feedback about</u> your new app?
關於你們的新應用程式，我能提供一點回饋意見嗎？

③ <u>A possible solution to this issue would be</u> putting up a sign.
此問題可能的解決辦法是設置告示。

④ Doing things a different way <u>might produce better results</u>.
改變做法，也許會得到更好的結果。

1 Copy the following paragraphs into the body of this complaint letter in the correct order.

Spark Electronics

326 Jurong East Street 31
Singapore 600326
Tel: 65 65 646163 Fax: 65 65 646164

November 21, 2023

Matthew Lau
Prosperity Entertainment Devices
28 Fung Yi Street
Ma Tau Kok, Kowloon
Hong Kong

Ref: PO 0785B

Dear Mr. Lau:

Ⓐ Please send replacements as soon as possible and arrange for collection of the damaged goods.

Ⓑ I regret to inform you of a problem with your recent shipment of printers (PO 0785B), which arrived today.

Ⓒ If you need to discuss the matter further, please contact me on +65 65-646163 ext. 3.

Ⓓ Ten of the printers had signs of damage. And as a result, we are not able to sell them. I hope you can understand how inconvenient this is for us.

❶ ....

❷ ....

❸ ....

❹ ....

Sincerely,

James Chew

James Chew
Purchasing Manager, Spark Electronics

2 Now do the same for this suggestion letter.

Green Cloud Technology
66 Ceres Street
San Francisco, CA 94124
USA
Tel: +1 415 822-4712

March 12, 2023

Yoichi Fujita
Tech PCO
18-20 Nihonbashi Koami-cho
Chuo-ku
Tokyo 103-0016
Japan

Dear Mr. Fujita:

Ⓐ While my hotel was comfortable, I would have liked a larger room and one on a higher floor.

Ⓑ Thank you once again for the chance to be one of your guest speakers and for your openness to feedback.

Ⓒ May I suggest that in the future you send out a preferences checklist to your speakers beforehand? I believe this would greatly improve their experience.

Ⓓ Thank you for inviting me to be a speaker at the conference in Tokyo last week. I enjoyed the experience, but I do have a small suggestion about hotel arrangements for your speakers.

❶ ....

❷ ....

❸ ....

❹ ....

Kind regards,

Sandra Lee

Sandra Lee
Chief Operating Officer, Green Cloud Technology

Lesson 12 客訴信、建言信回覆
Responses to Complaint and Suggestion Letters

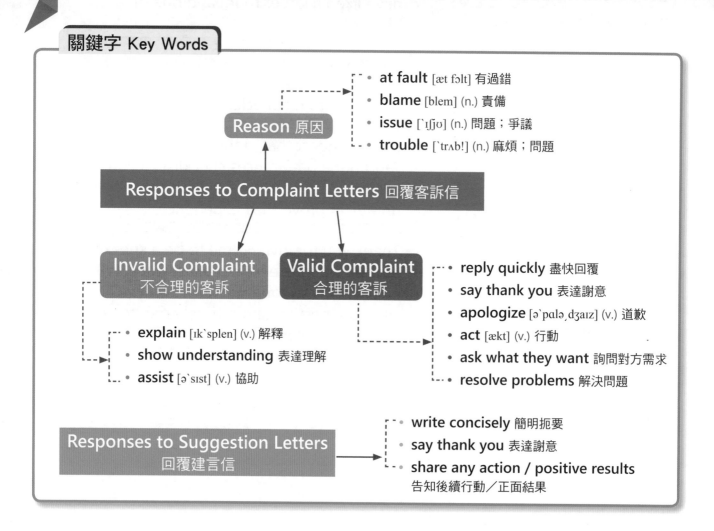

關鍵字 Key Words

Reason 原因
- **at fault** [æt fɔlt] 有過錯
- **blame** [blem] (n.) 責備
- **issue** [ˋɪʃʊ] (n.) 問題；爭議
- **trouble** [ˋtrʌb!] (n.) 麻煩；問題

Responses to Complaint Letters 回覆客訴信

Invalid Complaint 不合理的客訴
- **explain** [ɪkˋsplen] (v.) 解釋
- **show understanding** 表達理解
- **assist** [əˋsɪst] (v.) 協助

Valid Complaint 合理的客訴
- **reply quickly** 盡快回覆
- **say thank you** 表達謝意
- **apologize** [əˋpɑləˏdʒaɪz] (v.) 道歉
- **act** [ækt] (v.) 行動
- **ask what they want** 詢問對方需求
- **resolve problems** 解決問題

Responses to Suggestion Letters 回覆建言信
- **write concisely** 簡明扼要
- **say thank you** 表達謝意
- **share any action / positive results** 告知後續行動／正面結果

1-1 Replying to a Complaint Letter（回覆客訴信）

撰寫客訴的**回覆（response）**之前，應先仔細**檢視**公司的**客訴規章（complaints policy）**。顧客會希望公司採取**確切的步驟**來處理客訴，因此應對任何問題時，了解哪些事情可以做、哪些事情不能做，是非常重要的。

有了這個觀念後，即可開始**草擬（draft）**回覆信。若公司**已採取措施處理（deal with）**客訴，就應**告知顧客**。若無，就要清楚告知**未來會如何處理客訴**，以及處理的**時程**。有時，處理客訴前可能還需要釐清更多詳細情形，在這種狀況下，請在回應客訴時明確告知。若是客訴的**解決（resolve）方法不只一種**，可以列出各種方法，向顧客**清楚說明**，並等待顧客回覆後再做後續處理。

為了維繫與顧客長遠的良好關係，**回覆客訴信時應遵循以下步驟：**

1 **Reply Quickly（盡快回覆）**：回應客訴務必盡快，別讓顧客久候，以免使對方觀感更加惡劣。

2. **Say Thank You**（表達謝意）：當公司的產品和服務發生問題時，即時掌握問題所在相當關鍵，因此當顧客接洽回報問題時，務必表達感謝。

3. **Apologize**（道歉）：**開頭第一段**就要表達歉意，並在**最後一段**再次致歉，坦承問題已對顧客造成困擾。表達歉意有助於緩解顧客對於公司的不滿情緒。

4. **Give Them Action**（展現行動力）：告知顧客公司為了解決問題，已採取哪些行動、或未來會有哪些作為，說明時務必明確具體。**清楚告知行動內容**能贏得顧客的好感，有助於維持信任感。

5. **Ask What They Want**（詢問對方需求）：當客訴有不同的處理選項時，要**詢問顧客偏好哪一種解決方式**。**把顧客放在首要考量**，有助維繫雙方的正向關係。

6. **Resolve Problems**（確實解決問題）：回覆客訴信後，若承諾提供補償或採取行動，務必**確認後續有確實達成**，切勿表面致歉、空口白話，以免使對方更加失去信任。

1-2 **Replying to an Invalid Complaint**（回應不合理的客訴）

收到客訴信時，**仔細核對事實**非常重要。有時，對方可能有所過失、或找錯咎責（blame）對象，但此時仍應**禮貌回覆並解釋（explain）狀況，將每項不合理的客訴都視為合理的客訴**，並妥善回應、處理。雖然公司未必有錯（at fault），**表達善意理解（show understanding）的態度**依然重要，不要讓顧客覺得困窘尷尬，並應在能力範圍內盡量協助（assist）顧客。畢竟無論如何，顧客都是顧客，而提供協助會為公司留下良好印象。

2 **Replying to a Suggestion Letter**（回覆建言信）

收到建言信後，需要鄭重加以回覆。回覆信**不必太長**，但內容中要**感謝對方的回饋意見（feedback）**，並告知公司為此採取的**後續行動**，展現出公司樂於聽取並斟酌顧客的想法。當顧客覺得自身意見獲得傾聽時，就會對這家公司產生更深厚的感情。

為了確保妥善回覆顧客建言，請遵守以下原則：

1. **Write Concisely**（簡明扼要）：信件務求簡短並兼顧禮貌即可。

2. **Say Thank You**（表達謝意）：在**信件開頭**與**結尾處**向顧客致謝，感謝他們願意花費時間和心思。即使他們的建言未獲採納，也要讓對方知道，公司很感謝這些好意協助。

3. **Share Any Action**（告知後續行動）：告知顧客針對他們提出的建言，**公司有何後續動作**，例如可能已轉交給相關部門處理，或者已付諸實行。就算目前無法以具體動作回應，也要告知已將他們的**意見記錄下來**，留作未來參考。

4. **Share Positive Results**（告知正面結果）：讓顧客知道他們的建言提供了哪些幫助，可以簡短說明建議所帶來的**正面效益（benefit）**，這會讓顧客對自己的貢獻（contribution）感到與有榮焉。

以下是針對前一課（Lesson 11）客訴信和建言信的範例，所做出的回覆信範例：

訂單客訴的回覆信 Response to a Complaint About an Order

Prosperity Entertainment Devices

28 Fung Yi Street
Ma Tau Kok, Kowloon
Hong Kong
Tel: 852-36821820   Fax: 852-36821820

March 19, 2023

James Chew
Spark Electronics
326 Jurong East Street 31
Singapore 600326

Ref: PO 040127

Dear Mr. Chew:

Thank you for **bringing** this **to** my **attention**[1]. I am so sorry for the trouble caused by this error.

I checked the details of your order. Our shipping team is usually very **reliable**[2]. But they made a mistake this time. I spoke to our shipping manager today. He will meet with his staff and make sure that it does not happen again.

This morning we sent the missing products **via**[3] **express**[4] shipping. They should arrive within five **business days**[5]. I have also authorized a 15% refund to your company's account. This should also go through within five business days.

Again, I am deeply sorry for this mistake. Your company is one of our best customers. If there are any more problems, please don't wait to **get in touch**[6]. I will be very happy to help.

Sincerely,

Matthew Lau

Matthew Lau, Sales Manager
Prosperity Entertainment Devices

Key Terms 核心字彙片語

1 **bring (sth.) to (sb.'s) attention**
   [brɪŋ tu ə`tɛnʃən] 使（某人）注意到（某事）
2 **reliable** [rɪ`laɪəb!] (a.) 可靠的
3 **via** [`vaɪə] (prep.) 透過……
4 **express** [ɪk`sprɛs] (n.) 快遞
5 **business day** [`bɪznɪs de] (n.) 工作天
6 **get in touch** [gɛt ɪn tʌtʃ] 聯繫

2 商品損壞的回覆信 Response to a Complaint About Damage

Ruby Textiles, Inc.
39 Abdul Rehman Street
Mumbai 400003
India
Ph: +91 22-24935374　Fax: +91 22-24935375

10 May 2023

Nit Kaouthai
Deluxe
P.O. Box 876
Bangkok 10200
Thailand

Ref: PO 12L15

Dear Mr. Kaouthai:

Thank you for your letter. I know how **frustrating**[1] it is to receive damaged goods.

However, my records show that this order arrived with you three months ago on 1 February 2023. So it seems that the **goods**[2] were with you for some months before you opened them.

We check our **stockroom**[3] weekly for any signs of **damp**[4]. And all other **deliveries**[5] of these slippers have been received without any **issue**[6]. It is possible, then, that the goods were damaged during the three months they have been with you unopened. As a result, I am sorry but we cannot offer you a refund this time.

We do understand the problem this has caused you, however. So we would be happy to give you 5% off your next order with us. We **value**[7] your business and hope that this issue will not stop you ordering from us again.

If there is any other way I can help, please give me a call at the above number.

Yours faithfully,

Divya Manda

Divya Manda, Sales Manager
Ruby Textiles, Mumbai

Key Terms 核心字彙片語
1 **frustrating** [ˋfrʌstretɪŋ] (a.) 令人惱怒的
2 **goods** [gʊdz] (n.) 貨物
3 **stockroom** [ˋstɑkˏrum] (n.) 倉庫
4 **damp** [dæmp] (n.) 潮濕；濕氣
5 **delivery** [dɪˋlɪvərɪ] (n.) 交付；投遞
6 **issue** [ˋɪʃʊ] (n.) 問題
7 **value** [ˋvælju] (v.) 重視

TECH PCO

18-20 Nihonbashi Koami-cho, Chuo-ku

Tokyo 103-0016, Japan

Tel: +81 3 3661 9087　Fax: +81 3 3661 9088

September 21, 2023

Kevin Miller
Saturn Systems
1176 N. Ventura Avenue
Oak View, CA 93022
USA

Dear Mr. Miller:

Thank you for taking the time to write to me with your feedback about the recent data systems event in Tokyo. I am glad the hotel was **to your liking**[1]. I hope you had some time to **explore**[2] the city while you were here.

Your ideas about schedules are **well received**[3]. I **passed** them **along**[4] to our staff in a meeting this morning. They will make sure that in the future, there will be plenty of paper schedules **available**[5] at all our events. Our web team will also **post**[6] the information online. I am sure this will create a better event experience for both guests and speakers.

Thank you once again for sharing your thoughts with us. I hope we can have the pleasure of working together again soon.

Yours truly,

Yoichi Fujita

Yoichi Fujita, Executive Vice President
Tech PCO, Tokyo

Key Terms 核心字彙片語

1 **to (sb's) liking** [tu `laɪkɪŋ] 符合⋯⋯的喜好
2 **explore** [ɪk`splor] (v.) 探索
3 **well received** [wɛl rɪ`sivd] 收悉；充分接受
4 **pass along** [pæs ə`lɔŋ] 轉達
5 **available** [ə`veləb!] (a.) 可取得的
6 **post** [post] (v.) 張貼

1 為錯誤或服務不佳致歉 Apologizing for a Mistake / Poor Service

① I am so sorry for the trouble caused by one of our employees.

由於我們一名員工造成您的困擾，我深感抱歉。

② We deeply regret the inconvenience brought about by the computer error.

因為電腦故障造成您的不便，我們深表歉意。

③ We are surprised and very sorry to hear that one of our drivers acted violently

toward you.　聽到我們一名司機對您暴力相向，我們驚訝之餘也深感抱歉。

④ We sincerely apologize for this mistake.　關於這次錯誤，我們誠摯表達歉意。

2 提供解決方案或換貨 Offering Resolution or Replacement

① We will send a replacement right away.　我們將馬上寄送替換品。

② We will ship your replacement immediately.　我們會馬上寄出替換品。

③ We would like to offer you a 10% discount on your next order.

我們願意在您下一筆訂單提供九折優惠。

④ We will provide you with a full/partial refund.　我們會提供全額／部分退款。

3 回覆對方建議 Replying to a Suggestion

① Thank you for taking the time to offer your feedback.

感謝您撥冗提供意見。

② Thank you for your excellent ideas regarding how to make the process

more efficient.　謝謝您就如何讓流程更有效率，提出的良好意見。

③ Your suggestions about schedules are well received / received with

gratitude.　您對日程表事宜提出的建議我們充分接受／我們滿心感激地接受您就日

程表事宜提出的建議。

④ Thank you for sharing your thoughts with us.　謝謝您跟我們分享您的想法。

1 The letter on the next page is a response to a complaint from a customer. Fill in each blank using one of the four options provided.

1
- offer you my warmest congratulations
- invite you to our company's anniversary dinner
- sincerely apologize for his unacceptable behavior
- place an order for three crates of French wine

2
- this staff member will not be working with us again
- we can offer you a very good deal on shipping
- the event will be held on the 31st of March at 8 p.m.
- I have many years of experience in this area of work

3
- As you chose express delivery, you should receive it by the end of next week
- Having worked with you for many years, I know it is very well deserved
- Our product will certainly help improve your company's efficiency
- I hope you will accept it as compensation for this unfortunate situation

4
- I wish you all the success for the future
- please accept my sincere apologies
- feel free to get in touch if you have any questions
- thank you for considering my application

Delish Catering Co.

4253 St George Street, Vancouver BC, V5T 1Z7

T: 604-643-4327

May 23, 2023

Gloria Wang
483 Robson Street
Vancouver BC
V6B 3K9

Dear Ms. Wang:

Thank you for getting in touch about the problems you experienced with one of our staff members at your recent event. I would like to ❶ .... I know that it must have caused you great distress.

Please rest assured that ❷ .... Also, we will be having a special training day next week to remind all our staff about the importance of correct behavior. I am authorizing a 20% refund of our fee to your account. ❸ ....

Once again, ❹ ....

Kind regards,

Cecile Arquette

Cecile Arquette
Owner, Delish Catering Co.

2 The email on the next page is a response to a suggestion from a customer. Fill in each blank using one of the four options provided.

①
- Enclosed is a brochure
- I would like to place an ad
- I am writing to request a refund
- Thank you for your ideas

②
- I placed an order on the 1st of this month.
- I researched the alternatives you suggested.
- we received letters of praise from several customers
- we will try hard to improve the speed of our deliveries

③
- your application
- your excellent advice
- your years of hard work
- attending our event

New Message

From: cecile@delishcatering.ca

To: regina.guelph@fastmail.com

Subject: Re: Some alternatives to plastic

Dear Ms. Guelph,

❶ _____ regarding our use of plastics. After reading your email, ❷ _____ _____ . I have now decided to phase out plastics within the year.

Thank you once again for ❸ _____ .

All best,

Cecile Arquette

Owner, Delish Catering

Lesson **13**　致歉信 Apology Letters

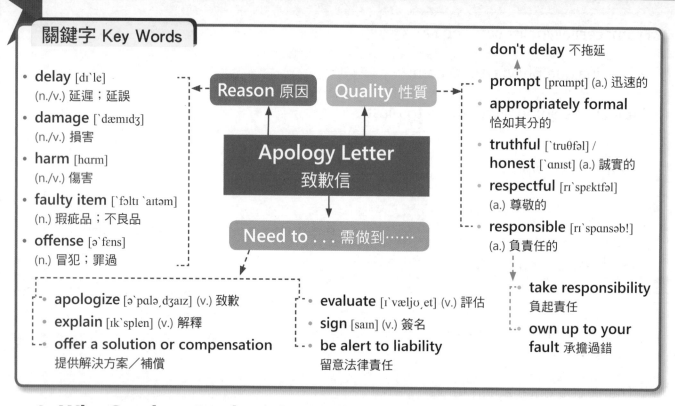

關鍵字 Key Words

- **delay** [dɪˋle]
  (n./v.) 延遲；延誤
- **damage** [ˋdæmɪdʒ]
  (n./v.) 損害
- **harm** [hɑrm]
  (n./v.) 傷害
- **faulty item** [ˋfɔltɪ ˋaɪtəm]
  (n.) 瑕疵品；不良品
- **offense** [əˋfɛns]
  (n.) 冒犯；罪過

Reason 原因　Quality 性質

Apology Letter
致歉信

Need to . . . 需做到……

- **don't delay** 不拖延
- **prompt** [prɑmpt] (a.) 迅速的
- **appropriately formal**
  恰如其分的
- **truthful** [ˋtruθfəl] /
  honest [ˋɑnɪst] (a.) 誠實的
- **respectful** [rɪˋspɛktfəl]
  (a.) 尊敬的
- **responsible** [rɪˋspɑnsəb!]
  (a.) 負責任的

- **take responsibility**
  負起責任
- **own up to your**
  fault 承擔過錯

- **apologize** [əˋpɑləˏdʒaɪz] (v.) 致歉
- **explain** [ɪkˋsplen] (v.) 解釋
- **offer a solution or compensation**
  提供解決方案／補償

- **evaluate** [ɪˋvæljʊˏet] (v.) 評估
- **sign** [saɪn] (v.) 簽名
- **be alert to liability**
  留意法律責任

1　Why Send an Apology Letter?（為何要寄致歉信？）

　　各家公司都會盡力避免出錯，但失誤在所難免（inevitable）。若是發生錯誤，企業應寫信**道歉（apologize）**，表示認知到自身過錯，也表示對於自身業務相當重視。若企業犯錯卻不願寫信致歉，客戶將來可能會轉而和其他公司往來合作。

　　反過來說，危機即是轉機，企業若能**勇於承擔（own up to）**並處理失誤，反而可以藉此與客戶建立更良善的關係。以下為幾種須撰寫致歉信的常見原因：

1 **Delay**（時程延誤）	若發生送貨時間延遲、任務進度延宕等情形，應為耽誤對方時間致歉。
2 **Damage / Harm**（造成損失或傷害）	因為業務過失造成對方金錢或人員的損失或傷害時，應對此疏失致歉。
3 **Faulty item**（產品瑕疵）	若公司產品存在瑕疵，應向消費者致歉。
4 **Offense**（言行冒犯）	若自己或公司員工有言行失當，應向受影響者致歉。

2　What Is a Good Apology Letter（致歉信的要點）

　　欲使致歉信達到使對方恢復信任、進而原諒過錯的目標，致歉信應確保滿足以下特質：

1 Prompt（迅速不拖延）	發現失誤發生時，切勿拖延（don't delay），要**即刻寫信道歉**，不要讓客戶生氣久候。
2 Appropriately formal / Respectful（恰如其分、展現尊重）	使用商業書信**恰當的正式結構、措辭**來寫道歉信函，顯示公司尊重對方、對該項失誤嚴肅看待。
3 Truthful / Honest（態度誠懇）	即使顧客對於錯誤相當不滿，公司若能**以誠實（honesty）的態度面對**，則有助挽回好感。
4 Responsible（負責任）	讓對方知道**你們會負起責任（take responsibility）、承擔過錯（own up to your fault）**，並且今後不會重蹈覆轍。

3 How to Write（致歉信要怎麼寫？）

1 **Apologize First**（一開頭就先道歉）
信裡要**儘早致歉**，這表示你將讀信者的感受放在第一位。

2 **Explain After Apologizing**（道歉完要說明原因）
請幫助讀信者理**解錯誤是如何發生的**。簡單扼要地告知事情的來龍去脈，但不要以藉口推託。

3 **Offer a Solution or Compensation**（提供解決辦法或補償方案）
告訴客戶你會**如何解決（solve）**此項錯誤，或是告知你會如何彌補他們的損失；常見的解決或補償措施包括**退款**、在**下筆訂單提供折扣優惠**、或是**修改公司政策（policy）**。

4 **Evaluate the Problem**（理解有些問題是無法解決的）
如果你的失誤讓客戶蒙受重大損失，他們可能會**不願意對此視而不見（overlook）**，甚至可能會被你所提供的折扣優惠觸怒。請根據實際狀況**隨機應變**。

5 **Sign Your Name**（道歉信要親筆簽名）
花點時間**親自為信件簽名**，以示對客戶的**尊重（respect）**。

6 **Be Alert to Liability**（留意法律責任）
致歉信在法庭上可能被視為**承認過失**的表現，因此若該次過錯有**引發法律行動（legal action）**的風險，信中轉達歉意的措辭最好**婉轉含蓄**，例如可以藉由**將焦點從自身錯誤轉移到顧客的體驗上**，來達到間接致歉的效果。試比較下列兩個句子：

❶ ❷ 著重顧客體驗；未提及失誤者何人，避免暗示問題是己方的責任。

❶ We are sorry that you did not receive your order.
很抱歉，您未能收到訂單貨品。
❷ I am sorry your computer was damaged.
很遺憾您的電腦壞了。

❸ ❹ 直接描述錯誤；坦承自身或公司犯錯，承認問題是我方造成的。

❸ We are sorry that we did not send your order.
很抱歉，我們未將您訂購的貨物寄出。
❹ I'm sorry I dropped your computer.
很抱歉，我把您的電腦摔壞了。

為延遲到貨致歉 Apology for Late Delivery

Muldoon Books

887 Helleck Avenue
Vancouver, VC B7Y 2K6

March 6, 2023

Zahra Aljumma
14/9 Solidarity Place
Vancouver, VC B5K 1L8

Dear Ms. Aljumma:

My records show that your recent order of books did not arrive by the agreed date. I am very sorry for this error. I also want to **reassure**[1] you that it will not happen again. The mistake was due to a computer error. This has now been **fixed**[2]. I hope the delay did not cause too much inconvenience.

I also hope that, as one of our **long-term**[3] customers, you can forgive this mistake. I would like to offer you a 30% discount on your next order as a goodwill **gesture**[4]. To **claim**[5] this, simply enter the **code**[6] COMP30 on the online order form.

If I can help you with anything else, please get in touch with me directly at noah@muldoonbooks.ca.

Yours sincerely,

Noah Ford

Noah Ford
Team Leader
Customer Relations Department

Key Terms 核心字彙片語

1 **reassure** [ˌriəˋʃʊr] (v.) 使……放心
2 **fix** [fɪks] (v.) 修理
3 **long-term** [ˋlɔŋˌtɝm] (a.) 長期的
4 **gesture** [ˋdʒɛstʃə] (n.) 表示；姿態
5 **claim** [klem] (v.) 索取
6 **code** [kod] (n.) 代碼

❷ 為產品瑕疵致歉　Apology for Defective Goods

Prosperity Entertainment Devices

28 Fung Yi Street
Ma Tau Kok, Kowloon
Hong Kong
Tel: 852-36821820 Fax: 852-36821820

13 October, 2023

Robert McBan
Zips and Zaps
4 Mount Macarthur Blvd.
Sydney, NSW 4723
Australia

Ref: PO100222a

Dear Mr. McBan:

We are very sorry that our latest shipment came with **faulty**[1] **items**[2]. You rightly expect only **high-quality**[3] goods from us. We regret that we **let you down**[4] this time.

Here, we **take** great **pride in**[5] our strict quality-**control**[6] system. We are now busy looking into how this issue was not **spotted**[7] by our team. When we find the cause of the error, we will take steps to make sure it does not happen again.

A replacement order will be shipped **free of charge**[8] to you by the end of today. When it arrives, our shippers will also **collect**[9] the faulty items from you. I would also like to offer you 15% off your next order from us. I hope this will make up for any trouble caused by this error.

Once again, please accept our deepest apologies.

Yours sincerely,

Sally Leung

Sally Leung, Head of Client Relations
Prosperity Entertainment Devices

Key Terms 核心字彙片語

1 **faulty** [ˈfɔltɪ] (a.) 有問題的
2 **item** [ˈaɪtəm] (n.) 品項
3 **high-quality** [ˈhaɪ͵kwɑlətɪ] (a.) 高品質的
4 **let (sb.) down** [lɛt daʊn] 使……失望
5 **take pride in . . .** [tek praɪd ɪn]
　 對……感到驕傲
6 **control** [kənˈtrol] (n./v.) 控制
7 **spot** [spɑt] (v.) 發現
8 **free of charge** [fri ʌv tʃɑrdʒ] 免費地
9 **collect** [kəˈlɛkt] (v.) 收取；收集

121

Ruby Textiles, Inc.

39 Abdul Rehman Street
Mumbai 400003
India
Ph: +91 22-24935374 Fax: +91 22-24935375

June 27, 2023

Kate Young
Fashion First
34 Christopher Mills Dr
Mount Laurel, NJ 08054
U.S.A.

Dear Ms. Young:

I am writing to apologize for the recent problems with your **account**[1]. I am also sorry for the delay in reply. It took us some time to **pinpoint**[2] the **exact**[3] issue.

Your **payment**[4] for your last order was indeed received on time. But a new member of our payments team **assigned**[5] it to an account with a name similar to yours. That is why you began getting late **notices**[6] even though you had, in fact, paid on time.

We will now be looking closely at our payments system to make it less **prone**[7] to this type of error. You have been a valued customer for a long time and we deeply regret **putting** you **through**[8] this **ordeal**[9]. By way of apology, I would like to offer you 5% off your next order from us. And please be **assured**[10] that this error will not happen again.

Yours faithfully,

Divya Manda

Divya Manda, Sales Manager
Ruby Textiles, Mumbai

Key Terms 核心字彙片語

1 **account** [əˋkaʊnt] (n.) 帳戶
2 **pinpoint** [ˋpɪnˏpɔɪnt] (v.) 精準確定
3 **exact** [ɪgˋzækt] (a.) 確切的
4 **payment** [ˋpemənt] (n.) 支付，付款
5 **assign** [əˋsaɪn] (v.) 分配；指定
6 **notice** [ˋnotɪs] (n.) 通知
7 **prone** [pron] (a.) 易於……的
8 **put (sb.) through . . .** [pʊt θru] 讓（某人）經歷……
9 **ordeal** [ɔrˋdiəl] (n.) 不愉快的經驗
10 **assure** [əˋʃʊr] (v.) 保證；確保

4 為變更致歉 Apology for Making a Change

TECH PCO

18-20 Nihonbashi Koami-cho, Chuo-ku

Tokyo 103-0016, Japan

Tel: +81 3 3661 9087　Fax: +81 3 3661 9088

Jan 21, 2023

Chan-yeol Kim

New Day Electronics

521 Teheran-ro

Samseong 1(il)-dong

Gangnam-gu

Seoul

South Korea

Dear Mr. Kim:

I am writing to **inform**[1] you that the Next Gen Electronics Conference in Tokyo, at which you were invited to speak next month, has been **postponed**[2]. My sincere apologies for this **last-minute**[3] change.

The postponement is due to the **venue**[4] being damaged by a recent earthquake. For safety, we must delay the event while **repairs**[5] **take place**[6]. It will now be held on March 3–5.

I understand if you will no longer be able to attend the event as a speaker. If this is the case, I am still happy to offer you 20% of your agreed **fee**[7]. If you can attend on the new dates, please let me know. I will then re-**book**[8] your travel tickets and hotel. I can also offer you a 10% rise on your fee as an apology for the trouble caused.

Thank you for your **patience**[9].

Kind regards,

Arata Murakami

Arata Murakami, Chief Liaison Officer
Tech PCO, Tokyo

Key Terms 核心字彙片語

1 **inform** [ɪnˋfɔrm] (v.) 通知

2 **postpone** [postˋpon] (v.) 延期

3 **last-minute** [ˏlæstˋmɪnɪt] (a.) 最後一刻前的

4 **venue** [ˋvɛnju] (n.) 場地

5 **repair** [rɪˋpɛr] (n./v.) 修理（工作）

6 **take place** [tek ples] 發生；進行

7 **fee** [fi] (n.) 費用

8 **book** [bʊk] (v.) 預定

9 **patience** [ˋpeʃəns] (n.) 耐心

123

Tara's Tasty Treats

89 Victoria Street
London
W70 4TJ

12 July 2023

Lina Chan
39 Mill Lane
London
W63 1YS

Dear Ms. Chan:

Subject: Our sincere apologies

I am writing to apologize for the **hurtful**[1] **social media**[2] **post**[3] **referenced**[4] in your letter dated 5 June 2023. We at Tara's Tasty Treats see how wrong it was. And we are very sorry for the **harm**[5] it caused.

The post was taken down right away after we received your letter. And the person who created it has been **reprimanded**[6]. I am now taking steps to make sure that this does not happen again. I will also be holding a special training day to teach my staff about this **sensitive**[7] topic.

As a gesture of goodwill[8], I would like to donate £100 to a **charity**[9] of your choice. Please let me know where you would like me to send it.

Once again, I am very sorry for the **offence**[10] caused. I hope we can do better in the future.

Yours sincerely,

Tara McDonald

Tara McDonald
Owner, Tara's Tasty Treats

Key Terms 核心字彙片語

1 **hurtful** [ˈhɝtfəl] (a.) 有害的
2 **social media** [ˈsoʃəl ˈmidɪə] (n.) 社群媒體
3 **post** [post] (n.) 貼文
4 **reference** [ˈrɛfərəns] (v.) 指出
5 **harm** [hɑrm] (n./v.) 傷害
6 **reprimand** [ˈrɛprəˌmænd] (v.) 訓斥
7 **sensitive** [ˈsɛnsətɪv] (a.) 敏感的
8 **as a gesture of goodwill**
　 [æz ə ˈdʒɛstʃɚ əv ˌgʊdˈwɪl] 為表達善意／誠意
9 **charity** [ˈtʃærətɪ] (n.) 慈善團體
10 **offence** [əˈfɛns] (n.) 冒犯；罪過（美式拼法為 offense）

常用句型及用語 Common Sentence Patterns and Phrases

1　道歉的用語 Apologizing

① I am very sorry for the error.　我對這次錯誤深感抱歉。

② I am writing to apologize for the late delivery.　我寫此信是為了延遲到貨致歉。

③ My sincere apologies for any offense caused.
我真誠地為任何造成的冒犯道歉。

④ Please accept my deepest apologies for our negligence.
請容我為我們的疏忽致上最深切的歉意。

⑤ We regret that we let you down this time.　很遺憾，這次我們讓您失望了。

⑥ We deeply regret that you received damaged goods.
我們非常抱歉您收到損壞的商品。

2　提供解釋說明 Explaining

① The error/mistake was caused by a fault in our computer system.
這次的錯誤／失誤是我們電腦系統故障造成的。

② The error/mistake was due to an unexpected power outage.
這個錯誤／失誤發生的原因是意外停電。

③ I assure you it will not happen again.　我向您保證，這種情況不會再發生。

④ We are taking steps to ensure this never happens again.
我們正採取相關措施，以確保此事不會再發生。

⑤ I assure you that the problem has now been fixed.
我向您保證，這個問題現在已經解決。

3　提議後續補償方案 Suggesting the Next Action

① I would like to offer a 20% discount on your next order.
我將提供您下筆訂單八折優惠。

② By way of apology, I would like to offer you 5% off your next order.
為了表示歉意，我將提供您下筆訂單享有5%折扣。

③ As a gesture of goodwill, I would like to offer you free shipping on your
next order.　為表達誠意，特此提供您下筆訂單免運費。

④ If you have any further questions, please get in touch.
若您有任何進一步的問題，請與我們聯繫。

1 Choose three of the sentences in the box below to complete the apology letter.

> * We wish you all the best with your two new stores and hope that everything goes smoothly with the openings.
> * We are currently checking the washing instructions on the rest of the product line.
> * I am writing to apologize for the problems you experienced with our shirts.
> * This is just a short note to thank you for speaking at our event last week.
> * We are happy to refund you the cost of the items and offer you 10% off your next purchase.

Fashion First
34 Christopher Mills Drive
Mount Laurel, NJ 08054

September 9, 2023

Alice Daughtrey
6707 Normandy Dr
Mount Laurel, NJ 08054

Dear Ms. Daughtrey:

1 ....

.... We pay close attention to the quality of our clothes. However, on this rare occasion this problem slipped our notice. Thank you for making us aware of it. **2** ....

....

3 ....

.... Please bring the shirts along with this letter to the store at any time and ask for Jane Russo, the manager. I will deal with the matter personally.

Sincerely,

Jane Russo

Jane Russo, Manager, Fashion First

2 You were recently notified that one of your orders arrived several days later than promised. Write a letter of apology to the customer.

Explain that you are investigating the cause of the delay and will take steps to ensure it doesn't happen again. Then offer the customer free express delivery on their next order.

Garment World
1263-7, Sanggye 1(il)-dong
Nowon-gu, Seoul
Rep. of Korea 139-838

May 4, 2023

Jane Russo
Fashion First
34 Christopher Mills Drive
Mount Laurel NJ 08054
USA

Dear Ms. Russo:

❶ ....
.... I understand that timely delivery is very important to our customers and that late delivery can cause all sorts of problems.

❷ ....
When the cause is found, ❸ ....
....

As compensation for the inconvenience caused, ❹ ....
....
Please use the code FD-1342 when placing your order.

Once again, I offer my sincere apologies.

Kind regards,
Joseph Park
Joseph Park
Manager, Garment World

3 Read the following email from a customer.

From: helgas567@fastmail.com

To: customerservice@londonlifetours.co.uk

Subject: Offensive jokes told by tour guide

To Whom It May Concern,

I recently attended a half-day city tour with your company. I was saddened to hear the tour guide, whose name was Joe, make some offensive jokes about people from my country. I had hoped to experience an educational tour of the city, but instead I felt very insulted. I hope you can take action on this matter and ensure that this kind of thing does not happen again.

Yours sincerely,
Helga Schmidt

Write back to the customer with an apology. Remember to do the following:

1 Apologize   2 Say what action you have taken

3 Offer a refund   4 Apologize again and ask for forgiveness

From: manager@londonlifetours.co.uk

To: helgas567@fastmail.com

Subject: Re: Offensive jokes told by tour guide

Dear Ms. Schmidt,

I was recently forwarded your email by my customer service department. 1 ....
....

This type of behavior is not encouraged or accepted by the company. 2 ....
....
.... As compensation, 3 ....
....

Our accounts department will be in touch shortly to process this.

Once again, 4 ....

Yours sincerely,

Toby James
Manager, London Life Tours

4 The following email is from a customer who is reporting a billing error.

New Message

Dear Mr. Walsh,

I recently reviewed my accounts and discovered an error regarding our recent transaction. The amount to be charged was $1,890; however, I seem to have been charged $1,980. I have attached a copy of the invoice along with a screenshot of the amount deducted from my account. I believe there must have been some kind of error in the billing process. I hope this matter can be resolved quickly.

Kind regards,

Margaret Liu

Now, **with a partner**, brainstorm and write an apology message to the customer.

Lesson 14 求職信 Employment Application Letters / Cover Letters

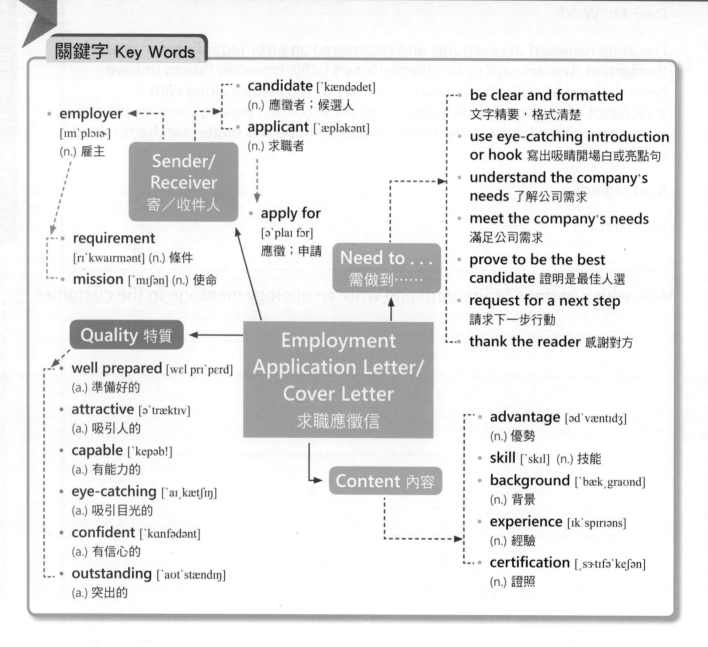

關鍵字 Key Words

Sender/Receiver 寄／收件人

- employer [ɪmˋplɔɪɚ] (n.) 雇主
- candidate [ˋkændədet] (n.) 應徵者；候選人
- applicant [ˋæpləkənt] (n.) 求職者
- apply for [əˋplaɪ fɔr] 應徵；申請
- requirement [rɪˋkwaɪrmənt] (n.) 條件
- mission [ˋmɪʃən] (n.) 使命

Employment Application Letter/ Cover Letter 求職應徵信

Need to . . . 需做到……
- be clear and formatted 文字精要，格式清楚
- use eye-catching introduction or hook 寫出吸睛開場白或亮點句
- understand the company's needs 了解公司需求
- meet the company's needs 滿足公司需求
- prove to be the best candidate 證明是最佳人選
- request for a next step 請求下一步行動
- thank the reader 感謝對方

Quality 特質
- well prepared [wɛl prɪˋpɛrd] (a.) 準備好的
- attractive [əˋtræktɪv] (a.) 吸引人的
- capable [ˋkepəb!] (a.) 有能力的
- eye-catching [ˋaɪ͵kætʃɪŋ] (a.) 吸引目光的
- confident [ˋkɑnfədənt] (a.) 有信心的
- outstanding [ˋaʊtˋstændɪŋ] (a.) 突出的

Content 內容
- advantage [ədˋvæntɪdʒ] (n.) 優勢
- skill [ˋskɪl] (n.) 技能
- background [ˋbæk͵graʊnd] (n.) 背景
- experience [ɪkˋspɪrɪəns] (n.) 經驗
- certification [͵sɝtɪfəˋkeʃən] (n.) 證照

1 What Is an Employment Application Letter?（求職信是什麼？）

　　求職信（employment application letter）是求職者寄給欲應徵公司的信，**是簡歷或履歷表（resume or CV）的開場白**，因此常稱為 cover letter（履歷封面信）。

　　求職信是你給企業的第一個印象，是**求職的第一封自我推薦信**，主要的功能是向對方**自我介紹**，信中應展現自己應徵這份工作的誠意，說明你**為什麼適合就職於該公司**，並重點**強調你是該工作的最佳人選（candidate）**。

2 **How to Write**（如何撰寫求職信）

1 **Be Clear and Formatted**（文字簡短精要，格式清楚）：求職信要簡短精要，它不是「履歷表自傳」，不宜長篇大論，200–400 字尤佳。**文字應明確好讀**、能打動人，**格式清楚**，讓你的求職信從人海中脫穎而出（stand out），吸引人資的目光，而有機會打開履歷自傳審閱。

求職信屬正式書信，信件的稱呼語務必正確，可用「**Dear Mr. /Ms.＋姓氏**」稱呼對方；若不確定收件人姓名，則可**使用對方職稱**，如「Dear Hiring Manager:」。若需使用同一封信當模板寄給多家公司（並不建議此做法），則務必確認有**修改稱謂**。結尾敬辭則可使用「**Sincerely,**」等，並簽上全名。

2 **Use Eye-Catching Introduction or Hook**（寫出吸睛的開場白或亮點句，簡短介紹自己）：求職信的**開頭幾行字**很重要，是足以讓你脫穎而出的關鍵文句。除了可以精簡提及寫信動機、想要應徵的職位、如何得知職缺相關資訊外，也要簡潔地自我介紹、**說明你個人特質、優勢**（advantage）**及經驗**，展現個性，強調**你為何比他人出眾**（outstanding），展現出寫作與溝通表達的卓越能力。

❶ 簡短說明有意爭取的職位，❷ 並且快速地說明自己的優勢所在，以便吸引審閱者的目光。

❶ I am writing with great interest to apply for the sales representative position in your company. ❷ As a capable salesperson with many years of solid experience, I can't wait to help your sales soar, just like I did for the many companies I previously worked for.

3 **Understand the Company's Needs**（證明你了解公司需求）：對於要應徵（apply for）的公司和職位，**事先做調查研究**，查詢**公司的使命**（mission）**和目標**，並在信中簡短描述公司，以及公司凸出的特色何在，讓公司充分了解你應徵這份職缺的熱忱以及誠意，並且知道你已經對這份工作有所了解，若錄取後能快速進入狀況。

❶ 展現已經對該企業進行過研究了解，並且 ❷ 知道未來職位的工作內容、目標與方向。

❶ From my research, I understand that your company is trying to develop energy-saving products that help slow down global warming. I appreciate that mission very much.
❷ Environmental protection is where my passion lies too, so I am very interested in taking part in your efforts.

131

4 Meet the Company's Needs（證明你能滿足公司需求）：信中必須展現你的**專業知識**和**教育背景**（educational background）如何能與公司需求和所應徵的職位相輔相成。如果過去的學經歷有和目前該公司所追求的目標相符合者，就可加以凸顯、強調（highlight），說明**你具備哪些專業知識和能力**，未來**可以為公司帶來什麼價值**。但切勿為了擴充信件篇幅，而多提與職缺無關的學經歷，以免審閱者判斷你不了解公司需求，造成反效果。

✅ **❶** 展現過去的求學和工作經驗，**❷** 如何和應徵中的工作能相輔相成。

> **❶** My master's thesis is about the development of artificial intelligence (AI). When I was in college, I also interned at a renowned AI developer in Silicon Valley for six months. **❷** I am sure I am well prepared for your AI engineer position.

❌ **❷** 強調描寫的工作經驗，和 **❶** 應徵的職位需求並無直接相關，可能讓審閱者難以判斷是否適任。

> I am very interested in **❶** working at your café. I may not have much experience in making coffee and sandwiches, but **❷** I worked as a food delivery driver for more than two years after graduating from college. The job was challenging, and I think I have memorized the name of every road in the city.

5 Prove You Are the Best Candidate（證明你是這份工作的最佳人選）：盡可能多**了解該職缺及其工作條件**（requirement）**的要求**。可以說明過去的**類似工作經驗**，以及任職期間有何**令人刮目相看的成果**，以證明你的專業能力。如果你是求職新鮮人（new to the workforce），可說明你過去參與過哪些**相關活動**，以展現未來能勝任這份工作所需的能力。此部分通常會跟上述第四點同時提出。

❶描述先前相關工作經驗，**❷**且指出工作期間所達成的亮眼成就，讓審閱者了解你的專業能力可以如何具體貢獻未來的雇主。

> When I served as **❶** an English tutor for senior high school students during my college years, **❷** their average test scores usually improved by about 30 percent. Many of them eventually got accepted by some of the best universities in the country thanks to their excellent exam results. That makes me believe I will be a great fit for your teaching position.

6 Request for a Next Step and Thank the Reader（結尾請求下一步行動，感謝對方閱讀信件）： 在結尾時呼籲對方有所行動也很重要。可以有禮貌且有自信地提出面試要求，此時可以用 **at your convenience**（在您方便時）說明公司可以有哪些後續行動，以及你會如何回應。

信中也務必要留下個人資料，包含姓名、住址、電話、email 信箱等聯絡資訊，以便公司能聯繫職缺事宜。最後，也要感謝對方抽空閱讀求職信。

❶ 有禮貌地向審閱者表明面試意願，並且 ❷ 提供充分聯絡方式供對方進行下一步動作，最後也不忘 ❸ 感謝審閱者抽空讀信。

Enclosed are my CV and a selection of my past work. In them you will learn more about my previous work experience and the certifications I acquired. ❶ If you wish to have an interview with me after reading this material, ❷ please call 0900-000-000 at any time. ❸ Thank you for taking the time to read this letter.

以上介紹的是一般求職信的寫作要點。為了展現誠意，信件具體內容可**根據應徵的公司加以變化**，並須**避免使用制式的罐頭信**，更切勿嘗試「一信闖天下」，用相同內容應徵不同性質的職位。最後，求職信的重要目標是吸引對方，使其有興趣打開你的簡歷或履歷表，因此也不需將個人經歷全數寫出，而過度重複簡歷／履歷、自傳和推薦信的內容。

求職信範例 1 Employment Application Letter 1

Michelle Wang

8468 East Sherwood St.
East Elmhurst, NY 11370
(+1) 646 555-1314

June 1, 2023

Attn: Mr. Timothy Hazlett
Human Resources Manager
Roosevelt Communications
1321 Main Street
New York, NY 10009

Dear Mr. Hazlett:

I am writing to apply for the role of junior editor. As a strong writer with **ample**[1] experience, I believe I would be a great **fit**[2].

Currently, I am finishing my **master's degree**[3] in English at NYU. Over the past two years, I have served as editor of the college newspaper. During this time, I have written over a hundred **pieces**[4] and edited many more. **Under my wing**[5], the paper's readers have more than doubled.

From my **research**[6], I see that the company is growing. I would love to be a part of that growth, and I believe my skills would make me a real **asset**[7]. I enclose a resume along with some pieces that show my **range**[8] as a writer. I look forward to hearing from you and talking about my fit with the company.

Sincerely,

Michelle Wang

Michelle Wang

Enc. (5)

> **Key Terms 核心字彙片語**
>
> 1 **ample** [`æmp!] (a.) 充足的
> 2 **fit** [fɪt] (n.) 合適
> 3 **master's degree** [`mæstɚz dɪ`gri] (n.) 碩士學位
> 4 **piece** [pis] (n.) 作品；報導
> 5 **under (sb.'s) wing** [`ʌndɚ wɪŋ] 在……的主責下
> 6 **research** [rɪ`sɝtʃ] (n.) 研究
> 7 **asset** [`æsɛt] (n.) 資產
> 8 **range** [rendʒ] (n.) （能力）範疇

2 求職信範例 2 Employment Application Letter 2

Allison Gonzalez

No. 11, Lane 200, Sec 4. Chung Shing Rd.
New Taipei City, Taiwan, 241
(+886) 909-123-321 • allisontheperson@gmail.com

October 24, 2023

Attn: Mr. David Burton
Principal
International School of Manila
University Parkway
Fort Bonifacio Global City
Taguig City, Philippines 1634

Dear Mr. Burton:

I am applying for the high school English teacher **position**[1] at ISM. I am **confident**[2] that my experience and **skill set**[3] make me a strong candidate for this position.

At present[4], I teach grades 7–12 at a **private**[5] English school in Taiwan. I also had a key role in creating the school's IB **program**[6]. I know your school is thinking of starting an IB program. I believe my experience in this area could be of great help.

At this **stage**[7] in my career, I would like to continue growing, and ISM would be a great place to do that. Please find my resume included. I would be glad to discuss with you how my experience meets your school's needs. I invite you to contact me **at your convenience**[8].

Sincerely,

Allison Gonzalez

Allison Gonzalez

Enc. (1)

Key Terms 核心字彙片語

1 **position** [pəˋzɪʃən] (n.) 職位

2 **confident** [ˋkɑnfədənt] (a.) 有信心的

3 **skill set** [ˋskɪl sɛt] (n.) （工作的）技能組合

4 **at present** [æt ˋprɛzənt] 目前；現在

5 **private** [ˋpraɪvɪt] (a.) 私立的；私有的

6 **program** [ˋprogræm] (n.) 課程

7 **stage** [stedʒ] (n.) 階段

8 **at your convenience** [æt jʊɚ kənˋvinjəns] 在您方便時

135

Peter Carlson

1999 Pike Street, San Diego, CA 92109

Mobile: 619-777-6688 | Email: petersoncarl@yarwho.com

February 11, 2023

Attn: Ms. Clary Chekov
Sales Manager
Acme Comedy Co.
1416 Meridian Ave.
Los Angeles, CA 33004

Dear Ms. Chekov:

It is with great interest that I read about the **open**[1] salesperson role at Acme. At present, I work in **marketing**[2], but I want a new challenge. As **a people person**[3] with strong communication skills, I think this role would be an ideal fit.

In the ad, you said that Acme is moving to Mexico. I speak Spanish **fluently**[4]. This would allow me to set up core sales deals early on. Also, with my many years in marketing, I could build a strong **bond**[5] between your marketing and sales teams. This would certainly **boost**[6] **profits**[7].

In short[8], I could help to make the move **smooth**[9] and successful. I have enclosed my resume and a recommendation from my employer. I look forward to meeting with you to talk more about my **potential**[10] in this role.

Sincerely,

Peter Carlson

Peter Carlson

Enc. (2)

Key Terms 核心字彙片語

1 **open** [ˋopən] (a.)（職位）空缺的

2 **marketing** [ˋmɑrkɪtɪŋ] (n.) 行銷

3 **a people person** [ə ˋpip! ˋpɝsn] 有人緣的人；人際關係強的人

4 **fluently** [ˋfluəntlɪ] (adv.) 流利地

5 **bond** [bɑnd] (n.) 聯結

6 **boost** [bust] (v.) 促進

7 **profit** [ˋprɑfɪt] (n.) 利潤

8 **in short** [ɪn ʃɔrt] 簡言之

9 **smooth** [smuð] (a.) 平穩的

10 **potential** [pəˋtɛnʃəl] (n.) 潛力

常用句型及用語 Common Sentence Patterns and Phrases

1 求職信的開頭 Writing an Opening to an Employment Application Letter

① I am exploring employment at the sales department in your company.
我正在尋求貴公司業務部的職缺機會。

② Your company is looking to expand to other parts of the country, and I will be of great help in the process.
貴公司正期望在國內擴點,而我將能在過程中成為極大助力。

③ It is with great interest that I am applying for the engineer position in your company.　我滿懷企盼地希望應徵貴公司工程師的職位。

④ I would be a great fit for your company.　我非常適合貴公司。

2 在求職信中介紹自己 Writing About Yourself in an Employment Application Letter

① I completed my MA degree in political science last month and am now looking to put my learning into practice.
我在上個月完成政治學碩士學位,現在希望能學以致用。

② I have experience in making a variety of French desserts to meet different customers' needs.　我擁有製作各式法式甜點的經驗,能滿足不同顧客需求。

③ My background includes serving as an airline attendant for one of the world's largest international airlines.　我的背景包括在全球大型的國際航空公司擔任空服員。

④ I have done many activities related to the position, such as creating illustrations for storybooks and magazines.
我從事過很多此職位的相關活動,例如為故事書和雜誌畫插畫。

3 求職信的結尾 Writing a Closing to an Employment Application Letter

① I look forward to hearing from you.　期待您的來信。

② Thank you for your time and consideration.　感謝您抽空審閱與考慮。

③ I have enclosed my resume for you to look over.　我已附上我的簡歷供您查閱。

④ I would be glad to discuss the position with you.　我將樂於與您討論這個職位。

1 Choose three of the sentences in the box below to complete the cover letter.

- I want to thank you for your great customer service.
- I am very interested in your food sales director position, and I have over 10 years' experience in the food industry.
- Please feel free to contact me for any reason at 952-926-8855 or by email at johnb@gmail.com.
- I am sorry that I have to return my purchase and would like a refund.
- I work as a food sales manager at Rainbow Foods.

60 E Broadway
Bloomington, MN 55425

March 12, 2023

Attn: Ms. Kai-Ying Lo
Human Resources Manager
Cub Foods
421 3rd St South
Stillwater, MN 55082

Dear Ms. Lo:

❶ _____

_____ I know I would be a great fit for your company.

Currently, ❷ _____

I have included a copy of my resume and recommendation letters from two of my supervisors.

❸ _____

_____ I look forward to hearing from you soon.

Sincerely,

John Bishop

John Bishop

Lesson 15 簡歷／履歷表 Resumes and CVs

關鍵字 Key Words

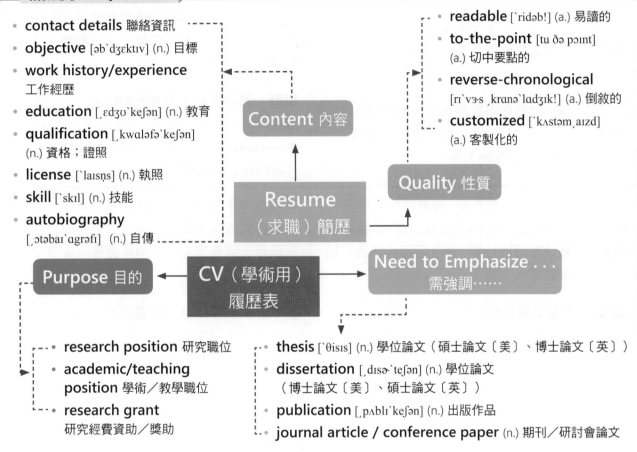

- **contact details** 聯絡資訊
- **objective** [əb`dʒɛktɪv] (n.) 目標
- **work history/experience** 工作經歷
- **education** [ˏɛdʒʊ`keʃən] (n.) 教育
- **qualification** [ˏkwɑləfə`keʃən] (n.) 資格；證照
- **license** [`laɪsns̩] (n.) 執照
- **skill** [`skɪl] (n.) 技能
- **autobiography** [ˏɔtəbaɪ`ɑgrəfɪ] (n.) 自傳

- **readable** [`ridəb!] (a.) 易讀的
- **to-the-point** [tu ðə pɔɪnt] (a.) 切中要點的
- **reverse-chronological** [rɪ`vɝ-s ˏkrɑnə`lɑdʒɪk!] (a.) 倒敘的
- **customized** [`kʌstəmˏaɪzd] (a.) 客製化的

Content 內容

Quality 性質

Resume （求職）簡歷

Purpose 目的 ← **CV**（學術用）履歷表 → **Need to Emphasize . . .** 需強調……

- **research position** 研究職位
- **academic/teaching position** 學術／教學職位
- **research grant** 研究經費資助／獎助

- **thesis** [`θisɪs] (n.) 學位論文（碩士論文〔美〕、博士論文〔英〕）
- **dissertation** [ˏdɪsə`teʃən] (n.) 學位論文（博士論文〔美〕、碩士論文〔英〕）
- **publication** [ˏpʌblɪ`keʃən] (n.) 出版作品
- **journal article / conference paper** (n.) 期刊／研討會論文

1 What Is a Resume/CV?（簡歷〔resume〕和履歷表〔CV〕是什麼？）

「**履歷表**」的英文表達方式有「**resume**」和「**CV**」兩種，兩個詞彙在求職市場中，常被視為同義詞而混用（used interchangeably），但嚴格來說，這兩個詞彙可以代表兩種不同性質的文件。

細分而言，**resume 屬於求職者的「簡歷」**，篇幅依寫作者經歷而異，但理想為一頁，一般不會超過兩頁，內容為求職者為了**爭取工作職缺（opening）**，列舉自身的過去工作經驗（work history/experience）、技能（skill）、學歷（education）等相關資訊。簡歷應讓審閱者能夠快速瀏覽，了解求職者的背景和特長，決定**是否邀請對方面試**，進而**給予工作機會**。

CV 為拉丁單字 curriculum vitae 的縮寫，原意為「生涯經歷」，篇幅相對 resume（簡歷）**更長**，且內容更加完整。在**美式用法**中，CV 常用來指稱申請**高等學術（academic）或教學（teaching）職位**，以及研究經費資助／獎助（research grant）時所需的履歷文件，因此內容會更著重學術成就（如學歷、研究著作成果）和學術相關職位（如教師、期刊編輯等）經驗。

139

Resume 和 CV 的主要差別可見下表。本課將首先介紹用途較廣的 **resume** 寫作方法，接著說明 **CV** 的寫作要點。

	Resume（源自法語，亦寫作 résumé）	**CV**（curriculum vitae；為和 resume 區別，可稱「academic CV」學術履歷）
目的	簡述個人專業上的**學、經歷背景**，以爭取特定職缺的面試和就職機會。	讓審閱者詳細了解求職者學術背景和相關經歷，主要為爭取**學術、研究類職缺機會**。
重點	特定職位所需經驗和技能、學位，以及其他和工作相關的**資格或證照**（certification）等。	**學歷、教學經歷、過去學術研究成果**（如簡述學位論文〔thesis / dissertation〕* 大要、曾發表的**論文**〔article / paper〕等）。
內容編排	可先說明求職目標，接著視個人情況，選擇先寫出工作經歷或學歷，之後補充職缺相關的技能、資格證照或活動經驗等細節。	可優先列出學歷背景，接著視情況先列舉研究成果（如申請研究員或大學教職時）或教學經驗（申請教學為主的職位時）。
篇幅	1 至 2 頁為佳	較簡歷長，可能至 3 頁或以上

（參考來源：Internship and Career Center, UC Davis; Purdue OWL; The Balance）

* 美式用法中，thesis 常指碩士論文，dissertation 指博士論文；英式用法則相反，thesis 常指博士論文，dissertation 指碩士論文。

2 Information in a Resume（簡歷應該有什麼內容？）

簡歷篇幅有限，以一頁最為理想，因此只需列出與**應徵職缺（job opening）相關的資訊**。撰寫簡歷和寫一般信件一樣，務必站在讀者角度思考，讓資訊清楚易讀（readable），才能讓審閱的主管快速完整地了解你的學經歷和專業能力，並在面試時幫助面試官提問、進一步了解應徵者。

一般來說，簡歷應包含以下資訊：

1 Contact Details（詳細聯絡方式）	你的全名、住址、電話號碼、電子郵件地址。
2 Objective（求職目標）	此部分請以簡短兩三句話，大略介紹自己和你的**職涯目標（career goals）**，讓讀者了解你的能力可以為公司創造何種效益。「求職目標」**屬於選填欄位**，但會有助於吸引審閱者的注意。對**職場新人**或**打算轉換跑道（changing careers）的人**來說，填寫這個欄位可能有所幫助。
3 Work History/Experience（工作經歷）	列出**主要、長期**的工作經驗，或任何**與職缺相關**的經歷。

4 Education / Educational History / Educational Background （教育背景）	列出大學、研究所學歷。如果有與工作相關的**證照**（qualifications）、**執照**（licenses）**或受訓經驗**，也可以列上。
5 Skills（技能）	列舉任何**工作可能會用到的技能**，如電腦或語言能力等。
6 Awards, Volunteer Work, Interests （獲獎紀錄、志工、興趣）	如果有**與工作相關**，或會**令人眼睛一亮**的得獎紀錄、志工經驗或興趣，就一併列上。

3 **Resume Structure & Format**（簡歷的結構與格式）

聯絡方式（contact details）需置於**頁面頂端**，如果有填寫**求職目標**就一併置於上方，也可以摘要說明簡歷重點，並強調**個人特質**（personal qualities）。其餘欄位的結構安排上，應力求**凸顯求職強項**（strengths），例如若你有豐富相關工作經歷，就列在前面；如果你才剛畢業，那就以學歷作為開頭。

以下為**撰寫簡歷的要點**：

1 Keep It Short（簡潔）

簡歷的理想長度是一頁。大型企業的職缺可能會吸引到上百份以上的簡歷，因此讓簡歷**保持簡短、重點分明**（to-the-point），會讓審閱者方便查閱。

2 Use Headings（使用標題）

簡歷上的**每個欄位**都應該有**清楚標示**說明，方便審閱者快速找到相關細節。

3 Use Reverse-Chronological Order（時間由近而遠排列內容）

每個欄位中，各項事件的排列應**從時間最近的開始**列舉，最久遠的經歷排在最後。各項工作經歷和求學過程的**起迄時間**，也務必明確列出。

4 Use Correct Verb Tenses（留意動詞時態）

務必使用正確的動詞時態：描述**過去的工作或活動**經驗時，要使用**過去式**動詞，而描述**目前仍在進行的工作、職務**等內容時，則使用**現在式**，以免使審閱者感到困惑。

5 Use Appropriate Fonts（使用適當字型）

使用**清楚、外觀專業的字型**（font），例如 Times New Roman，避免使用太有個性、不易閱讀的字型，例如 Comic Sans。字型色彩選擇**黑色**，字級設 **11 或 12 級**。

6 Use Bullet Points（使用項目符號條列）

以條列方式列出每項工作或經驗，描述該項**工作的主要職責**（key responsibilities），以及你從中**學習到的技能**（skill learned），方便審閱者快速閱讀消化（digest），抓到重點。

4 How to Write a Good Resume（如何撰寫成功的簡歷）

除了上述各項基本要點，求職者也要打造出自身的品牌價值和特色，才能受到徵才主管的青睞（favor），在廣大勞動市場（labor market）中脫穎而出。求職者可將自己看成待價而沽的商品，**針對企業和職缺要求將簡歷內容進行「客製化」（customize）**，以吸引對方的目光，讓簡歷使企業一見傾心。

客製化簡歷時，需要參考的因素包括：

1 Corporate Culture and Characteristics（企業文化及特性）

各家企業都有屬於自己的組織文化（organizational culture）和業務特性，因此撰寫簡歷前，**務必對應徵對象的企業特性有所研究及了解**，藉此決定簡歷寫作的內容與風格口吻，讓審閱者認為你的個人特色與該企業的文化氛圍（atmosphere）可以一拍即合。

2 Job Requirements and Content（職位需求及內容）

每項職缺對於應徵者所要求的學、經歷、個人特質和專業技能往往不同，例如業務人員（salesperson）和企劃人員（planner）相比，理想特質就會有所差異，因此寫作簡歷時，**需圍繞在（center on）當下所應徵職缺的要求及工作內容**，避免使用相同簡歷應徵不同工作。

5 How to Write a Career Autobiography（如何撰寫生涯自傳）

簡歷常會在最下方附上**「生涯自傳」（career autobiography）**，透過文章讓求職者介紹自己的學經歷背景及個人特質。自傳**最忌諱寫成流水帳（dull description）**，從家庭成長背景開頭、冗長地介紹與職缺無關的（irrelevant）個人細節，而無法聚焦重點。

為了讓自傳內容有效讓主管辨別（recognize）你的個性和專業能力，可在**自傳中著重說明以下幾點：**

- **個人特質**以及**專業經歷**
- 曾經從過往工作或求學經驗中，獲得什麼樣的**成長（growth）**或**益處（gain）**
- 過去的活動和職場表現，曾對雇主或其他人有什麼**主要貢獻（contribution）**
- 解釋為何這些個人特質和相關經歷，足以**證明你能適任（fit）工作**

除了過去經驗的敘述外，自傳也可以提及**自身未來生涯規畫（career plan）**。若身為求職新鮮人，尚不了解所應徵的職缺未來可以有哪些發展空間，以提供生涯規畫的方向，可以多向從事相關工作的親友、學長姊或師長請教，也可以透過報章或網路搜尋相關資訊，作為自傳寫作的參考。

自傳撰寫時也應使用強而有力的動詞，讓審閱者感受到求職者**具備強烈工作動機**（motivation）。以下彙整自傳中用來**描述各項個人特質的常見動詞**，供參考運用：

1 組織企劃與 創造能力	organize 組織；establish 建立；formulate 規劃；create 創造；develop 發展；plan 計劃；arrange 安排；launch 發起；introduce 引介；propose 提案；present 做簡報；release 推出
2 統整分析與 判斷能力	integrate 結合；coordinate 協調；reorganize 重整；restructure 重組；analyze 分析；discover 發現；estimate 預估；identify 辨識；recognize 識別；indicate 指出
3 管理領導與 培訓能力	manage 管理；lead 領導；guide 引導；assign 交付任務；pilot 帶領；steer 指導；oversee 監督；direct 指導；improve 提升；elevate 提升；inspire 啟發；train 訓練
4 溝通協商與 諮詢能力	communicate 溝通；negotiate 談判；convince/persuade 說服；collaborate/partner 合作；discuss 討論；resolve/settle 解決；advise/recommend/suggest 建議；consult 諮詢
5 目標執行與 成就能力	finalize 敲定；execute/perform/conduct 執行；complete 完成；demonstrate 展現；reach/attain 達到；succeed 成功；achieve/accomplish 成就；realize 實現；fulfill 履行

6 How to Write a CV（如何撰寫〔學術性〕履歷表）

CV 和 resume 的主要差別，在於 CV 大多用於爭取**在學術圈**（academia）**任職**，因此內容也會往建立學者威望的方向鋪陳。CV 常包含的細項說明如下：

1 **Personal Information** （個人資訊）	年齡、國籍（nationality）等**個人資訊**和完整的**聯絡方式**。
2 **Education /** **Educational History /** **Educational Background** （教育背景）	學歷背景和研究經歷等。學歷通常以**由近而遠**的方式列舉，也就是先寫出最後取得的學位，著重**高等學歷**，例如博士（doctor）、碩士（master）和學士（bachelor）等。若未選擇就讀大學，則可列舉國、高中或小學學歷。
3 **Work History/Experience** （工作經歷）	CV 由於篇幅較長，可列出**所有從事過的工作**，因此可能包含義工或榮譽性質的經歷，但仍應**視目標職位**，選擇經歷的著重項目和納入與否，安排上也可如學歷一樣，依時間由近而遠列出。

4 **Memberships** （會員資格）	由於 CV 目標為學術職位，通常還可以列出求職者**參與的社群**、**團體**，例如學術協會或專業協會等。
5 **Publications** （發表或出版著作）	亦可列出職位所屬領域相關的**發表／出版著作**，如期刊論文、專書著作、研討會論文等。
6 **Awards**（獎項）	可列舉在學術、專業或其他領域獲得的**獎項**。
7 **Special Certifications** **or Training**（特殊資格、 證照或培訓經驗）	若已取得和**目標職位有關的資格**、**證照**，或接受過相關**培訓**，不妨也列舉出來。
8 **Interests**（興趣）	如果跟應徵的工作相關，也可在 CV 簡述求職者有哪些**獨特的興趣**。

雖然目的和結構有所差異，寫作 CV 和 resume 仍有許多共通的要點，例如皆要**以欲徵求的職位為核心**，選擇要在履歷中呈現或強調何種內容。本課第 3 節提到的各項 resume 寫作重點技巧，也都可以適時應用於撰寫 CV。

要提醒的是，如本課開頭所述，未必所有企業或單位都會仔細辨別 resume 和 CV 兩種文件的用語差別，因此當對象企業向你索取 resume/CV 時，如果不確定對方指的是何種類型的履歷，**建議進一步詢問確認**，以便提供對方真正需要的內容。

1　剛畢業的職場新鮮人的簡歷 A Resume From a Recent Graduate

David Chang
143 Rockland Street, Brooklyn, NY 11223
Tel: 212-590-2695 @: david.chang@fastmail.com

Objective

A top-scoring computer science graduate looking for an entry-level position in an exciting tech **start-up**[1]. Eager to put into practice skills gained as an **undergraduate**[2] and summer **intern**[3] at a **high-profile**[4] software development company.

Education

State University of New York, Albany　　　　　　　　　　　　　2018–2022
BSc Computer Science
GPA 4.0

Related Coursework

- Computer Architecture & Assembly Language
- Web development
- Software Engineering I, II
- **Analysis**[6] of **Algorithms**[7]

- **Programming**[5] Languages and Translation
- Usability Engineering
- Data Structures
- File Structures and **Database**[8] Systems

Core Skills

Programming: HTML/CSS, JavaScript, Python, SQL, C++, C#

Database Development: MySQL, Distributed Data Warehouses, Storage Capacity Management, SSRS, ETL, Relational Data, Data Models

Work Experience

Phase 3 Software Inc., New York　　　　　　　　　　　　Jun.–Aug. 2021
Software Development Intern

- Gained practical experience using computer science knowledge in a professional setting
- Improved **coding**[9] abilities by being introduced to new tools and programming languages
- Created documentation for and tested new software applications
- **Collaborated**[10] with senior leaders to investigate and fix a wide range of technical issues
- Researched current technology trends to help with product innovations

Key Terms 核心字彙片語

1. **start-up** [`stɑrt͵əp] (n.) 新創公司
2. **undergraduate** [͵ʌndɚˋgrædʒʊət] (n.) 畢業生
3. **intern** [ˋɪn͵tɝn] (n.) 實習生
4. **high-profile** [ˋhaɪˋprofaɪl] (a.) 備受矚目的
5. **programming** [ˋprogræmɪŋ] (n.) 程式設計
6. **analysis** [əˋnæləsɪs] (n.) 分析
7. **algorithm** [ˋælgə͵rɪðəm] (n.) 演算法
8. **database** [ˋdetə͵bes] (n.) 資料庫
9. **coding** [ˋkodɪŋ] (n.) 編碼；撰寫程式
10. **collaborate** [kəˋlæbə͵ret] (v.) 合作

② 資深專業人士的簡歷 A Resume From an Experienced Professional

Jacob Green
70 School Lane, London, E90 3XR
Tel: 020 7946 0422 | Email: jacob.green23@supermail.com

WORK EXPERIENCE

2019 to present	**Sales Manager**
	Lion Games
	London

- Lead a sales team of five to **reach**[1] sales targets
- Hire and train sales team members to a high standard
- Analyze sales data in order to develop **strategies**[2]
- Identify new markets and market **shifts**[3]
- Increased sales by 20% in the 2020–2021 **financial year**[4]

2017 to 2019	**Sales Representative**
	Gadget World
	Manchester

- **Generated**[5] **sales leads**[6]
- **Negotiated**[7] contracts with potential clients
- Provided monthly sales reports
- Gave sales presentations to a number of clients

2016 to 2017	**Sales Intern**
	Gadget World
	Manchester

- Assisted the manager and senior staff with **administrative**[8] duties
- Was offered sales representative job after completion of internship due to excellent performance

---

EDUCATION

| 2016 to 2017 | **BSc**[9] **Business Management** |
| | University of Leeds |

SKILLS

Soft skills: Leadership, communication, problem solving, **teamwork**[10]

Languages: English (Native), French (Fluent), Japanese (Intermediate)

Computer: Salesforce CRM, Microsoft Office, SQL language

Key Terms 核心字彙片語

1 **reach** [ritʃ] (v.) 達到；與……交流

2 **strategy** [ˋstrætədʒɪ] (n.) 策略

3 **shift** [ʃɪft] (n./v.) 轉移；轉變

4 **financial year** [faɪˋnænʃəl jɪr] (n.) 會計年度

5 **generate** [ˋdʒɛnəˏret] (v.) 產生

6 **sales lead** [selz lid] (n.) 銷售商機

7 **negotiate** [nɪˋgoʃɪˏet] (v.) 協商

8 **administrative** [ədˋmɪnəˏstretɪv] (a.) 行政的

9 **BSc** (n.) 理學學士（**Bachelor of Science**的縮寫）

10 **teamwork** [ˋtimwɝk] (n.) 團隊合作

3 欲轉換跑道者的簡歷 A Resume From a Professional Wanting to Change Careers

Jenny Tripp
2F, No.86, Lane 119, Sec.3, Heping E. Road, Taipei City, Taiwan
Tel: 0909623400   Email: jenny_tripp@firemail.com

Objective

Experienced **journalist**[1] with excellent communication skills seeking a new challenge. Interested in working in an advertising role. **Possesses**[2] many transferable skills from previous career. Eager to **demonstrate**[3] ability to craft exciting, well-written advertisements and marketing-related content.

Professional Experience

Features Writer 2018 to present
English News Taiwan — Taipei, Taiwan
• Regularly **come up with**[4] interesting topics for stories
• Ensure that articles attract and hold reader interest
• Perform detailed research on a wide variety of topics

Writer / Assistant Editor 2015 to 2018
Fun Taipei Magazine — Taipei, Taiwan
• Produced exciting content for a young, **urban**[5] audience
• **Fact-checked**[6] and **proofread**[7] articles thoroughly
• Edited others' work to a high standard

Reporter 2011 to 2015
The Vancouver Evening News — Vancouver, Canada
• Wrote news pieces under strict deadlines
• Developed excellent communication skills by conducting regular interviews with members of the public

Relevant Certificates

• Google Ads Search **Certification**[8] (2020), Google
• Google Ads Display Certification (2020), Google
• **Viral Marketing**[9] (2019), Coursera
• **Content Marketing**[10] (2019), Hubspot

Education

University of Toronto 2007 to 2011
BA[11] Journalism

Key Terms 核心字彙片語

1 **journalist** [`dʒɝnəlɪst] (n.) 新聞記者
2 **possess** [pəˋzɛs] (v.) 具有；擁有
3 **demonstrate** [`dɛmənˌstret] (v.) 展示
4 **come up with** [kʌm ʌp wɪð] 想出
5 **urban** [`ɝbən] (a.) 都會的
6 **fact-check** [`fæk(t)ˌtʃɛk] (v.) 事實查核
7 **proofread** [`prufˌrid] (v.) 校對

8 **certification** [ˌsɝtɪfəˋkeʃən] (n.) 檢定；證明
9 **viral marketing** [`vaɪrəl `mɑrkɪtɪŋ] (n.) 病毒式行銷
10 **content marketing** [`kɑntɛnt `mɑrkɪtɪŋ] (n.) 內容行銷
11 **BA** (n.) 文學學士（**Bachelor of Arts** 的縮寫）

James Smith

Assistant[1] Professor[2] of Law, Columbia Law School[3]
123 Louis Lane, Hightown, USA
(555) 666-5544 / james.smith@email.com

EDUCATION

2013–2017	**Doctor[4] of Juridical Science** Yale Law School, New Haven, CT Dissertation: "The Impact of International Human Rights Law on Domestic Legal Systems: A Comparative Analysis"
2011–2013	**Master of Laws** Harvard Law School, Cambridge, MA Thesis: "The Intersection of Technology and Privacy Law: An Examination of Legal Frameworks in the Digital Age"
2007–2011	**Bachelor of Arts** (Political Science) University of California, Los Angeles, CA

PROFESSIONAL EXPERIENCE

2021–present	**Assistant Professor of Law** (Columbia Law School, New York, NY) • Teach courses on **constitutional**[5] law, **administrative**[6] law, and civil rights. • Conduct research on the impact of technology on privacy and civil liberties. • Published several articles in top law **journals**[7] on the intersection of technology and law. **Courses**[8] **Taught:** • Constitutional Law I: The Structure of Government • Constitutional Law II: Civil Rights and Civil Liberties • Administrative Law • Law and Technology: Privacy, Security, and Ethics • First Amendment: **Freedom of Speech and Press**[9]
2018–2021	**Associate Attorney** (WilmerHale, Washington, DC) • Represented clients in complex **litigation**[10] matters, including **antitrust**[11] and **intellectual property**[12] disputes. • Advised clients on regulatory **compliance**[13] and **corporate governance**[14]. • Contributed to several successful cases, resulting in significant client victories.
2017–2018	**Law Clerk, Honorable Ruth Bader Ginsburg, Supreme Court**[15] **of the United States** (Washington, DC)

- Conducted legal research and drafted memoranda on a variety of legal issues.
- Assisted Justice Ginsburg in preparing for oral arguments and drafting opinions.
- Gained insight into the workings of the highest court in the United States.

SELECTED[16] PUBLICATIONS

- Simth, J. (2023). Privacy and the **Internet of things**[17]. *Harvard Law Review, 154*(5), 20–36.
- Simth, J. (2022). Algorithmic bias and the Fair Housing Act. *Yale Law Journal, 130*(6), 32–50.
- Simth, J. (2022). Regulating big tech: Lessons from the past. *Stanford Law Review, 73*(3), 11–34.

CONFERENCES[18] & PRESENTATIONS[19]

- Lee, K. & Simth, J. (2023, Mar. 4). *The ethics of artificial intelligence in legal decision Making* [Paper presentation]. International Conference on Law and Technology, London, UK.
- Simth, J. (2022, Jun. 24). *Exploring the intersection of intellectual property and competition law* [Paper presentation]. Annual Conference of the International Association of Law Schools, New York, NY, USA.

HONORS AND AWARDS

| 2016 | **Order of the Coif, Yale Law School** |
| 2014–2015 | **Fulbright Scholarship, Italy** |

PROFESSIONAL MEMBERSHIPS[20]

- American Bar **Association**[21]
- Association of American Law Schools

Key Terms 核心字彙片語

1 **assistant** [əˋsɪstənt] (a.) 助理的
2 **professor** [prəˋfɛsɚ] (n.) 教授
3 **law school** [lɔ skul] (n.) 法學院
4 **doctor** [ˋdɑktɚ] (n.) 博士
5 **constitutional** [͵kɑnstəˋtjuʃən!] (a.) 憲法的
6 **administrative** [ədˋmɪnə͵stretɪv] (a.) 行政的
7 **journal** [ˋdʒɝn!] (n.) 期刊
8 **course** [kors] (n.) 課程
9 **freedom of speech and press** (n.) 言論出版自由
10 **litigation** [͵lɪtəˋgeʃən] (n.) 訴訟
11 **antitrust** [͵æntɪˋtrʌst] (a.) 反壟斷的

12 **intellectual property** [͵ɪnt!ˋɛktʃʊəl ˋprɑpɚtɪ] (n.) 智慧財產
13 **compliance** [kəmˋplaɪəns] (n.) （法令）合規
14 **corporate governance** [ˋkɔrpərɪt ˋgʌvɚnəns] (n.) 公司治理
15 **supreme court** [səˋprim kort] (n.) 最高法院
16 **selected** [səˋlɛktəd] (a.) 精選的
17 **Internet of things** (n.) 物聯網（常簡稱 IoT）
18 **conference** [ˋkɑnfərəns] (n.) 研討會；會議
19 **presentation** [͵prizɛnˋteʃən] (n.) （論文）發表
20 **membership** [ˋmɛmbɚ͵ʃɪp] (n.) 會員身分
21 **association** [ə͵sosɪˋeʃən] (n.) 協會

常用句型及用語 Common Sentence Patterns and Phrases

1 描述經歷的欄位名稱 Categories for Describing Experience

① Career History; Employment History; Work History
職涯經歷、任職經歷、工作歷程

② Experience; Work Experience; Professional Experience
經歷、工作經歷、專業經歷

③ Relevant Accomplishments; Selected Accomplishments
相關成就、相關成就摘列

2 描述技能的欄位名稱 Categories for Describing Skills

① Skills Profile　能力綜述

② Areas of Expertise　專業領域

③ Technical Skills　技術能力

④ Core Skills　核心技能

⑤ Soft Skills　軟技能（溝通、合作能力等）

⑥ Computer Literacy　電腦素養

⑦ Language Ability　語言能力

3 其他簡歷／履歷表上的常見項目 Other Possible Resume/CV Categories

① Relevant Courses　相關課程

② Certifications / Qualifications　證照／資格

③ Achievements　成就

④ Awards　獲獎紀錄

⑤ Activities and Interests　活動與興趣

⑥ Personal Information (age, date of birth, visa status, etc.)
個人資料（年齡、生日、簽證狀態等）

⑦ Internships　實習經歷

⑧ Volunteer Work (any other nonpaid work—e.g., charity work)
志工工作（任何其他不支薪工作，如慈善活動）

Lesson 15 Exercises

1 Here is an excerpt from Lewis Grant's cover letter. Use the information to complete the resume below.

In 2018, I earned a BSc degree in Business. After that, I worked for two years as Junior Manager at Strength Sports. There, I learned how vital it is to have a good team in place. And I often advised the senior managers when hiring new staff. Since 2020, I have been Warehouse Manager at Taste Italy Group. One of my key duties is to hire and train all warehouse and delivery staff. This experience, along with my strong people skills, makes me ideal for the role at your company.

Lewis Grant
30 Church Street, London, SW64 9WD
Tel: 020 7946 0612 | Email: lewis.grant37@speedmail.com

WORK EXPERIENCE

① .... to present   **Warehouse Manager**

② ....

London

- Oversee warehouse operations

- **③** ....

- Perform quality control on all products

- Communicate with global vendors

2018 to 2020   **④** ....

Strength Sports

Birmingham

- Supported the senior management team

- Evaluated staff and prepared performance reports

- Advised on hiring new staff members

EDUCATION

2015 to **⑤** ....   **BSc ⑥** ....

University of Sheffield

SKILLS

Core skills: leadership, organization, strong **⑦** ....

Languages: English (native), Italian (fluent)

2 Rodney Tsao is applying for a position at a university. Here is an excerpt from his cover letter. Use the information to complete the academic CV below.

I am currently an assistant professor of history at the National Nanman University in Taipei, Taiwan, and have previously worked as a postdoctoral research associate at the Wenting Academic Institute, also in Taiwan. I completed by PhD in 2018 in the Department of History at Goshborough University with a doctoral dissertation entitled, "The Steamworks of Mr. Darson: A Preliminary Investigation of Early Victorian Labour Management, 1840–1853," for which I was awarded the Lester Reeves Foundation Doctoral Fellowship in my final year.

My current research focuses on the intersection between Victorian fashions and technological ideas in the nineteenth century. I have also recently begun a project centred on fashion in the colonial discourse and presented a paper at the 2022 Meeting for Victorian Nostalgia Studies in Lostradale, Alberta, last December.

Rodney Tsao

Assistant Professor
Department of History, National Nanman University
No. 78, Sec. 3, Leien Rd., Pilei District, Taipei City 55555, Taiwan ROC
rodneytsao@nnmu.edu.tw

EDUCATION

2012–2018	**PhD, Goshborough University** Departments of History Dissertation: " ❶ .... "
2008–2011	**MA, University of Lidonia** Department of History & Literature Thesis: "Ruffpunk: Elizabethan Revivalists in 19th Century Britain"
2002–2007	**BA, University of Lidonia** History and Drama Studies

WORK EXPERIENCE

2021–Present	**Assistant Professor**
	Department of History

② .... Taiwan ROC

- Teach undergraduate history courses and create lesson plans.
- Conduct research on historical topics and present findings at academic conferences.
- Advise and instruct students in their academic pursuits.

2019–2021　③ ....

Research Center for Victorian Reception Studies

Wenting Academic Institute, Taiwan ROC

- Assisted senior researchers in conducting research.
- Collected and analyzed data and presented findings to the research team.

COURSES TAUGHT

Spring 2022	Special Topics to Victorian Pretentiousness, National Nanman University
Spring 2022	History of Science and Technology, National Nanman University
Fall 2021	Clothing and Culture in 18th Century England, National Nanman University
Fall 2021	Fashion and Modernity in Victorian England, National Nanman University

SCHOLARSHIPS & AWARDS

2017–2018	④ ....
2016	Lansat Library Travel Grant

CONFERENCES & PRESENTATIONS

- Tsao, R. (2022, Dec. 15). *What Richard Francis Burton wore when he was wandering through Central Africa* [Paper presentation].
  ⑤ ...., Lostradale, AB.
- Tsao, R. (2021, Nov. 29). *Forged love letters that should never have been found or read* [Paper presentation]. 2020 Annual Conference of the Degeneracy and Late Romanticism, October Town, Swesborg.

Lesson 16 電子郵件 Emails

關鍵字 Key Words

- **purpose** [ˋpɝpəs] (n.) 目的
- **audience** [ˋɔdɪəns] (n.) 讀者群
- **appropriateness** [əˋproprɪətnəs] (n.) 適當
- **reason for forwarding emails** 轉寄電郵的原因

- **sender's / receiver's address** 寄／收件人地址
- **Cc (= carbon copy)** （電郵）副本
- **Bcc (= blind carbon copy)** 密件副本
- **subject** [ˋsʌbdʒɪkt] (n.) 主旨

Need to Consider . . . 需考量……

Etiquette 禮儀

Format 格式

Need to Avoid . . . 需避免……

Email 電子郵件

Structure 結構

- **emoji** [iˋmodʒi] (n.) 表情符號
- **abbreviation** [əˏbrivɪˋeʃən] (n.) 縮寫
- **all capital letters** 全大寫字母
- **exclamation point** [ˏɛkskləˋmeʃən pɔɪnt] (n.) 驚嘆號

- **opening** [ˋopənɪŋ] (n.) 開場白
- **body** [ˋbɑdɪ] (n.) 正文
- **closing** [ˋklozɪŋ] (n.) 結尾
- **signature block** [ˋsɪgnətʃɚ blɑk] (n.) 簽名檔
- **attachment** [əˋtætʃmənt] (n.) 附加檔案；附件

電子郵件（email）是現在**最頻繁且廣泛使用的商務溝通方式**，可用來達成各種溝通目的，如本書介紹的推銷、感謝、投訴等。雖然使用的媒介不同，電郵的**基本寫作原則和紙本書信相同**，撰寫方式同樣取決於**信件目的**及**收信對象**。商務人士每天可能都需處理大量電子郵件，寫得好的信件可能收到即時回覆，因此務必**把焦點放在讀者身上**，注意他有什麼**需求**，回答他會提出的**問題**，並顧及**結構（structure）**和**禮儀（etiquette）**是否適當。

1 Email Header（電子郵件標頭）

商務電子郵件由很多個部分組成，寄件者先要填妥電子郵件最上端「標頭」（header）的部分，包括電子郵件地址、主旨和附件等。

寄件者	From:	此欄位顯示寄件者電子郵件地址。電子郵件帳號應該要正式而專業，**最好顯示全名**，不要用暱稱或具玩笑性質的帳號，如 hellokittyfan@xxx。
收件者	To:	輸入**收件者**的電子郵件地址。
副本	Cc:	如果信件要寄給**需要掌握信中所述的事件發展者**，就用副本的方式寄出。
密件副本	Bcc:	Bcc 是 blind courtesy copy 或 blind carbon copy 的縮寫。這欄地址**不會被其他收件人看到**，但 Bcc 收件人可看到其他收件人地址，希望保有隱私、不被其他收件者看到的收件者，應將其電子郵件地址輸入此欄。
主旨	Subject:	信件主旨要**簡潔具體**，涵蓋本次信件溝通的重要主旨，能讓收信者**快速掌握信件的討論重點**，而決定是否要打開信閱讀。主旨句未必是完整句子，不影響文意的單字可刪除，因此很像新聞標題。
附件	Attached:	顯示郵件**所附的檔案**。

2 **Effective Subject Line**（撰寫切中要點的主旨）

　　主旨欄（subject line）在電子郵件中非常關鍵，屬於讀信者首先會看到的資訊，因此必須有效（effectively）使用主旨欄，**以便對方願意或優先處理（prioritize）你的郵件**，並重視你的訊息。要寫出簡潔有力的主旨，可遵照以下建議：

1 **Be Informative and Specific**（清晰具體）：**清楚傳達（convey）郵件的主題**，避免籠統（general）或太過模糊（vague）的說法，以便對方能判斷（determine）信件內容重要性、及時處理你的郵件。可參照下列不同主旨寫法的對照：

❌ 內容籠統，無法判斷郵件性質和急迫性。

✅ 內容具體清晰，讀信者可以掌握郵件重要性。

❌ Business plan 商務計畫

✅ Revisions to business plan from 9/13 board meeting.
9 月 13 日董事會商務計畫修訂結果

❌ 若讀信者未事先得知首爾會議事宜，就可能判斷為無關的信件並加以忽略。

✅ 內容具體，讀信者可清楚了解信件目的和自己的關聯性。

❌ Conference in Seoul 首爾的會議

✅ Invitation: Keynote speaker at Seoul Conference
邀請：首爾會議主題演講者

2 **Be Brief**（簡短）：主旨這一行要簡短，否則太長可能會超過（run off）欄位。你不需要把郵件裡所有的資訊都寫進主旨欄，只要清楚點出主題即可：

❌ 內容過於冗長，讀信者難以掌握信件重點。

✅ 內容精簡，讀信者可快速抓到信件目的。

❌ Meeting requested for next week to discuss discrepancies in vacation policy, overtime policy, and salary
要求下週開會討論休假政策、加班政策與薪水的差異

✅ Meeting requested for next week to discuss job benefits 要求下週開會討論工作福利

3 **Mention Deadlines**（寫出期限）：若信件有具體回覆（respond）期限，應在主旨中標示清楚。商務人士每天都會收到眾多郵件，因此若信件主旨未表明有回覆期限，對方可能就不會立刻打開郵件，導致時限錯失。

4 **Use Proper Punctuation**（適用一般標點符號規則，但是句尾不需標點）：主旨應依照一般的規則，正確使用逗號（comma）、撇號（apostrophe）等標點符號來書寫，但是句尾不加上句號等其他標點符號。

主旨的寫法和新聞標題相似，並不完全遵守一般文法規則。若不影響文意（meaning），可以把不重要的字去掉，只須盡量符合文法即可，不一定需寫成具備主詞（subject）、動詞（verb）、受詞（object）的完整句子。

3 Structuring a Business Email（信件內容架構）

撰寫商務電子郵件時，應避免冗長的文字段落，而在段落間留白會讓整體訊息較清楚易讀。此外，須使信中訊息應盡量清楚、簡短，整體架構和其他注意事項如下：

From: Lynne Contra <lynne@bigorchid.com>

To: Andrew Lloyd <a.lloyd@catererspuls.com>

Cc: Ophelia Price <ophelia@bigorchid.com>

Subject: Flower selection for July 19 event—please respond by July 7

Attachment: bigorchidselections.doc

❶ **Opening**（開場白）：開場先寫出有禮貌的**問候語**（可稍微不正式），接著寫出**收件者的名字**，最後加上逗號。

Dear Mr. Lloyd,

❷ **Body**（正文）：為電郵主要內容，應直接**切入重點**，並遵守下列原則：
- 段落宜簡潔，各段間保留一行**空行**。
- 可用**編號**或**分項清單**。
- **言簡意賅**，避免無關資訊。
- 在信件收尾處，提出**明確的要求**。

Thank you again for confirming Big Orchid's services for the July 19 Tastebud Gala. I am writing to ask about your flower selection for the event. To ensure that your top choices will be in stock, we must have your flower selections by the end of this week. Below are three of our most popular options:

1. Happy Time (sunflowers, lilies, etc.)
2. Ice and Fire (cornflowers, roses, etc.)
3. Eastern Earl (orchids, peonies, etc.)

Please use the attached Word file to make your selections and email them to us no later than July 7.

We look forward to the Gala!

❸ **Closing**（結尾）：以有禮貌的**告別問候**或**致謝詞**作為結尾，後面接**逗號**，接著寫上**寄件者名字**。

Thank you,

Lynne Contra

❺ **Attachment**（附件）：如果有附件，記得**在信件本文提及**，並告知收件者要如何處理附件。忘記加上附件的意外也時常發生，因此最好在開始寫信時就**先把附件附上**。

❹ **Signature Block**（簽名檔）：簽名檔上應要附有寄件者的**全名**和**其他聯絡方式**，例如公司的電話號碼和網站。

Lynne Contra
Manager
Big Orchid Floral Design
www.bigorchid.com
lynne@bigorchid.com

4 **Etiquette**（禮儀）

撰寫商業電子郵件有許多因素要考慮。在動筆寫作前，請先**考量以下要點**：

1 Consider Your Purpose（寄信目的為何？）

每封商務電子郵件都應該有個**明確目的**。一封信最好只含括**一個主題**，以確保收件者了解內容重點，並能直接回覆你的訊息，另外這也有助於寄件者和收件者後續歸納郵件。

2 Consider Appropriateness（寄信是否適當？）

先判斷電子郵件是否是最好的溝通方式。如果**主題需要來回討論**，**打電話**也許是比較好的選擇。電子郵件的內容也是重要的考慮因素：如果**內容敏感**或**預計告知對方壞消息**，**當面表達**或打電話也許是最好的方式。

3 Consider Your Audience（收信對象是誰？）

商務電子郵件可以友善親切或很正式莊重。思考電子郵件的接收者是誰，有助於寄件者**決定信件的正式程度**。例如，員工寄給主管的電子郵件，語氣就會和發給同事的郵件不同。也請記得，使用**公務電子郵件（work email）**地址寄出的信都代表公司，特別是要寄信到組織外部時，更要尤其留意。

另外，為使電郵的**語氣保持專業**，可注意以下各點：

1 Avoid Emojis and Abbreviations（使用正式文字，避免使用表情符號和縮寫）：

網路聊天時常用的笑臉等**表情符號**，以及**縮寫或簡化字詞**，例如：U（You）、THX（Thanks）、Plz（Please）、OMG（Oh my God）、TTYL（Talk to you later）等，應**盡量避免**使用。不過商業書信中常用的縮寫字詞，則可適時使用，例如：CC（carbon copy）、BCC（blind carbon copy）、RE（referring to / regarding）、FYI（for your information）、PS（postscript）等，皆為常見電郵用語。

2 Avoid All Capital Letters（避免以全大寫字母書寫）：以全大寫字母行文時，看起來會像是寄件者在大吼說話。如要使特定資訊較為醒目，可用**斜體字（italics）**或**加粗（bold）字體**。

3 Avoid Too Many (or Any) Exclamation Points（避免使用過多、或不要使用驚嘆號）：
驚嘆號可用來表達友善的語氣，但**不宜過度使用**，非常正式的電子郵件則絕對不會出現驚嘆號。

4 Use a Grammar/Spell-Check Tool（使用文法／拼字檢查工具）：**文法**和**拼字錯誤**會讓你想傳達的訊息顯得不夠清楚、不夠專業。

5 Be Considerate When Forwarding Emails（轉寄信件時要考慮周到）：只有在必要時才轉寄郵件，而轉寄信件時，務必向收件者說明轉寄該封信的原因。

寄給同事的電子郵件 Email Sent to Colleagues

New Message

To: John Shafer <john.shafer@envirowise.com>, Jason Huang <jason.huang@envirowise.com>, Zhenxin Xu <jenxin.xu@envirowise.com>, Oscar Santos <oscar.santos@envirowise.com>, Amelia Johnston <amelia.johnston@envirowise.com>, Seojun Lee <seojun.lee@envirowise.com>

Cc: Colleen Fornier <colleen.fornier@envirowise.com>

Subject: Yesterday's **Staff Meeting**[1]

Attachment: professionalism[2]-in-the-workplace.doc

Good morning Team,

Thank you to those who **attended**[3] the staff meeting yesterday. A friendly **reminder**[4] that beginning next week:

- The lunchroom may only be used during the lunch break.
- You may **work from home**[5] on Fridays.
- If you will be **absent**[6] from the staff meeting, email me before the **workday**[7] begins.

Some staff members did not attend the meeting yesterday. Please note that staff meetings are on the second Tuesday of each month. Please see the attached file.

Many thanks,

Omar

————————————

Omar Hamid
Manager
Envirowise Paper Solutions
envirowisepapersolutions.com
879-919-3912

Key Terms 核心字彙片語

1 **staff meeting** [stæf ˋmitɪŋ] 員工會議
2 **professionalism** [prəˋfɛʃən!ˏɪzəm] (n.) 專業態度
3 **attend** [əˋtɛnd] (v.) 出席；參加
4 **reminder** [rɪˋmaɪndɚ] (n.) 提醒
5 **work from home** [wɝk fram hom] 在家（遠距）工作
6 **absent** [ˋæbsn̩t] (a.) 缺席的
7 **workday** [ˋwɝkˏde] (n.) 工作日

2 確認預約的電子郵件 Email to Confirm a Reservation

New Message

To: Pauline Walters <pauline.walters@biztech.com>

Cc: Brent Peters <brent.peters@pastacity.net>

Bcc: John Baker <john.baker@freemail.com>

Subject: **Reservation**[1]—please **confirm**[2] by July 18th

Attachment: pastacitymenu.pdf

Hello Pauline,

Thank you for choosing Pasta City for your company event on July 24th. As we discussed on the phone, the meal will cost $25 per **guest**[3]. Please see the attached **menu**[4] for details on what is included in the price.

I would appreciate if you could confirm the following by July 18th:

1. The number of guests who will be attending.
2. The number of guests requiring a **vegetarian**[5] option.
3. The time you would like your event to begin.

We look forward to **hosting**[6] your event!

Best regards,

Ryan

Ryan Wilson
Reservation Coordinator

Pasta City
pastacityrestaurant.com
573-198-7382
reservations@pastacity.net

Key Terms 核心字彙片語

1 **reservation** [ˌrɛzəˋveʃən] (n.) 預約；訂位
2 **confirm** [kənˋfɝm] (v.) 確認
3 **guest** [gɛst] (n.) 客人
4 **menu** [ˋmɛnju] (n.) 菜單
5 **vegetarian** [ˌvɛdʒəˋtɛrɪən] (a./n.) 素食的（人）
6 **host** [host] (v.) 主辦

New Message

To: Lori Patino <loripat1983@fastmail.net>

Cc: customerservice@beautifulyou.com

Bcc: Vivian Wang <sales005@beautifulyou.com>

Subject: Replying to refund request for Order #937012

Attachment: customerloyaltycoupon20.pdf
returnshippinglabel.pdf

Dear Ms. Patino,

Thank you for your email **regarding**[1] your order. I am sorry to hear that you were unhappy with the products.

We offer a full refund for orders made within the last 30 days. **Unfortunately**[2], 30 days have passed. It has been 90 days since you placed your order. In this case, we can offer you a **credit**[3] to our online store.

Thank you for being a **loyal**[4] customer. I have attached a discount code for 20% off your next **purchase**[5]. There will be new products added to our website soon.

I have also attached a return shipping **label**[6]. Please return the unused portions of the products you are unhappy with. **We will apply**[7] **the credit to your account once we have received the returned items.**

Sincerely,

Xiaoping

―――――――――

Xiaoping Zhu
Customer Service Representative
Beautiful You Skincare
729-900-1285
xiaoping.zhu@beautifulyou.com

> **Key Terms 核心字彙片語**
>
> 1 **regarding** [rɪˋgɑrdɪŋ] (prep.) 有關……
> 2 **unfortunately** [ʌnˋfɔrtʃənɪtlɪ] (adv.) 遺憾地；不幸地；可惜地
> 3 **credit** [ˋkrɛdɪt] (n.) 商品抵用金
> 4 **loyal** [ˋlɔɪəl] (a.) 忠誠的
> 5 **purchase** [ˋpɝtʃəs] (n.) 購買
> 6 **label** [ˋleb!] (n.) 標籤
> 7 **apply** [əˋplaɪ] (v.) 使……生效／起作用

1　主旨撰寫範例 Subject Lines

① October 19th reservation　10月19日訂位事宜

② Order # 892y71 – Shipping confirmation　訂單# 892y71—出貨確認

③ Order deadline for free shipping　訂單免運期限

④ Monthly sales report – due Friday　每月業務報告——週五交出

2　電子郵件的招呼用語 Polite Greetings in Emails

① Good morning team/all/everyone　各位團隊成員早安／大家早安／各位早安

② Hello/Hi (name)　哈囉／嗨＋（人名）

③ To the HR/Accounting/Sales department　致人資部／會計部／業務部

④ How are you (name)?　（人名）＋你好嗎？

3　說明電子郵件的來信目的 Explaining the Purpose of an Email

① I am writing to inform you about our recent changes to company policies.
這次寫信是想告知您有關我們近期公司政策的異動。

② We would like to discuss with you your suggestions regarding the design of our promotional materials.　我們想和您討論您對我們宣傳資料設計上的建議。

③ This email is to notify you that your subscription to our service will expire in one week.　此封電郵意在向您告知，您訂閱我們的服務將於一週後到期。

④ I am writing this email in response to your request to use footage from our films to produce videos for commercial use.
本信是為了回應您要求使用本公司電影片段，來製作商用影片的事宜。

4　結尾敬辭 Polite Closings

① Many thanks,　非常感謝

② All the best,　祝一切順利

③ Sincerely,　謹啟

④ Best/Kind regards,　致上最好／親切的問候

⑤ Respectfully yours,　敬上

1. Using the phrases provided, write an email to your colleagues explaining that you will be away from the office for a week.

The email should tell your colleagues who to contact while you are not working. Put the correct phrase in each numbered space. You will not use every phrase provided in the boxes below.

VACATION!!!!	Hello, sales team	I will return on July 4
please contact Cindy Cheng	Please enjoy the great weather	Out of office 27/6 – 3/7
I will be out of town next week	plz talk 2 Cindy Cheng	All the best

---

To: sales.team@premiumsales.com

From: m.wright@premiumsales.com

Subject: ❶ ....

❷ ....

I want to make sure you all know that ❸ ....

❹ .... If you have any questions about

sales projects while I am away, ❺ .... at

ccheng@premiumsales.com.

❻ .... ,

Miranda

Senior Associate
Premium Sales

---

2 Using the phrases provided, write an email to your manager to tell him that you have finished a new inventory checklist.

Ask for some feedback on your work. Put the correct phrase in each numbered space. You will not use every phrase provided in the boxes below.

A-OK	Newinventory.xls	Inventory
to organize a meeting to introduce the new system	I appreciate your concern	Let me know when you're free to discuss these changes
Attached is the new inventory file I've created	New Inventory Form Attached – Seeking Feedback	Please let me know what you think of

---

To: paul.dunbar@suppliesunchained.com

From: chloe.blake@suppliesunchained.com

Subject: ❶ ....

Attachment: ❷ ....

Hi Paul,

❸ .... As we discussed, I have added columns to show when new stock has been ordered and when it is expected to arrive.

❹ .... the new format and whether it needs any more changes. I also think it might be useful
❺ .... to the stock room team.

❻ ....

Best,

Chloe

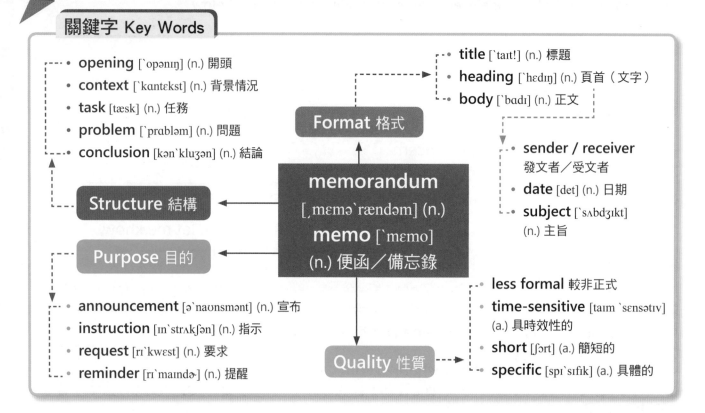

Lesson 17　便函 Memos

關鍵字 Key Words

- **opening** [`opənɪŋ] (n.) 開頭
- **context** [`kɑntɛkst] (n.) 背景情況
- **task** [tæsk] (n.) 任務
- **problem** [`prɑbləm] (n.) 問題
- **conclusion** [kən`kluʒən] (n.) 結論

Structure 結構

Purpose 目的

- **announcement** [ə`naʊnsmənt] (n.) 宣布
- **instruction** [ɪn`strʌkʃən] (n.) 指示
- **request** [rɪ`kwɛst] (n.) 要求
- **reminder** [rɪ`maɪndə] (n.) 提醒

Format 格式

memorandum [ˌmɛmə`rændəm] (n.)
memo [`mɛmo] (n.) 便函／備忘錄

Quality 性質

- **title** [`taɪt!] (n.) 標題
- **heading** [`hɛdɪŋ] (n.) 頁首（文字）
- **body** [`bɑdɪ] (n.) 正文

- **sender / receiver** 發文者／受文者
- **date** [det] (n.) 日期
- **subject** [`sʌbdʒɪkt] (n.) 主旨

- **less formal** 較非正式
- **time-sensitive** [taɪm `sɛnsətɪv] (a.) 具時效性的
- **short** [ʃɔrt] (a.) 簡短的
- **specific** [spɪ`sɪfɪk] (a.) 具體的

---

1 What Is a Memo?（何謂便函？）

「便函／備忘錄」的英文是 **memorandum**（**複數 memorandums / memoranda**），常簡稱為 **memo**，是在商業界裡用來**溝通資訊**、**傳遞訊息**的文書類型。便函幾乎都是公司、辦公室或團隊用來進行**內部溝通**、**交流**的文件，所以可以不必像其他的商業文書那麼正式（less formal）。便函常用於**宣布事項**（announcement）、**溝通問題**或**商討解決方案**，亦可用於要求讀者**採取行動**。便函傳遞的資訊通常具有**時效性**（time-sensitive）。

2 How to Write（便函該怎麼寫？）

便函要寫得**清晰**、**易讀**（clear and easy to read），使用**正確的格式與結構**（correct format and structure）十分重要。便函的內容最好**簡短**（short）、**具體**（specific），並使用與文中訊息內容相符的行文風格（style）來書寫。

1 Format（便函的格式）

公司大多有便函的樣板（template），其格式跟傳真封面頁（fax cover letter）樣板很類似。便函可分為三個基本要素：

1 Title（標題）：**便函的標題**應寫出 memo 或 memorandum。如果公司使用預先印有公司名稱的便函專用紙，則標題 memo 或 memorandum 應出現在公司名稱的下方。

2 **Heading**（頁首區）：頁首區位於便函正文的上方，內容應包括：

發文者（sender）	應寫出發文者的**全名**，亦可加上發文者**頭銜**或**職稱**。
受文者（receiver / distribution list）	完整寫出所有**受文者的姓名**，亦可包括其**頭銜**或**職稱**。
發文日期（date）	應標示發文日期，且為避免混淆，日期的月分不應以數字書寫，而是用**英文縮寫表示**，例如應寫出「Sept.」而非「09」來表示「九月」。
主旨句（subject）	便函的主旨句應簡短，但內容要具體明確。

3 **Body**（訊息正文）：正文部分是便函所要傳達的訊息。有些便函非常簡短，甚至只有一、兩句話，而有些便函的資訊較多，篇幅也較長。

2 **Structure**（正文的結構）

便函的正文通常可分為三個部分：

1 **Opening**（開頭）：便函的開頭**不需問候語（greeting）**，**直接陳述重點**即可。

❶ Beginning July 14th, staff are required to report absences through our new online system. 自 7 月 14 日起，全體員工皆須透過新的網路系統回報缺勤情況。

❷ All new employees must complete the health and safety training program by the end of the month.
所有新進員工必須在月底前完成健康暨安全培訓課程。

❸ We are happy to announce the addition of Sarah Waters as Senior Sales Manager. 我們很高興地宣布莎拉‧沃特斯加入本公司，擔任資深業務經理一職。

2 **Context/Task/Problem**（背景情況／任務／問題）：此部分應寫進更多與主旨有關的細節，像是解釋文中提到異動的原因，或作出相關決定的**理由（context 背景情況）**、告訴讀者該**做些什麼（task 任務）**，或是說明有什麼問題需要**解決（problem 問題）**。

背景情況 context	背景情況的說明，可讓讀者知道更多與**便函主旨有關的細節內容**。舉例來說，在說明公司活動取消的便函當中，可以說明導致取消的背景因素（經濟狀況、當前傳染病情形等）。
任務 task	便函若欲傳達工作任務，應提供如何完成任務的**詳細指示（instruction）**，並附上可協助者的**聯絡方式（contact information）**。
問題 problem	以便函說明問題時，應將**相關狀況解釋清楚**，包括該問題對公司會有什麼影響、需要何種解決辦法等。

3 **Conclusion**（結論）：結論**不需要**加上「Sincerely,」、「Best regards,」等結尾敬辭，應在此再次**提醒（remind）此便函重點**為何，也常會要求讀者**採取特定行動**。例如：

- 提醒員工有哪些任務必須完成。

- 針對在便函裡提出（present）的特定問題，要求（request）受文者擬定解決辦法。

1 通知福利的便函 Memo to Inform About Benefits

FAN Factory

MEMO

To: All Sales **Agents**[1]

From: Allan Wu, President

Cc: May Zhong, Vice President

Date: November 22, 2023

Re: Annual sales goal

It is almost the end of the year and I wanted to share some good news. We have **exceeded**[2] our **annual sales**[3] goal!

We have sold 10,000 more **ceiling fans**[4] than expected. Last year at this time, we were **forced**[5] to let some staff go. It is because of your hard work that we have been able to keep our business open. We hope our sales will continue to rise into next year.

To thank you for your excellent work, we will be adding a $100 **bonus**[6] to your next **paycheck**[7]. We will also **celebrate**[8] by hosting a pizza lunch for all sales agents next Thursday. Please let Maureen at the front desk know if you like one or two **slices**[9] by next Wednesday afternoon.

Key Terms 核心字彙片語

1 **agent** [`edʒənt] (n.) 仲介；代理人

2 **exceed** [ɪk`sid] (v.) 超越

3 **annual sales** [`ænjʊəl selz] (n.) 年度銷售額

4 **ceiling fan** [`silɪŋ fæn] (n.) （裝在天花板的）吊扇

5 **force** [fɔrs] (v.) 強迫

6 **bonus** [`bonəs] (n.) 獎金

7 **paycheck** [`pe͵tʃɛk] (n.) 工資

8 **celebrate** [`sɛlə͵bret] (v.) 慶祝

9 **slice** [slaɪs] (n.) （一）片

2 宣布異動的便函 Memo to Announce Changes

Memorandum

To: All Store Employees
From: Trish Williams, Owner
Cc: Bruce Williams, Owner
Date: April 19, 2023
Re: New store hours

Our **business hours**[1] will be changing at the beginning of next month. We will **postpone**[2] opening the store by one hour and close three hours later than **normal**[3]. Our new store hours will be 9:00 A.M. to 9:00 P.M. We will also begin opening on Saturdays with reduced hours from 9:00 A.M to 6:00 P.M.

As you know, we rarely receive customers before 9:00 A.M. Some customers have complained that our store closes too early. We cannot **afford**[4] to miss these potential sales. Our new store hours will hopefully bring more business to our store.

Please **note**[5] that the new **lunch break**[6] times will be 12:30–1:00 P.M. or 1:00–1:30 P.M. Kindly check with the manager on duty when you begin your **shift**[7] to find out which lunch break to take.

Many of you have families and I know it is not possible for everyone to work on the weekend. Please email me by this Friday at 3:00 P.M. if you are available to work on Saturdays. I know these changes **come as a surprise to**[8] many of you and I thank you **in advance**[9] for your **cooperation**[10].

Key Terms 核心字彙片語

1 **business hours** [ˈbɪznɪs aʊrz] (n.) 營業時間

2 **postpone** [postˈpon] (v.) 延後

3 **normal** [ˈnɔrml] (n.) 常態

4 **afford** [əˈford] (v.) 承擔得起⋯⋯

5 **note** [not] (v.) 注意到⋯⋯

6 **lunch break** [lʌntʃ brek] 午休時間

7 **shift** [ʃɪft] (n.) 輪班

8 **come as a surprise (to sb.)** [kʌm æz ə səˈpraɪz] 使⋯⋯大為驚訝

9 **in advance** [ɪn ədˈvæns] 預先地

10 **cooperation** [koˌɑpəˈreʃən] (n.) 合作

Artistic Designs Inc.

Memo

To: Sales Team
From: Brenda Reed, Sales Manager
Cc: Janice Huang, Vice President
Date: May 7, 2022
Re: **Funding**[1] for October **Conference**[2]

Senior **management**[3] has agreed to pay for all interested staff to attend the annual sales conference. The following costs will be **reimbursed**[4]:

• $100 meal **allowance**[5]

• Hotel room for 2 nights

• **Fuel**[6] (up to $200)

I know that many of you have been waiting to hear this news. It is a tradition for our team to attend this event. This year should be another great learning experience for all.

If you wish to attend, please let me know via email. There are many other events taking place **downtown**[7] that weekend. It is important to book your hotel room as soon as you can. Please **submit**[8] **receipts**[9] to the **head office**[10] by June 30th.

Key Terms 核心字彙片語

1 **funding** [ˈfʌndɪŋ] (n.) 經費；資金
2 **conference** [ˈkɑnfərəns] (n.) 會議
3 **management** [ˈmænɪdʒmənt] (n.) 管理階層
4 **reimburse** [ˌriːmˈbɜˑs] (v.) 報銷
5 **allowance** [əˈlaʊəns] (n.) 補貼；津貼
6 **fuel** [ˈfjʊəl] (n.) 油錢
7 **downtown** [ˌdaʊnˈtaʊn] (adv./a.) 市中心地／的
8 **submit** [səbˈmɪt] (v.) 繳交
9 **receipt** [rɪˈsit] (n.) 收據
10 **head office** [hɛd ˈɔfɪs] (n.) 總公司；總部

1 提供資訊的用語 Giving Information

① <u>This is to notify you of</u> the recent change to our restaurant's opening hours.　在此告知大家我們最近餐廳營業時間的變動。

② <u>We are pleased to announce that</u> we are holding a Christmas party this Friday afternoon in the company cafeteria.

我們很高興宣布，本週五下午將在公司餐廳舉行耶誕派對。

③ <u>We wish to inform you that</u> we are going to open new branches and hire more people in the coming months.

我們希望通知大家，接下來幾個月我們將會擴點並招募更多員工。

2 如何傳達好／壞消息 Sharing Good/Bad News

① <u>I am happy/pleased to tell you that</u> our sales have increased by over 50 percent in the past year.

我很高興／開心向大家告知，本公司業績過去一年成長了超過五成。

② <u>We are pleased to share with you that</u> our CEO will return to work in a week after recovering from surgery.

我們很開心跟大家分享，我們的執行長手術復原後，將於一週內回到崗位上。

③ <u>We regret to inform you that</u> we are shutting down the factory in Vietnam.　我們很遺憾地告知大家，我們將關閉在越南的工廠。

④ <u>Unfortunately/Sadly</u>, we are considering laying off unessential staff to cut costs for our company.

不幸／遺憾的是，我們正考慮裁減非必要人力，以降低公司支出。

3 便函結論用語 Concluding

① <u>Thank you for your support in</u> our decision to cancel the company trip due to health concerns.　感謝大家支持我們決定因為健康考量而取消員工旅遊。

② <u>We are confident this change will be</u> good news, especially to our female colleagues.　我們有信心這項異動將是好消息，尤其是對女性同仁來說。

③ <u>I am looking forward to your feedback on</u> our renovated break room on the second floor.　我很期待聽取大家對於二樓整修後員工休息室的回饋意見。

1 Using the phrases below, write a memo to your entire staff to tell them about a new hire. You will not use every phrase in the boxes.

We are confident that	Welcome our new team member	as a junior sales associate
We look forward to your feedback	It will not be possible to	We regret to inform you
We are pleased to announce that	Her first day in the office will be	You can reach her
Unfortunately	Notification	We are excited

Zinger Sales

Memorandum

To: All staff

From: Clarence Deng, VP for Sales

Date: August 15, 2023

Subject: ❶ _____

❷ _____ Claudia Chao will be joining the sales staff at Zinger. I know she will receive a warm welcome.

Claudia will join the Eastern Sales Team ❸ _____ . ❹ _____ August 20. ❺ _____ at chao.c@zinger.com and on her office line, (415) 444-3322.

❻ _____ to be expanding the sales team after our record-breaking sales last year. ❼ _____ Claudia will be a very valuable member of the team. Welcome aboard, Claudia!

2 Using the phrases below, write a memo to your entire staff to remind them that the office will be closed next week. Include all important information your staff will need. You will not use every phrase in the boxes.

please call Beverly Hong at (301) 245-5533	Sales tactics	Hours
We would like your feedback	All staff	work from home that week
	Met our annual goals	schedule any meetings or events at the office
let your clients know that you will be available from home	This is to notify you that	be available to handle any technical questions
	Office closed next week	

Atlantic Arts and Crafts

Memo

To: ❶ ....

From: Beverly Hong, Office Manager

Date: August 8, 2023

Re: ❷ ....

❸ .... the office will be closed for repairs next week, from August 14 to August 19. All staff should be prepared to ❹ ....
Our tech support team will ❺ ....
....

Please ❻ ....
Please do not ❼ ....
during that week.

If you have any questions, ❽ ....
....

其他商用書信種類
Other Types of Business Correspondence

1 Letter of Inquiry（詢價信簡介）

詢價信（letter of inquiry）為潛在顧客看到宣傳或促銷活動後，或有購買產品／服務的需求時，用來**詢問商品**或**服務價格**的信。通常各公司都會提供**詢價表格（inquiry form）**，請詢價者就其公司、產業、需求等回答問題，然後據此提供報價。若沒有找到詢價表格，就要自己寫詢價信，寄給對方的業務（sales）或行銷（marketing）部門。

詢價信主要目的是詢問每單位產品的價格，詢價信中的常見問題包括：

- 產品價格是？大量訂購有沒有可能得到折扣？
- 訂購手續完成後，什麼時候可以拿到產品？運送方式為何？
- 除了詢價的商品外，有沒有其他的產品更符合我的需求？

如果詢價目標是一項服務，信中問題可能包括：

- 服務如何收費？
- 按小時／按日／按月計費嗎？
- 透過此項服務所購買的產品，公司會從中收取佣金嗎？

2 Letter of Quotation（報價信簡介）

報價信（letter of quotation）就是**對詢價信給予的回覆**，用以**告知對方詢問的產品或服務價格**。報價信可以用來進行「**穩固報價**」（firm offer，或稱「**實盤**」）或「**非穩固報價**」（non-firm offer，或稱「**虛盤**」）。

穩固報價表示**承諾以固定價格出售特定產品**，而且通常是在一定期限內。對方一旦接受穩固報價，就不能撤銷（withdraw）。進行穩固報價的報價信應包含下列元素：

- 提及對方之前寄來的詢價信（或詢價表格）
- 產品名稱
- 每單位價錢，以及願意提供的折扣（若有）
- 下訂單的期限和方式
- 其他必要工作細節，如付費、交貨、包裝、運送方式和時間等

非穩固報價代表報價的內容仍可能變動，而非穩固報價信通常不會包含上述所有資訊，通常也會**表明報價相關條件尚未定案**，此時可使用「this quotation is subject to our final consideration」（此報價會依我們最後的考量進行調整）這類句型來表達。

3 **Order Letter**（訂貨信簡介）

訂貨信（order letter）為向對方公司索取商品或服務的信。許多公司訂有自己專用的訂貨信格式，格式內容應該提供讀信者所有訂購相關的所需資訊。

但是訂貨信有時也會以電子郵件、電話、傳真等其他形式寄發，這時讀信者就要留意對方是否提供所有需要的資訊；如果有缺漏，應馬上洽詢發信的客戶。

訂貨信常常會跟**訂單表格**（order form）一起寄出，有時候則是訂貨信本身就充當訂單，說明客戶想要訂購的商品內容。無論何種方式，讀信者收到訂貨信後，要立刻告知發信的客戶自己已經收到訂單，並開始準備出貨事宜。

4 **Resignation Letter**（離職信簡介）

離職信（resignation letter）為**員工有意提出辭職**（resign）**時**寫給公司的信。即使員工已經跟主管表明過辭職意願，還是應該寫封正式的離職信，以展現對公司與主管的尊重。

要注意的是，離職信可能會由原公司保留在員工檔案裡，留存很長一段時間，所以就算離職時對於工作有諸多不滿，也不可以任意寫出失禮、有失風度的離職信，而是應使用**客氣謹慎**（courteous and discreet）的語氣來書寫。

離職信中一般不需說明離職後的計畫或工作，但是如果覺得有必要，當然還是可以加以說明。一般說來，離職信的架構可如以下安排：

第一段	清楚說明離職意願，並寫出離職時間。如果無法提早預告離職、讓公司有足夠的緩衝時間做過渡安排，也應在信中為引起的不便致歉。
中間段落	可在此部分感謝雇主於在職期間的提攜，並對於將要離開公司表示遺憾（express regret）。若覺得有必要，可以提及離職理由。
最後一至兩段	最後可以表明你願意協助接替你的新進同事（new hire），讓他更順利接手工作。也或許可以提供未來的聯絡方式，並表示離職後也樂意回答任何問題。

5 **Reference Letter**（推薦信簡介）

　　推薦信（reference letter）是寫信者寄給被推薦人（正在求職者）未來的雇主，幫助其取得下一份工作。推薦信有兩種，一種是**就職證明書（employment reference）**，一種是**推薦信（letter of recommendation）**，兩種信件區別如下：

1 **Employment Reference**（就職證明書）：目的為證明被推薦者曾於該公司工作，會寫出其**工作起訖時間**、**薪酬**、**職位**等。就職證明書並非寫給特定個人，因此**稱謂不會寫出特定人名**。此類信薦篇幅**簡短**、語氣**客觀**，有時甚至是當事人先行草擬後再請主管簽名，內容一般會說明下列項目：

- 寫信人與當事人的關係（例如主管、企劃經理等）
  The writer's relationship to the employee

- 當事人於該公司的任職時間
  Beginning and ending dates of the person's employment at the company

- 當事人的職位與職務內容 Positions held and descriptions of each

- 當事人離職時的薪資（通常也會寫出起薪）
  Ending salary (and often the starting salary as well)

2 **Letter of Recommendation**（推薦信）：信中會詳述求職者優良的工作表現、個性、技能等**正面職場特質（quality）**。推薦信通常是針對特定的工作職位而寫，寄送對象常為特定的個人或公司，因此**稱謂可以寫出收件人名字**，或是至少寫出**收件機構名稱**。信中除了被推薦人過去**職務**、**薪資**、**工作起訖時間**等基本資訊外，也應該就被推薦人的下列特質寫出評語：

- 優點、技能、才能 Strengths, skills, and talents

- 主動、熱忱、正直、可靠等各項特質
  Initiative, dedication, integrity, reliability, or other qualities

- 工作態度與人際溝通技巧 Attitude and interpersonal skills

- 與團隊合作的能力 Ability to work with a team

- 獨立工作的能力 Ability to work independently

- 任何其他跟工作契合度有關的資訊
  Any other information relevant to his or her employability

① 詢價信範例 Letter of Inquiry

Lee Chef¹ Supply

65 Chien Hsing Road, San Min District

Kaohsiung City, Taiwan

March 25, 2023

Blumenschein, Inc.

Adickesallee 3

94855

Frankfurt am Main

Germany

Dear Sirs:

We have noted your advertisement in *Appetite* magazine and are interested in your **assortment**² of **utensils**³, particularly knives. We would appreciate a **quote**⁴ for the entire Blumenschein Large Knife Collection, the Braun Standard Kitchen Line, and the Modern Quality Chef's Set. Please **indicate**⁵ prices **C.I.F.**⁶ Kaohsiung, Taiwan. Please indicate your earliest delivery date, terms of payment, and discounts for regular **purchases**⁷. We would also appreciate receiving your catalog.

Respectfully,

Lee Wen

Lee Wen

Lee Chef Supply

Key Terms 核心字彙片語

1 **chef** [ʃɛf] (n.) 主廚；廚師

2 **assortment** [əˋsɔrtmənt] (n.) 各式各樣

3 **utensil** [juˋtɛns!] (n.)（家用、廚房）器具

4 **quote** [kwot] (n.) 報價

5 **indicate** [ˋɪndəˏket] (v.) 指明

6 **C.I.F** 到岸價格（即包含貨物成本 **cost**、運送保險費 **insurance** 和運費 **freight** 的報價方式）

7 **purchase** (n.) 購買

Blumenschein, Inc.

Adickesallee 3, 94855
Frankfurt am Main, Germany

April 4, 2023

Attention: Lee Wen
Lee Chef Supply
65 Chien Hsing Road, San Min District
Kaohsiung City, Taiwan

Dear Mr. Lee:

Thank you for your **inquiry**[1]
of March 25. The prices you requested
are as follows:

- Blumenschein Large Knife Collection:
  $240.00
- Braun Standard Kitchen Line: $275.00
- Modern Quality Chef's Set: $300.00

Key Terms 核心字彙片語

1 **inquiry** [ɪn`kwaɪrɪ] (n.) 詢價；詢問
2 **expedited shipping** [`ɛkspɪˌdaɪtəd `ʃɪpɪŋ] (n.) 快捷運送
3 **insurance** [ɪn`ʃʊrəns] (n.) 保險（費）
4 **total** [`tot!] (n.) 總額
5 **(be) subject to** [`sʌbdʒɪkt tu] 尚待……而定
6 **constitute** [`kɑnstəˌtjut] (v.) 被視為；構成
7 **wire (bank) transfer** [`waɪər trænsfɚ] (n.) 電匯；匯款
8 **payment in advance** [`pemənt ɪn əd`væns] 預先付款
9 **negotiation** [nɪˌgoʃɪ`eʃən] (n.) 協商
10 **case-by-case** [kes baɪ kes] (a.) 依個案決定的

Expedited shipping[2] plus **insurance**[3] to Kaohsiung, Taiwan, is estimated at $230, bringing the **total**[4] to an estimated $1,045. Please understand that this offer is **subject to**[5] the final quote from our shipping partner and does not **constitute**[6] a firm offer.

Orders are filled and shipped the day after they are received. Using Globe Ship expedited service, we can deliver an order to Taiwan within 3 days of the order's placement. For first-time customers, we require **payment in advance**[7] through an international **wire bank transfer**[8]. We offer a 2% cash discount. Orders over $1,500 are subject to **negotiation**[9]. We offer discounts for large orders on a **case-by-case**[10] basis. To discuss a large order, please call me at +49 69 674561 or fax a completed order form from the enclosed catalog to +49 69 670002.

Sincerely,

Karl Blumenschein

Karl Blumenschein
Sales Director, Blumenschein Inc.

Enclosure: catalog

3 訂貨信範例 Order Letter

Lime Tree Fashion

33 Miter **Industrial Estate**[1]

Toronto, Ontario M3B 2W6, Canada

March 12, 2023

Yu-pao Yang
Fit **Garment**[2] Equipment
37 Yungnan St.
Taichung 402
Taiwan

Reference: PO 359/25

Dear Mr. Yang:

Thank you for sending us your latest catalog. Please find enclosed our purchase order for 150 **sewing**[3] machines. We agree to your **terms**[4] of payment.

Please note that we have chosen **express shipping**[5]. It is **vital**[6] that we receive these items before the end of the month. Please let us know as soon as possible if this is not an option.

Sincerely,

Paula Holdroyd

Paula Holdroyd
Purchasing Manager, Lime Tree Fashion

Enc. (1)

Key Terms 核心字彙片語

1 **industrial estate** [ɪnˋdʌstrɪəl ɪsˋtet] (n.) 工業區
2 **garment** [ˋgɑrmənt] (n.) 衣服
3 **sew** [so] (v.) 縫製
4 **term** [tɝm] (n.) 條款；條件
5 **express shipping** [ɪkˋsprɛs ˋʃɪpɪŋ] (n.) 快遞；快速貨運
6 **vital** [ˋvaɪt!] (a.) 重要的

Saturn Systems

1176 N. Ventura Avenue, Oak View, CA 93022, USA
Tel: +1 719 392-9068 Fax: +1 719 392-9069

June 22, 2023

Stanley Price
R&D[1] Manager
1176 N. Ventura Avenue
Oak View, CA 93022

Dear Mr. Price:

It is with regret that I inform you that I will **resign**[2] from my role as junior engineer on Friday, July 22.

I would like to thank you for your support during my two years here. The decision to leave has not been an easy one. I have enjoyed my time with the R&D team. I have learned a lot from you and the **senior**[3] engineers. And I am proud of the work I have done.

However, I have decided to return to university full-time this year to **pursue**[4] a master's degree in **finance**[5]. As a result, I will no longer be able to remain in my position at Saturn Systems.

If I can **assist**[6] in any way with the hiring or training of my **replacement**[7], please let me know. I am happy to help however I can.

Sincerely,

Laurie Lau

Laurie Lau

Key Terms 核心字彙片語

1 **R&D** [ˌɑr ən ˈdi] 研發（= research and development）

2 **resign** [rɪˈzaɪn] (v.) 辭職

3 **senior** [ˈsinjɚ] (a.) 資深的；高級的

4 **pursue** [pɚˈsu] (v.) 追求

5 **finance** [ˈfaɪnæns] (n.) 財務；金融

6 **assist** [əˈsɪst] (v.) 協助

7 **replacement** [rɪˈplesmənt] (n.) 代替者

5 推薦信範例 Reference Letter

R&J Financial Services

9 Windsor Road

Leeds

LS34 7LQ

6 January 2023

To Whom It May Concern:

Sophie Trent was a junior financial **planner**[1] at my company from May 2020 to June 2022. Her starting salary was £27,000 annually. At the end of her employment, she earned £32,000 annually.

During her time here, she worked with several key clients. She took steps to make sure their investments stayed **profitable**[2] in this tough **economic climate**[3]. She showed a talent for analyzing financial data, and she was able to share her **findings**[4] with her clients in simple terms. Because of this, they always spoke very highly of her.

I saw Ms. Trent as a key part of our team. She always worked hard and achieved **excellent**[5] results. I know that she will benefit any business she is a part of, so I recommend her without **hesitation**[6]. Please feel free to call me on 0113-9496-0970 ext. 2 if you have any more questions.

Yours faithfully,

Timothy Rossiter

Timothy Rossiter
Director, R&J Financial Services

Key Terms 核心字彙片語

1 **planner** [ˋplænɚ] (n.) 規劃師
2 **profitable** [ˋprɑfɪtəbl̩] (a.) 有盈利的
3 **economic climate** [͵ikəˋnɑmɪk ˋklaɪmɪt] (n.)（經濟）景氣
4 **finding** [ˋfaɪndɪŋ] (n.) 發現
5 **excellent** [ˋɛksələnt] (a.) 傑出的
6 **hesitation** [͵hɛzəˋteʃən] (n.) 猶豫

1 詢價與詢問資訊 Making Inquiries and Asking for Information

① I am interested in your new air fryer and would like more information about it, including a quotation.

我對貴公司的新款氣炸鍋非常有興趣，希望能得到更多的相關資訊，包括報價。

② I would like to receive pricing information about your catering service.

我希望就貴公司的外燴服務得到價格相關資訊。

③ Please tell me the current price of your maple syrup.

請告知貴公司的楓糖漿目前的價格。

④ Please send me more information about your products.

請您就貴公司產品寄來更多資訊。

⑤ Please send me a quotation for the work specified below.

請您就下列工作內容提供報價。

⑥ Please explain how you would charge for the work detailed in this letter.

請您就信中工作內容如何收費提出說明。

2 進行穩固／非穩固報價 Making a Firm/Non-firm Offer

① We are pleased to provide you with the information you requested in your letter. 我們非常樂意提供您來信詢問的資訊。

② I hope the information enclosed answers your questions.

希望附上的資訊能夠回覆您的問題。

③ This offer is good for the next 20 days. 此報價於即日起 20 日內有效。

④ This offer will not be valid after June 30. 此報價在 6 月 30 日後就不適用。

⑤ This letter constitutes a firm offer. 本信之報價為穩固報價。

⑥ In order to give you an accurate quote, we need the following information.

為了提供您正確的報價，我們需要下列資訊。

⑦ Please send us the following information to help us prepare a correct quotation. 請寄來下列資訊，以協助我們提供正確的報價。

⑧ The prices quoted here are subject to change. 此處的報價仍可能變更。

⑨ This quote is subject to consideration and does not represent a final offer.

此報價可能調整，並非最終報價。

3 下訂單並交代相關事宜 Placing Orders and Making Requests

① We herewith order the following items. 　我方在此訂購下列產品。

② Enclosed please find our order. 　訂單已隨信附上。

③ We would appreciate it if you could deliver the order as soon as possible.
若你們能盡速出貨，我們將不勝感激。

④ Packing should be strong enough to ensure sufficient protection.
包裝方式應要能提供足夠的保護。

⑤ Goods of inferior quality will be returned at the supplier's risk and expense.
品質不佳的產品將退回，由供應商承擔相關風險與費用。

4 表達離職意願 Announcing Your Resignation

① Please accept this letter as my formal resignation from my role at ONE Inc.
謹以此信正式辭去我在ONE公司的職位。

② The purpose of this letter is to announce my resignation from my position
at Macrobook. 　此信意在向您知會，我將辭去我在Macrobook的職位。

③ Please accept this letter as notice that I will be resigning in mid-February.
請容我以此信向您告知，我將於二月中離職。

④ I hereby tender my resignation from my role as sales manager.
在此辭去本人業務經理的職務。

5 撰寫推薦信的用語 Writing Reference Letters

① I am only too happy to recommend Mr. Tom Smith for the position of
research assistant. 　我很樂於推薦湯姆‧史密斯先生擔任研究助理的職務。

② His/her performance indicates that he/she is ready for a new level of
responsibility. 　他／她的表現顯示他／她已做好準備，承擔更進一步的責任。

③ Ms. Johnson is more than capable of handling the workload of a software
engineer. 　強森女士勝任軟體工程師的工作綽綽有餘。

④ In my years of working with Tina, she has shown herself to be a capable
manager / brilliant problem solver, etc.
在我與蒂娜共事的這幾年，她已充分展現自己是能力出眾的經理／出色的問題解決
專家等。

字彙表 Vocabulary

Lesson 1

accurate (a.) 精確的
business letter (n.) 商業書信
feature (n.) 特性
formal (a.) 正式的
functional (a.) 實用取向的
helpful (a.) 有幫助的
informative (a.) 資訊充足的
liability (n.)（法律上的）責任；義務
practical (a.) 實用的
professional (a.) 專業的
quality (n.) 性質

Lesson 2

apology letter (n.) 致歉信
complaint letter (n.) 客訴信
congratulation letter (n.) 恭賀信
cover letter (n.) 求職信
CV (n.) 履歷表（= curriculum vitae）
email (n./v.) 電子郵件
invitation letter (n.) 邀請信
letter of inquiry (n.) 詢價信
letter of quotation (n.) 報價信
letter of resignation (n.) 離職信
memo (n.) 便函（= memorandum）
order letter (n.) 訂貨信
reference/recommendation letter (n.) 推薦信
resume (n.) 簡歷（= résumé）
sales letter (n.) 推銷信
suggestion letter (n.) 建言信
thank-you letter (n.) 感謝信

Lesson 3

attachment (n.)（電子）附件
body (of letter) (n.) 信件正文
closing (n.) 結尾
closing line / complimentary close (n.) 結尾敬辭
copy to 副本註明
date (n.) 日期
enclosure (n.) 附件
greeting (n.) 問候語
heading (n.) 信首
letterhead (n.) 信頭
name (n.) 姓名
opening (n.) 開頭

recipient's address (n.) 收件人地址
reference number (n.) 參考文號
salutation (n.) 稱謂
sender's address (n.) 寄件人地址
signature (n.) 簽名（親筆）
subject (n.) 信件主旨
title (n.) 職稱／單位

Lesson 4

abstract (a.) 抽象的
clear (a.) 清楚明確的
cohesive (a.) 流暢連貫的
complete (a.) 詳實完整的
complex (a.) 複雜的
concise (a.) 言簡意賅的
concrete (a.) 言之有物的
considerate (a.) 體貼周到的
correct (a.) 正確無誤的
courteous (a.) 客氣有禮的
fragmented (a.) 破碎凌亂的
incomplete (a.) 不完整的
inconsiderate (a.) 不體貼的
incorrect (a.) 不正確的
repetitive (a.) 重複的
rude (a.) 無禮的的

Lesson 5

action (n.) 行動
attention (n.) 注意力
capital (a.)（字母）大寫的
capitalization (n.) 使用大寫字母
careless (a.) 粗心的；草率的
desire (n.) 欲望
edit (v.) 編輯
formatting (n.) 格式安排
grammar (n.) 文法
impolite (a.) 不禮貌的
interest (n.) 興趣
persuasive (a.) 有說服力的
plan (v.) 規劃
punctuation (n.) 標點符號
review (v.) 檢查
spelling (n.) 拼字
tone (n.) 適當的語氣
word choice (n.) 用字遣詞
write (v.) 寫作

Lesson 6

a good/wide choice of (sth.) 各式……可供選擇
appeal (to sb.) (v.)（對……）有吸引力
appealing (a.) 有吸引力的
call to action (n.) 行動呼籲；行動指示
carrier (n.) 運輸業者
carry (v.)（商店）販售（某物）
catalog (n.)（商品）目錄（英式拼法為 catalogue）
client (n.) 客戶
core (n.) 核心
deliver (v.) 運送
entire (a.) 整個的
extend (v.) 提供；給予
flexible (a.) 有彈性的
from door to door 從路程開始到結束（此處指貨品從寄貨者送到收貨者）
inform (v.) 告知
informative (a.) 資訊充足的
motivate (v.) 使……產生動機
of (great/no) interest (to sb.) 使……（很／不）感興趣
operation (n.) 營運
option (n.) 選項
order/reply form (n.) 訂購／回覆單
package (n.) 套裝方案
partner (v.) 和……搭檔合作（+ with）
persuade (v.) 說服
product (n.) 產品
promote (v.) 推廣
promotional (a.) 宣傳的；推銷的
remain (v.) 保持……
sample (n.) 樣品
server (n.) 伺服器
service (n.) 服務
shipment (n.) 運輸（的貨品）
software (n.) 軟體
solution (n.) 解決方案
stock (n.) 存貨；庫存
variety (n.) 各種；多樣化
with (sth.) in mind 考量到……

Lesson 7

additional (a.) 額外的
annual (a.) 年度的
board of directors (n.) 董事會
charity (n.) 慈善（事業）
collection (n.) 收集物

commitment (n.) 必須處理的事情
company (n.) 陪伴
declination (n.) 婉拒
decline (v.) 婉拒
directions (n.)〔複〕（交通）路線指引
due to 由於……
event (n.) 活動
fundraiser (n.) 募款活動
guest (n.) 賓客
hold (v.) 舉行；主持
host (n.) 主辦方；主持人 (v.) 主辦；主持
invitation card (n.) 邀請卡
launch (n.) 發布會
location (n.) 地點
occasion (n.) 場合
on hand （因特定目的）在場的
organizer (n.) 籌辦者
out-of-town (a.) 出城外的
presentation (n.) 簡報發表
preview (n.) 預展
prior (a.) 先前的
prior commitment (n.) 預定行程
product line (n.) 產品線（同家廠商推出的一系列類似產品或服務）
purpose (n.) 目的
reason (n.) 原因
regret (v.)（因……）抱歉或遺憾
RSVP (v.)（縮寫）敬請回覆
showing (n.) 展覽
time (n.) 時間
unable (a.) 不能夠的
unfortunately (adv.) 遺憾地
valued (a.) 貴重的
with pleasure 非常樂意

Lesson 8

advance (v.) 推進
afford (v.) 負擔
appreciate (v.) 感謝
audience (n.) 對象
board (n.) 董事會；委員會
commend (v.) 稱讚
compliment (v.) 讚美
contract (n.) 合約
contribution (n.) 貢獻
direct (a.) 直接的
discuss (v.) 討論

donation (n.) 捐款；捐贈
genuine (a.) 真誠的
grateful (a.) 感激的
immediate (a.) 立即的
impact (v.) 影響
input (n.) 投入
interview (n./v.) 面試
investment (n.) （時間、精力）投入；（金錢）投資
make time 空出時間
meet with (sb.) 和……見面
mission (n.) 任務；使命
pipe (n.) 管線；水管
plumbing (n.) 水管工程
praise (v.) 稱讚
project (n.) 專案；工程
recent (a.) 近期的
recommend (v.) 推薦
relationship (n.) 關係
scholarship (n.) 獎學金
sincere (a.) 誠懇的
solve (v.) 解決
specific (a.) 具體的
supply (n.) 用品；供給品
task (n.) 任務；工作
thankful (a.) 感謝的
timely (a.) 及時的

Lesson 9

auto (n.) 汽車（automobile 的簡稱）
automatic (a.) 自動的
beauty (n.) 美麗
community (n.) 社區；社群
corporate (a.) 公司的
cosmetics (n.) 〔複〕化妝品
customer (n.) 顧客
cyclist (n.) 單車騎士
donor (n.) 捐贈者
earn (v.) 贏得
express (v.) 表達
fill out 填寫
form letter (n.) 制式信件
honored (a.) 備受榮幸的
mass (a.) 大批的
milestone (n.) 里程碑
neighbor (n.) 鄰居
newspaper (n.) 報紙
participant (n.) 參與者

press release (n.) 新聞稿
public (a.) 公開的
race (n.) 比賽
satisfaction (n.) 滿意
smoothly (adv.) 平穩地
social media (n.) 社群媒體
take part (in an event) 參與（活動）
unspecified (a.) 未特定的
when it comes to . . . 說到……

Lesson 10

achievement (n.) 成就
admiration (n.) 敬佩
anniversary (n.) 週年紀念日
appropriate (a.) 得體適當的
(be) down to (sb.) 〔英〕（某事是）仰賴、歸功於（某人）
benefit (v.) 得益
business relation (n.) 業務關係
capable (a.) 有能力的
care (n.) 關心
catch up 聊聊近況；敘舊
certainly (adv.) 絕對地
compliment (n.) 讚美
concise (a.) 簡潔的
congratulation (n.) 祝賀（詞）
coworker (n.) 同事
dealing (n.)（商業）往來
dedication (n.) 奉獻
deserve (v.) 值得
distracting (a.) 令人分心的
effusive (a.) 過度熱情的
end (n.) 方面；部分
expansion (n.) 擴張
factor (n.) 因素
fast (a.) 快速的
firm (n.) 公司
firsthand (adv./a.) 第一手地（的）
from strength to strength 日益茁壯；蒸蒸日上
further (adv.) 另外
impress (v.) 使……印象深刻
in no small part 在不小程度上
in safe hands 令人覺得安心可靠
invitation (n.) 邀請
issue (n.)（報刊的）期
key (a.) 關鍵的
leadership (n.) 領導（能力）
loyalty (n.) 忠誠

marketing (n.) 行銷

milestone (n.) 里程碑

monthly (a.) 每月的

newsletter (n.) 通訊

on behalf of 謹代表……

passion (n.) 熱情

positive (a.) 正面的

profile (n.) 傳略；人物簡介

promotion (n.) 升遷

reader-focused (a.) 聚焦讀者的

retirement (n.) 退休

reward (v./n.) 回報

sarcastic (a.) 諷刺的

sense (n.) 判斷力

settle in 安頓下來

shrewd (a.) 精明的

sincere (a.) 真誠的

take over 接任

talent (n.) 才能

transition (n.) 過渡（期）

vital (a.) 極重要的

work ethic (n.) 工作態度；職業道德

yearly (a.) 每年一度的

Lesson 11

access (v.) 取用

advice (n.) 忠告

arrange (v.) 安排

clear (a.) 明確的

compensation (n.) 補償

complaint policy (n.) 客訴規章

contact (v.) 聯繫

damage (n.) 損害

discount (n.) 折扣

enclose (v.) 隨信附上

error (n.) 錯誤

evidence (n.) 證據

fact (n.) 事實

fault (n.) 過失

feedback (n.) 回饋

follow (it) up 後續追蹤

for your reference 供你參考

friendly (a.) 友善的

If you don't mind, . . . 如果你不介意……

inconvenience (n.) 不方便

inform (v.) 通知

invoice (n.) 請款帳單；發貨單；發票

meet (one's) demands 達成……的要求

opinion (n.) 意見

partial (a.) 部分的

PO (= purchase order) (n.) 訂購單

practical (a.) 切實的

present (v.) 發表

professional (a.) 專業的

put (sth.) on sale 將……推出販售

quality (n.) 品質

refund (n.) 退款

regret (n./v.) 遺憾

repair (n.) 維修

replacement (n.) 換貨；更換

response (n.) 回覆

rot (n.) 腐蝕；長霉

schedule (n.) 時程表

Lesson 12

act (v.) 行動

apologize (v.) 道歉

assist (v.) 協助

at fault 有過錯

available (a.) 可取得的

blame (n.) 責備

bring (sth.) to (sb.'s) attention
使（某人）注意到（某事）

business day (n.) 工作天

damp (n.) 潮濕；濕氣

delivery (n.) 交付；投遞

explain (v.) 解釋

explore (v.) 探索

express (n.) 快遞

frustrating (a.) 令人惱怒的

get in touch 聯繫

goods (n.) 貨物

invalid (a.) 不合理的

issue (n.) 問題；爭議

pass along 轉達

post (v.) 張貼

reliable (a.) 可靠的

reply (v.) 回覆

resolve (v.) 解決

stockroom (n.) 倉庫

to (sb's) liking 符合……的喜好

trouble (n.) 麻煩；問題

understanding (n.) 理解

valid (a.) 合理的

value (v.) 重視
via (prep.) 透過……
well received 收悉；充分接受

Lesson 13

account (n.) 帳戶
apologize (v.) 致歉
appropriately formal 恰如其分的
as a gesture of goodwill 為表達善意／誠意
assign (v.) 分配；指定
assure (v.) 保證；確保
book (v.) 預定
charity (n.) 慈善團體
claim (v.) 索取
code (n.) 代碼
collect (v.) 收取；收集
compensation (n.) 補償
control (n./v.) 控制
damage (n./v.) 損害
delay (n./v.) 延遲；延誤
evaluate (v.) 評估
exact (a.) 確切的
explain (v.) 解釋
faulty (a.) 有問題的
faulty item (n.) 瑕疵品；不良品
fee (n.) 費用
fix (v.) 修理
free of charge 免費地
gesture (n.) 表示；姿態
harm (n./v.) 傷害
high-quality (a.) 高品質的
honest (a.) 誠實的
hurtful (a.) 有害的
inform (v.) 通知
item (n.) 品項
last-minute (a.) 最後一刻前的
let (sb.) down 使……失望
long-term (a.) 長期的
notice (n.) 通知
offense (n.) 冒犯；罪過（英式拼法為 offence）
ordeal (n.) 不愉快的經驗
own up to . . . 承擔……（過錯等）
patience (n.) 耐心
payment (n.) 支付，付款
pinpoint (v.) 精準確定
post (n.) 貼文
postpone (v.) 延期

prompt (a.) 迅速的
prone (a.) 易於……的
put (sb.) through . . . 讓（某人）經歷……
reassure (v.) 使……放心
reference (v.) 指出
repair (n./v.) 修理（工作）
reprimand (v.) 訓斥
respectful (a.) 尊敬的
responsible (a.) 負責任的
sensitive (a.) 敏感的
sign (v.) 簽名
social media (n.) 社群媒體
solution (n.) 解決方案
spot (v.) 發現
take place 發生；進行
take pride in . . . 對……感到驕傲
take responsibility 負起責任
truthful (a.) 誠實的
venue (n.) 場地

Lesson 14

a people person 有人緣的人；人際關係強的人
advantage (n.) 優勢
ample (a.) 充足的
applicant (n.) 求職者
apply for 應徵；申請
asset (n.) 資產
at present 目前；現在
at your convenience 在您方便時
attractive (a.) 吸引人的
background (n.) 背景
bond (n.) 聯結
boost (v.) 促進
candidate (n.) 應徵者；候選人
capable (a.) 有能力的
certification (n.) 證照
confident (a.) 有信心的
employer (n.) 雇主
experience (n.) 經驗
eye-catching (a.) 吸引目光的
fit (n.) 合適
fluently (adv.) 流利地
in short 簡言之
marketing (n.) 行銷
master's degree (n.) 碩士學位
mission (n.) 使命
open (a.) （職位）空缺的
outstanding (a.) 突出的

piece (n.) 作品；報導
position (n.) 職位
potential (n.) 潛力
private (a.) 私立的；私有的
profit (n.) 利潤
program (n.) 課程
prove to be 證明是……
range (n.)（能力）範疇
requirement (n.) 條件
research (n.) 研究
skill (n.) 技能
skill set (n.)（工作的）技能組合
smooth (a.) 平穩的
stage (n.) 階段
stand out (from . . .)（從……）脫穎而出
under (sb.'s) wing 在……的主責下
well prepared (a.) 準備好的

Lesson 15

academic / teaching position 學術／教學職位
administrative (a.) 行政的
algorithm (n.) 演算法
analysis (n.) 分析
antitrust (a.) 反壟斷的
assistant (a.) 助理的
association (n.) 協會
autobiography (n.) 自傳
BA (n.) 文學學士（Bachelor of Arts 的縮寫）
BSc (n.) 理學學士（Bachelor of Science 的縮寫）
certification (n.) 檢定；證明
coding (n.) 編碼；撰寫程式
collaborate (v.) 合作
come up with 想出
compliance (n.)（法令）合規
conference (n.) 研討會；會議
conference paper (n.) 研討會論文
constitutional (a.) 憲法的
contact details 聯絡資訊
content marketing (n.) 內容行銷
corporate governance (n.) 公司治理
course (n.) 課程
customized (a.) 客製化的
database (n.) 資料庫
demonstrate (v.) 展示
dissertation (n.) 學位論文（博士論文〔美〕、碩士論文〔英〕）
doctor (n.) 博士
education (n.) 教育
fact-check (v.) 事實查核

financial year (n.) 會計年度
freedom of speech and press (n.) 言論出版自由
generate (v.) 產生
high-profile (a.) 備受矚目的
intellectual property (n.) 智慧財產
intern (n.) 實習生
Internet of things (n.) 物聯網（常簡稱 IoT）
journal (n.) 期刊
journal article (n.) 期刊論文
journalist (n.) 新聞記者
law school (n.) 法學院
license (n.) 執照
litigation (n.) 訴訟
membership (n.) 會員身分
negotiate (v.) 協商
objective (n.) 目標
possess (v.) 具有；擁有
presentation (n.)（論文）發表
professor (n.) 教授
programming (n.) 程式設計
proofread (v.) 校對
publication (n.) 出版作品
qualification (n.) 資格；證照
reach (v.) 達到；與……交流
readable (a.) 易讀的
research grant 研究經費資助／獎助
research position 研究職位
reverse-chronological (a.) 倒敘的
sales lead (n.) 銷售商機
selected (a.) 精選的
shift (n./v.) 轉移；轉變
skill (n.) 技能
start-up (n.) 新創公司
strategy (n.) 策略
supreme court (n.) 最高法院
teamwork (n.) 團隊合作
thesis (n.) 學位論文（碩士論文〔美〕、博士論文〔英〕）
to-the-point (a.) 切中要點的
undergraduate (n.) 畢業生
urban (a.) 都會的
viral marketing (n.) 病毒式行銷
work history/experience 工作經歷

Lesson 16

abbreviation (n.) 縮寫
absent (a.) 缺席的
apply (v.) 使……生效／起作用

appropriateness (n.) 適當
attachment (n.) 附加檔案；附件
attend (v.) 出席；參加
Bcc (= blind carbon copy) 密件副本
Cc (= carbon copy) (電郵) 副本
confirm (v.) 確認
credit (n.) 商品抵用金
emoji (n.) 表情符號
etiquette (n.) 禮儀
exclamation point (n.) 驚嘆號
forward (v.) 轉寄
guest (n.) 客人
label (n.) 標籤
loyal (a.) 忠誠的
menu (n.) 菜單
professionalism (n.) 專業態度
purchase (n.) 購買
regarding (prep.) 有關……
reminder (n.) 提醒
reservation (n.) 預約；訂位
signature block (n.) 簽名檔
staff meeting (n.) 員工會議
subject (n.) 主旨
unfortunately (adv.) 遺憾地；不幸地；可惜地
vegetarian (a./n.) 素食的 (人)
work from home 在家 (遠距) 工作
workday (n.) 工作日

Lesson 17

afford (v.) 承擔得起……
agent (n.) 仲介；代理人
allowance (n.) 補貼；津貼
announcement (n.) 宣布
annual sales (n.) 年度銷售額
bonus (n.) 獎金
business hours (n.) 營業時間
ceiling fan (n.) (裝在天花板的) 吊扇
celebrate (v.) 慶祝
come as a surprise (to sb.) 使……大為驚訝
conclusion (n.) 結論
conference (n.) 會議
context (n.) 背景情況
cooperation (n.) 合作
downtown (adv./a.) 市中心地／的
exceed (v.) 超越
force (v.) 強迫
fuel (n.) 油錢

funding (n.) 經費；資金
head office (n.) 總公司；總部
heading (n.) 頁首 (文字)
in advance 預先地
instruction (n.) 指示
lunch break (n.) 午休時間
management (n.) 管理階層
normal (n.) 常態
note (v.) 注意到……
paycheck (n.) 工資
postpone (v.) 延後
problem (n.) 問題
receipt (n.) 收據
reimburse (v.) 報銷
request (n.) 要求
shift (n.) 輪班
short (a.) 簡短的
slice (n.) (一) 片
submit (v.) 繳交
task (n.) 任務
time-sensitive (a.) 具時效性的
title (n.) 標題

Appendix

assist (v.) 協助
assortment (n.) 各式各樣
(be) subject to . . . 尚待……而定
C.I.F 到岸價格 (即包含貨物成本 cost、運送保險費 insurance 和運費 freight 的報價方式)
case-by-case (a.) 依個案決定的
chef (n.) 主廚；廚師
constitute (v.) 被視為；構成
economic climate (n.) (經濟) 景氣
excellent (a.) 傑出的
expedited shipping (n.) 快捷運送
express shipping (n.) 快遞；快速貨運
finance (n.) 財務；金融
finding (n.) 發現
garment (n.) 衣服
hesitation (n.) 猶豫
indicate (v.) 指明
industrial estate (n.) 工業區
inquiry (n.) 詢價；詢問
insurance (n.) 保險 (費)
negotiation (n.) 協商
payment in advance 預先付款
planner (n.) 規劃師
profitable (a.) 有盈利的
pursue (v.) 追求

quote (n.) 報價
R&D 研發（= **research and development**）
replacement (n.) 代替者
resign (v.) 辭職
senior (a.) 資深的；高級的
sew (v.) 縫製
term (n.) 條款；條件
total (n.) 總額
utensil (n.)（家用、廚房）器具
wire (bank) transfer (n.) 電匯；匯款

必學
英文商業
書信寫作
快速上手

作　者	Owain Mckimm / Michelle Witte / Shara Dupuis (Lessons 16–17) / Brian Foden (Lesson 6) / Richard Luhrs (Lesson 7) / John Calhoun (Lesson 14) / Laura Phelps (Lesson 13 部分)
譯　者	黃詩韻／陳依辰
審　訂	Helen Yeh
企劃編輯	葉俞均
編　輯	高詣軒
校　對	陳彥臻
主　編	丁宥暄
內文排版	洪伊珊／林書玉
封面設計	林書玉
製程管理	洪巧玲
發 行 人	黃朝萍
出 版 者	寂天文化事業股份有限公司
電　話	+886-(0)2-2365-9739
傳　真	+886-(0)2-2365-9835
網　址	www.cosmoselt.com
讀者服務	onlineservice@icosmos.com.tw
出版日期	2023 年 6 月 初版

國家圖書館出版品預行編目(CIP)資料

必學英文商業書信寫作快速上手/Owain Mckimm等著；黃詩韻, 陳依辰譯. -- 初版. -- [臺北市] : 寂天文化事業股份有限公司, 2023.06
　面；　公分
ISBN 978-626-300-194-7(菊8K平裝)

1.CST: 商業書信 2.CST: 商業英文 3.CST: 商業應用文
4.CST: 寫作法

493.6　　　　　　　　　　　　112008407